DREAM O

When Marcus O'Neill came into Laurel's Long Island bookshop, she had no idea of the new road he would open for her. Only when Marcus picked up a copy of her father's latest novel did premonition strike her.

Clifton York had left her mother when she was a small child. She had pretended she didn't care, but fed her own secret anger by reading his books, following his career, keeping old pain alive.

When Marcus explained that her father was his friend, that Cliff York now lived in the Florida keys and was in need of help. Laurel was forced to a decision. Laurel finds herself drawn into intrigue involving sunken treasure, modern piracy, and a burgeoning new love. She must not only deal with a surprising new family but with the strange and evil orchids that threaten her new love and will eventually lead to nightmare.

**Also by the same author,
and available from Coronet:**

Blue Fire
Emerald
Flaming Tree
The Quicksilver Pool
Rainsong
The Window on the Square

About the author

Phyllis A. Whitney was born in Yokohama,
Japan, of American parents. The A in her name
stands for Ayame, the Japanese word for Iris.
The family returned to live in the USA when
she was fifteen. She published her first book in
1941 and has been a bookseller, librarian,
reviewer and writing teacher. Her many novels
have made her an international bestseller.

Dream of Orchids

Phyllis A. Whitney

CORONET BOOKS
Hodder and Stoughton

The characters and situations in this book are entirely imaginary and bear no relation to any real person or actual happening.

First published in Great Britain in 1985 by Hodder and Stoughton Ltd.

Coronet Edition 1988

British Library C.I.P.

Whitney, Phyllis A. (Phyllis Ayanne), *1903–*
Dream of orchids.
I. Title
823'.52[F]

ISBN 0-340-42848-1

Printed and bound in Great Britain for Hodder and Stoughton Paperbacks, a division of Hodder and Stoughton Ltd., Mill Road, Dunton Green, Sevenoaks, Kent TN13 2YA (Editorial Office: 47 Bedford Square, London WC1B 3DP) by Richard Clay Ltd., Bungay, Suffolk.

ACKNOWLEDGMENTS

My special thanks to Joar and Wright Langley for their books on Key West, and for their advice. I am grateful to Joan for her careful reading of my manuscript.

The Monroe County Public Library was hospitable and helpful during my visit to Key West, and later in sending me material. Betty Bruce and Sylvia Knight of the research department answered endless questions, and assisted with introductions to those who might help me.

Several residents generously opened their homes to me so that I could "build" my own house authentically in the story. I want to thank Joan and Edward Knight, Rita Sawyer, Marcia Herndon, and Richard Lischer for allowing me "back of the scenes."

I am grateful as well to my friend Don Reed, of Marine World, in California, for helping with my scuba-diving scenes.

Dream

of Orchids

1

The bookstore had emptied, and we were nearly ready to close. Stan Neese, my assistant, was working at the back, and I had just set down my record of sales for the day when a man walked into the shop—a stranger.

He caught my attention, not only because of his bright red hair, but also because a deep tan doesn't often appear in March in our part of Long Island. Bellport is a quiet village, especially before the summer people arrive. His manner suggested barely suppressed energy, even when he stood quite still beyond my semicircle of counter and regarded me searchingly in a way that seemed almost a challenge.

Under one arm he carried a small, square florist's box tied with green ribbon, and as he rested the box on the counter, Ernest, my bookstore cat, padded across to examine it. The stranger made friends, scratching behind Ernest's tawny ears and smiling at the loud purr that resulted. His smile came easily, relaxed, amused—until he looked at me again with a question in his eyes that I couldn't answer, since I didn't know what the question was.

I tried the standard phrase. "May I help you?"

"I hope so," he said, and walked away between book tables, looking around with a more intense interest than the average customer was apt to show. I gave up watching him and returned to my work. If he wanted something, he'd have to let me know.

When I glanced at him again, I saw that he'd stopped before some paintings of Bellport scenes that I'd hung on the wall. They clearly interested him, and since I'd painted them myself, I began to watch him more closely.

After a time he turned back to me. "Are these houses local?" he asked.

I told him they were, and he smiled as if to himself. "That's interesting, and rather curious."

That was a remark I didn't understand, but now I was beginning to feel curious myself about who this man was, and what he wanted.

He gave me no clue until, moving about, he found a table of books near the front of the shop and picked up a copy of Clifton York's new suspense novel, *Caribbean Gold*. The moment he took the book into his hands, I felt as though a warning bell had rung—though with no logical reason, since the pile of books was there to attract customers, and people picked them up every day. Yet something told me this was different.

Stan came forward to wait on him, knowing I was busy closing out the register. We'd had a disagreement earlier that day, and Stan was still miffed and hardly speaking to me. Something had to be done about him sooner or later. He not only wanted to buy out the store and take it over, he wanted to take me over as well, and he had no idea of the rebellion that had begun to seethe beneath the smooth surface I tried to offer the world. My safe disguise!

I noticed how strikingly tall the stranger seemed beside Stan and again how vividly red his hair was. He considered Stan's earnest, spectacled face and said, "No, thanks." Then he stared openly at me again. Not caring for a challenge I didn't understand, I stared back and became aware for the first time of the deep gray-blue of his eyes. They were the color of the bay with the sun shining on it—and that was a completely irrelevant thought.

Stan went back to the cartons he was unpacking, and the red-haired man turned the Clifton York novel over in his hands to examine the photograph on the back panel. Then he looked at me again.

"Of course you're Laurel York. You look remarkably like your father—thick black hair, blue eyes, squarish chin. I expect you've been told that before."

I'd been told it more often than I liked, since I didn't want to look like my father, and I hated being caught off guard like this.

"Who are you?" I asked. "What do you want?"

"My name is Marcus O'Neill. Sometimes I help your father with his research. I dug up some of the background scoop for *Caribbean Gold.*"

I reached for the stool behind me and perched on it, hooking my heels over a rung to steady myself. An excitement I didn't welcome was rising in me, and I needed to hold it back, give nothing away. If ever I let it go, I didn't know what would happen.

"I know very little about Clifton York," I said coolly. A statement that was scarcely true, since I never missed anything about him that came my way. I'd always read his interviews and studied his book jackets, and I'd followed all the movies made from his books. Two or three times in the past I'd even caught him on television—without my mother knowing. Of course I had read every word he'd written with a contradictory mix of curiosity, longing, and resentment that had been hard for me to live with. Somehow I'd always managed to conceal what seemed to me a morbid interest. After what he had done to my mother—and to me—I had no business thinking of him at all. My mother had been hurt for as long as I could remember, and I'd never wanted to add to her anguish. Now that she was gone, there was no more need for suppression, but old feelings died hard.

"I haven't seen my father since I was three years old," I told Marcus O'Neill. "As far as I'm concerned, I have no father."

"Perhaps that's partly your own fault." He continued to study me, considering, judging, while my indignation grew.

"What do you want, Mr. O'Neill?" I asked.

"Not to quarrel with you. But I'm no diplomat, and I suppose there's no graceful way to ease into this."

I didn't know what he wanted to ease into, and because of his connection with my father, I meant to resist, no matter what it was.

"I'm sorry about your mother's death," he went on.

"Why should you be sorry? I don't suppose he is."

"He could be, you know, though probably in a remote sort of way. His wife—his second wife—died nearly a year ago. He's a lonely, driven, unhappy man."

"He has two other daughters to keep him company, hasn't he?"

"He was talking about you a few days ago—just wondering out loud. That's partly what brought me here."

"Long Island's a whole coastline from Key West! Did he send you?"

"I'm afraid not. He doesn't know I've come—it was my own idea."

"Why?" I wished the shaking inside me would stop.

His look softened a little. "I wanted to learn something about Laurel York. Is there a place where we could talk?" He used my name easily, as though he'd spoken it in the past.

I was all too aware of Stan's listening presence at the back of the store. Another late customer came into the shop, and when Stan hurried forward again I led the way up wide wooden steps to my browsing gallery. A rocker and comfortable armchair waited there, and a table stood ready to receive books pulled down from the shelves. This was where I kept more expensive art books in various categories. The lighting was good, but soft, and the brown wooden shelves and floor gave a subdued feeling of quiet and serenity to the long room. I still believed in browsing space for readers. Stairs at the rear led down to the children's section.

He chose the armchair and I the rocker, though I kept my feet solidly on the floor, so the chair wouldn't move. I was still in a tense, suspended state of waiting. I had no questions to ask. There was nothing I wanted to know . . . and everything.

"I met Cliff York about ten years ago when I was twenty-two," he said. "I was breaking in as a free-lance writer—I'd sold a few articles to magazines. Cliff gave me a research job that helped me to survive, and he sent other opportunities my way. I'd come to Key West to write about the island, and I liked it enough to stay. My home was in Wisconsin, but I had no more ties there, and I'd been wandering around since I got out of college."

His tone was conversational now, but I was still on guard, and he made me increasingly uneasy. I would listen to him, but whatever he asked of me, the answer would be no.

He'd brought the florist's box with him, and now he set it on the floor beside his chair.

"Haven't you been curious about your father?" he asked, suddenly direct. "Or about your two half sisters?"

I gripped the arms of the rocker. The old longing that I wanted to deny seemed stronger than ever and impossible to deal with.

"He treated my mother horribly. He just left—walked out on us both! In all these twenty-five years since I was three, he has never sent me one single birthday card, or one letter, or called me on the phone. After my mother divorced him, he married that—that woman!—and we never heard from him again. I'm not to blame for any of that. How could I possibly want to get in touch with him?"

"I'm sorry. He's not an easy man to understand, and I'm not trying to excuse anything he did in the past. Of course I don't know what your mother was like. It's just that he's having a rough time right now. His older daughter, Iris, is only twenty-four, and she's going determinedly into a marriage her own mother was very much against. Fern, your younger sister, is a delicate little thing, and their mother's death has hit her hard. Your father has lost his grip completely since Poppy died. He was very much in love with his wife right to the end, you know."

I didn't want to hear how much Cliff York had loved another woman instead of my mother.

"So what is all this to me?" I knew I sounded defiant, but I couldn't help that. I'd been holding everything back for too long—years too long.

"Perhaps nothing. That's what I've come to find out. I care about what happens to Cliff. I owe him."

"Are you suggesting that I go to Key West?"

The appraising look had returned. "I expect it was a mistake for me to come here. A wild chance I had to take. But there's nothing I can ask of you. There's no real reason why you should consider what he may need."

"No, there isn't," I said quickly. "But you might at least have phoned before you walked in on me like this."

"Would you have seen me if I had?"

I tried to be honest. "Probably not. I can't forget all the times when I needed him and he wasn't there."

"Of course I don't blame you for the way you feel."

He spoke stiffly and I knew he *was* blaming me, and that made me angry. Let him go back to Key West! Let him carry word to Clifton York that he had an older daughter who would never forgive him for what he had done.

My chair was rocking furiously, and he reached out one brown hand, quieting me and the chair. Then he picked up the florist's box and handed it to me. "This is for you."

I didn't want to take the box. I didn't want flowers from him, or from anyone in Key West.

"Your half sister Fern sent it. Fern is the only one who knew I was coming here."

In spite of my reluctance, I had to take the box and slide the green ribbon off. When I lifted the lid and spread back white tissue, I found a lovely miniature orchid inside. It was a pale greenish-bronze, edged with a band of deep crimson around the fluted petals with speckles of darker bronze cast like confetti upon satin. There was a card in the box, and I took it out. *From Fern* had been penned across it in a small, firm hand.

I held the delicate blossom—my first orchid from Key West —and a certain presentiment stirred in me. I couldn't know it then, but this was the beginning of the dream that was to haunt me for so long.

To hide an emotion I didn't want to show, I spoke a bit tartly.

"If that woman's name was Poppy, how could she possibly call her daughters Iris and Fern? How could she do anything so silly?"

"Poppy York was never a silly woman," he said quietly. "A bit dramatic and breathtaking, perhaps. Completely enchanting—but never foolish. She was a lady to be reckoned with—and she still is. She held that house together for a long time, and you can still feel her influence all through it. Her death was tragic and senseless."

I put the orchid back in its nest of tissue and set the open box on the table near me. I didn't dare to think about the half sister who had sent me this flower. Or of why she had sent it, and what she was like. I didn't want to weaken in my resistance.

Marcus stood up, and I rose with him. "Fern wanted you to know that she grew this flower herself. I'll go along now. I'm staying overnight with friends in East Patchogue, and I'll be flying home tomorrow. Thanks for talking with me."

I went down the stairs with him to the front door of the shop. In a moment he would be gone, and I would never hear from Key West again. My angry instinct to resist, coupled with all the longings that I'd suppressed, made miserable companions, and suddenly I wanted to dismiss one and satisfy the other.

"I need time to think," I told him in a rush. "Let me have tonight. Can you stop here at the shop tomorrow morning before you leave? I can be here as early as you like."

He stood two steps down on the sidewalk and looked up at me in that strange way that made me uneasy, uncertain. It was as though some unexpected current flowed between us, quickening a new awareness in me, making me feel suddenly more alive than I had in a long while.

His smile was warm, kind—as though he understood, which of course wasn't possible. This man could be appealing when he chose, but I didn't want to trust him.

"Why did you come?" I demanded. "You haven't really explained that."

"One reason I've come is because there may not be a lot of time left. Cliff's had one heart attack, and he doesn't always take care of himself. Besides, there's an anniversary coming up in April. The anniversary of Poppy's death—and such dates can be dangerous."

"Dangerous?"

He answered too quickly. "To emotional health. Or haven't you lived long enough to find that out?"

"How did she die?"

"Perhaps your father would tell you about that. Otherwise, it's not important to you, is it?"

I couldn't deal with his directness.

He went on. "Would you care to have dinner with me tonight? We can't stand here talking on your doorstep."

I was already backing into the shop. "Thanks, but—no. I need to be alone. I need to think."

"You need to stop being scared of your own shadow," he said. "Good night, Laurel. I'll be back in the morning. Say, eight o'clock."

I watched him stride off down the street with a vigorous, purposeful walk. He was a man who knew where he was going and what he wanted, and I wasn't going to tag after him or be pushed into anything I didn't really want to do. I wasn't that scared.

I went inside, feeling troubled. The store had emptied, and I tried to shake off the peculiar spell I'd fallen under.

Questions were about to pour out of Stan, and I stemmed

the tide quickly. "His name is Marcus O'Neill. He helps my father in his research, and he wanted me to come to Key West."

"That's idiotic! Of course you won't go," Stan said in his most outraged tone.

"Of course I won't," I repeated, feeling unreasonably irritated. "Just go home, Stan. I'll close up. I want to be by myself for a while."

At least Stan had never accused me of being scared of shadows—my own or anyone else's—and sensing my angry mood, he got out of the shop as fast as he could.

I locked the back door, clicking the bolt firmly, and began to turn out lights. One thing I knew—I loved this shop. It had rescued me from aimlessness after college, and I had worked hard for its success. I was at home with books and with people who enjoyed reading as much as I did. My mother had loaned me the money to buy it, and it had done well enough so that I'd been able to pay her back. But it wasn't my whole life. It couldn't satisfy the dreaming and the make-believe that went churning on inside me, even though I kept them hidden. I was supposed to be capable and sensible. All those dull virtues! No one suspected the wild dreams that sometimes pushed against a trap my mother had built around me and that I had helped her to build. But I didn't like the emotion that had surged up in me when a stranger from Key West had suddenly sprung the trap.

Walking among the book tables and turn stands, I touched a bright jacket here and there and knew I was among my friends. Trusted friends who never let me down—and who encouraged my dreaming. I'd always loved the very smell and feel of books —even before I opened the covers to see what was inside. I read about the authors and knew all their titles, and I knew my customers' tastes and how individual the matter of a "good book" was. This was my world—and it ought to be enough.

It wasn't.

Halfway down the shop, I paused before several paintings on the wall. If I had a creative talent, it was this, though I'd never worked at it steadily. That was another dream I had no place for. The seascape I had painted on Fire Island. Another was a watercolor of a white clapboard house with a picket fence —a typical old Bellport house. This was the picture that had caught Marcus O'Neill's attention, and I wondered why.

Ernest, whose home was in the shop, stretched, yawned, and came to rub his head against my ankle. I picked him up and stood looking at the third picture. It was an imaginative water-color scene of a tropical beach. An island beach—somewhere. Women in native dress walked on wet sand with baskets on their heads. I smiled, remembering the fantasy I'd really been painting—a jacket for one of my father's books. How foolish could I be!

I put on my coat, but before I left I went up to the gallery and took the orchid from its box. Marcus O'Neill had said that my half sister Fern had grown it. She wasn't real for me, and I didn't know what had prompted her to send me this flower. Nevertheless, I pinned it to my lapel and went quickly down-stairs. Without a glance, I walked past the stack of *Caribbean Gold,* told a purring Ernest good night, and let myself out the door, leaving a single light burning inside.

Along Main Street, store lights shone in the windows. It was a very short Main Street that turned at each end into South Country Road. In March the days were longer, so it wasn't dark yet—just a bit dusky—though there was still a snap to the air. I walked briskly down Bellport Lane toward the bay.

An unexpected feeling of vitality flowed through me—something I'd caught from Marcus O'Neill?—and I moved fast, needing to use it up. I was still upset, but I hadn't felt this alive since my mother had died. Maybe, if I could be honest with myself, I wanted to go to Key West.

For too many years I'd relied on hidden dreams and make-believe—always about exotic and faraway places. I'd read my father's books and often envied his luxurious, flamboyant style, even while I resented him. Now I had an opportunity to take a large, risky step that might result in a good deal of pain. Yet I knew that romantic "elsewhere" still drew me.

The idea of my father drew me. There'd been times when I felt that I must be like him in some ways—because I was so different from my mother. Even while I often hated the difference, it made me want to know all that I'd missed, all that had been withheld from me.

I walked past white clapboard houses like the one in my painting, past white picket fences that were typical of an older Long Island. These houses were more than a hundred years old, and their dignity and grace gave the area a special flavor that had attracted writers and artists and musicians since the last century. Some old families still lived in them.

I followed the street to the edge of the bay and turned down a narrow lane, leaving the marina and dock area behind. When I reached a place near a seawall, I looked across rolling water to the long, low strip of Fire Island that stretched for thirty miles on the near horizon, protecting this part of the South Shore from Atlantic storms. For the moment I didn't want to think or feel, and the endless motion of gray water had a soothing effect.

As the evening grew dark, the temperature dropped, and I turned to climb to a side street and the small house that I had shared with my mother. She had bought it with her savings after my father left, and she'd continued to work in a real estate office until her recent illness.

The house seemed painfully quiet as I turned my key in the door and stepped into the hall. I'd had this feeling ever since Mother had died. Only now something new laced through the emptiness—a sense of freedom that I'd never felt before. Almost a guilty feeling. If I chose I could go anywhere I pleased, do anything I liked.

I spoke ruefully aloud to Marcus O'Neill. "What are you doing to me? How can you come here and stir me up, make me furious, change everything?" I could imagine his smile, with that challenge behind it. A challenge I wanted to fling back in his face.

These days I avoided the dining room where Mother and I had always eaten together. I ate instead in the generous kitchen, sitting beside a back window that looked out on a great beech tree whose branches were still bare. Lately I'd taken to reading while I ate, since that made the meal seem less lonely.

Again I remembered Marcus O'Neill's words. I wasn't "so young" that I didn't understand about the anniversaries connected with death. I'd already gone through the phase of "one week ago today . . ." and "one month ago," "two months ago." I could understand that the year's anniversary of a death would be painful. But Marcus had used the word "dangerous." Why? I didn't believe his answer. I didn't altogether believe his reason for coming to see me. That my father was troubled by a heart problem was undoubtedly true and must be considered. Yet I'd sensed there was something else worrying Marcus that he hadn't touched on and that I didn't in the least understand.

Tonight oyster stew would do for my supper, and when I sat down to eat I placed the orchid from Key West beside my place. How beautiful it was in all its tiny detail, how delicate—and somehow artificial as well. Orchids had never been my favorite flower, and I found it impossible to imagine the sister named Fern who had sent this to me.

Tonight I didn't feel like reading. All the questions I'd been holding back had surged up, brought to the surface by Marcus O'Neill. I knew very well what I must do before another night went by. This was something I'd postponed for too long.

When I'd rinsed my dishes, I went upstairs to Mother's front room. Between looped organdy curtains I could see the water, though our house was not on its edge. Few lights shone on the bay, and except for a street lamp, the night was thick and dark, the sky clouding over. "Weather" blowing in.

Key West was an island too, but it was the tropics. At this time of year the climate should be perfect. A relief from the long winter we'd had in the North. Though spring was nearly here, and I hated to miss the first budding. There would be dogwood, azaleas, lilacs, and flowering cherry. In Key West— palm trees!

Enough, I told myself sternly. No more dreaming. I went to my mother's desk and sat down. One side drawer held an envelope marked with my name. I hadn't been willing to read what was inside until now. These weren't business papers, but something more personal. I had taken the sheets out only once, to find a long letter, handwritten, the lines sometimes wavering across the pages because of her tremor. I'd put it away quickly, not ready to face the pain it would bring when I read it.

Now I followed the words all the way through twice, and then I carried the sheets into my own room and sat down in my favorite reading chair, turning on no lights. This must be a time for quiet thinking, for reorienting. "Truths" that I'd believed in all my life might not be true, after all, and that was both shocking and hard to accept.

My father, it seemed, had sent money for my support until I was through college. Mother had refused alimony, but she'd never told me where the fund came from. Anger began to stir in me—futile anger, because there was no outlet for it.

Her bitterness against him had never faded, and it showed beneath every word of her letter. At least she had tried to be honest with me, even though it came too late. In words that wavered on the page she'd confessed to the terrible bargain she'd made with my father. He'd been infatuated—"be-witched" by that "awful woman from Key West"—and he had wanted a divorce so he could marry her. My mother's marriage to Clifton York had not been a good one—probably a mistake from the first, for all that she'd loved him so deeply. Yet she would have clung to it if he had been willing to stay.

She told him that she would divorce him on one condition. He must never try to see or get in touch with his daughter again. At that point in her writing my mother's words had tumbled raggedly across the paper with a touch of hysteria. She saw now that this had been a cruel pact as far as I was concerned. She'd felt that she must protect me from the man my father had turned into—she had fooled herself with this argument. But with her own death so near, she had to tell me the truth, make me understand that what she had done had supposedly been for my good. Cliff had let me go when he made his choice. He had let me go deliberately, choosing the woman named Poppy over Janet, his wife, and Laurel, his flesh-and-blood daughter.

My hand shook as I held the letter. When had either one tried to see the viewpoint of a small, abandoned daughter, who had grown into a woman who still felt rejected? I wasn't sorry for myself—I was just angered by these two blind, stubborn people who had injured me and taken away my own birthright.

I would forgive my mother, of course. I was already stronger than she had been. But how could I forgive my father, and why should I ever want to see him again? Why should there be this sense of yearning for something I'd never known and could never possibly have at this late date?

Just the same, those two whom I resented had felt something that had never touched me. I had never been in love like that. Not as Mother had loved Clifton York, or as he had loved the woman named Poppy. Perhaps until such a love happened to me, I couldn't judge either of them fairly. But I still had a right to my anger.

There was another terrible revelation in the letter. Nearly a year ago my mother had gone away for a week—ostensibly to visit an old friend in Tennessee. By that time she knew she was going to die, and she went to Key West without telling me. In the end she hadn't seen my father because he wouldn't see her. Another score against him! Poppy had just died, and he was too depressed, too distraught to see his first wife. Alida Burch, who was my father's secretary, had talked to my mother. Mrs. Burch had said that everything was too upset in the house, and it would be better if she came another time. The secretary was apparently a strong, determined woman, and my mother couldn't deal with her in her own weakened state.

I switched on a lamp beside my chair and read this part of the letter again.

> I saw no one else, but I knew there was something terribly wrong in that house. I caught several hints of it. That woman's death—not even I could wish her such a way of dying—had shaken them all. Mrs. Burch couldn't be rid of me fast enough.

Of course I never tried again. I don't have that kind of courage, and I lacked the strength to make another trip.

She'd had plenty of courage to go there at all. Her one hope must have been to mend some of the damage she had caused between me and my father. Probably hopeless in the first place. She had her own blame, but part of it lay with him. He hadn't needed to hold to so cruel a pact forever. He could have broken it at any time in later years—if he had really wanted to. Nor could I forgive him the unkindness of refusing to see my mother, when she had come all that distance.

I got up and rummaged in my desk for an album of snapshots. In one of them Clifton York held me in his arms—a far younger man than the author on the book jackets, dark-haired and smiling. My arms were wound tightly about his neck—a loving picture. While I couldn't remember him except in the vaguest way, I had a sense of enfolding warmth when I looked at the snapshot; an illusion of security that I'd never felt in my growing-up years as the daughter of a father who had rejected me so completely.

At the very end she had written one line that burned in my mind: *Go to see him, Laurel. You'll need him now, and perhaps he needs you.*

I slept very little that night, and sometimes in those long, tossing hours, I thought not about the father I couldn't remember, but of the younger man, Marcus O'Neill, who had so suddenly upset my life. With my eyes closed, I could see him all too vividly. His fiery hair with a slight curl to it, the gray-blue eyes that looked through me and seemed to find me wanting, the mouth that could smile almost tenderly as he stroked the fur of a cat. The images in my mind sharpened an awareness I didn't welcome, tantalizing and much too provocative.

I still wasn't sure what I would tell him in the morning, and it was nearly daylight by the time I fell asleep.

When I opened the bookshop well ahead of Stan, I found Marcus O'Neill waiting for me on the sidewalk.

"I won't keep you long," he said, following me through the door. "I have a plane to catch at LaGuardia, and friends are driving me there." He nodded toward a car waiting at the curb. "I won't ask you questions you aren't ready to answer. Here's my address, and I hope you'll write when you make up your mind. There's a phone number there too."

He was brusque, hurried, and he seemed to have a faculty for taking the wind out of my sails. Whatever I might have said flew out of my mind because he gave me no time to say it. In one sweep he'd postponed everything, and all but dismissed me.

For a moment longer he stood looking about the shop, while Ernest, recognizing him as a friend, came and rubbed his head against a trouser leg.

Then the same watercolor he'd noticed before seemed to catch Marcus O'Neill's eyes, and he was suddenly in less of a hurry. He moved closer to look up at it—the painting of a Bellport house with a white picket fence. My name was in one corner, and this time he found it.

"You painted this? Is it for sale?"

I had sold some of my pictures through the shop, and I nodded hesitantly.

"It strikes a chord," he said. "You'll understand why if you come to Key West. I'd like to buy it and take it with me."

I wasn't entirely pleased. There's always a pang when I part with work that holds so much of me. In this case, he would show it to my father—leaving me altogether vulnerable. Yet I couldn't refuse Marcus's request, and a small defiant voice at the back of my mind whispered, *Let him take it! Let him show Clifton York that he has another daughter!*

I wrapped the framed picture for him in corrugated paper and sealed it with brown tape. When he'd tucked it under his arm, he stood for a moment at the door.

"You could fly to Miami, and I'd meet you there with my car. There's an airport on the island, but you'd need to change planes to reach it. Key West is pretty special, and if you come, you should get the feeling of it first by the drive over the keys. Thanks for letting me talk with you, Laurel. You may not need your father now, but he needs you more than even he realizes. So I hope you'll come." He looked suddenly thoughtful—not very happy—and I realized again that something he hadn't told me was troubling him.

When he went off, moving with a quick assurance that seemed typical, he left the shop quiet in his wake. Too quiet, too empty, too filled with books instead of life.

I wasn't accustomed to indecision, to wavering back and forth. I'd always been able to make up my mind to do whatever had to be done. In fact, I was better known for behaving impulsively than for waiting to make judicious moves.

When Stan came into the shop, he took one look at my face and sighed. "You're going, aren't you? I was afraid of that. Well—I suppose you'd better get it out of your system. Then maybe you'll come home and we can settle a few things."

"I'm not burning any bridges," I told him. "My father has a bad heart, and I'd better try to see him in time. I shouldn't be gone very long."

It was a hard day to get through because of Stan's disapproval and my own wavering state of mind.

I waited until evening and then called the number Marcus had left with me. He had arrived back home and answered the telephone. I would come to Key West, I told him, and would let him know the date and time of my plane to Miami as soon as I made my reservations. It would be April by then.

He said, "That's fine, Laurel. I'll tell Cliff you're coming. Of course he'll want you to stay at the house."

That, I felt, was something to leave open, but before I could object, Marcus had rung off. I wondered if his abruptness was a way of leaving me no choice.

Just the same, I felt a strange exhilaration because I'd taken the first step toward meeting my father and entering a world that seemed totally new and exotic to my northern eyes. Clifton York might very well hate my coming, but I'd have to take that risk. For him I could only belong to an unhappy time that was past. For me—? How was I to know until I met him?

Perhaps what I'd said to Stan wasn't true. Perhaps I really would be burning my bridges. The idea brought a certain excitement in spite of my doubts. I was still angry about a lot of things—and I wanted to be. I had some debts to pay off. But I was ready now to savor as well, to taste and experience. I didn't altogether mind the scent of smoke rising from those bridges.

2

On the way to Miami I felt more fully alive than I could ever remember being, and I was eager to meet head-on whatever experiences lay ahead of me. Yet there were still butterflies and a good many uneasy questions.

Part of my uneasiness concerned Marcus O'Neill. He was the one link with my father, but I'd felt some hostility between us, and I didn't know what to expect now. I mustn't let my imagination take off when it came to meeting my father and two half sisters. And I must never forget the hurt to my mother, the indifference toward me. And let Marcus make what he would of that.

He was waiting in the terminal when I came off the plane, and I saw him before he saw me. He stood apart from a group that was meeting our flight, and his height and red hair made him stand out from any crowd. He looked much too somber, I thought, and his very expression added to my uncertainty.

When I reached him he greeted me gravely. "Hello, Laurel. I was wondering if you might back out at the last minute."

So he meant to go right on challenging me.

"I don't back out of things," I told him evenly.

He steered me toward the baggage area, where we waited for my suitcase to come through, exchanging the usual uninspired comments about the flight down. I listened more to what he wasn't saying than to his words, and my conviction grew that matters weren't going well in Key West—there was some kind of trouble. So perhaps there would be no welcome for me there at all.

When my bags appeared on the conveyor belt, Marcus picked them up and led the way outdoors into balmy Florida sunshine. Today, in light slacks and a green shirt with an open collar to accommodate the climate, he looked more easygoing.

"This is your father's car," he explained as he let me into the passenger seat of a blue Mercedes. "Mine's having problems at the moment."

We drove into Miami traffic, heading south, and I was sharply aware of the man beside me. I knew so little about him, and I sensed so much that was unsettling. His long, tanned hands relaxed comfortably on the wheel, and the driver's seat had been pushed well back to allow for his stretch of long legs. I was more conscious of him than I wanted to be.

Since I'd had lunch on the plane, there was no need to stop, and we drove toward Homestead, the last town before the keys. It would be at least an hour before we reached the first key, and I tried to formulate the questions that kept seething up in me. In the face of Marcus's continued silence, I finally burst out with the uppermost question.

"How does my father feel about my coming?"

Marcus glanced at me and then back at the road. "Why don't you just relax for now, and I'll tell you all about everything later. We're going to follow a pretty interesting road, and you ought to know something about it."

Clearly it would be useless to push him, and even though the questions still seethed, I tried to listen as he talked about the Overseas Highway to Key West. The flat, sandy landscape and endless palm trees flowed past the car window.

It would be a drive of several hours, he told me, since the keys stretched more than a hundred miles along a reef that separated the Gulf of Mexico from the Atlantic Ocean. The island of Key West was at the tip of the "scorpion's tail" that curved into waters where ocean and gulf met in swirling currents.

"A lot of the highway is built over water," Marcus said. "Though I wish I'd been around when the keys weren't connected with bridges. The way into Key West used to be only by boat. Just the same, the highway is a miracle in its own right."

His voice warmed as he told me the story—a voice that carried color and vibrancy, and I found myself once more listening to its sound as well as to his words.

The reason the Overseas Highway existed at all, he said, was because of one man's obsession. Long before this project, Henry Flagler had built a railroad to open Palm Beach. Later he determined to run the tracks all the way down the keys to isolated little Key West—a gigantic undertaking that took years of planning before a single piling was put in. Everything had to be brought in by boat at first, and there were endless complications and disasters.

"A lot of people said he was crazy, but Flagler paid no attention. Obsessions never count the cost. In a way, I suppose he was running a race with time because he wanted to see his railroad completed in his own lifetime. He brought in hundreds of workers to build huge concrete pilings and bridges from key to key, and a good many of those men died during the years of construction. There were accidents, explosions, hurricanes. They called the railroad Flagler's Folly in those days, and it lasted for just twenty-three years.

"In 1912 when the first train whistle sounded in Key West, the whole town went crazy. There are pictures of that celebration. I remember one of a little girl handing Henry Flagler a bouquet of flowers, and there are tears on his cheeks."

"Why did it last only twenty-three years?"

"In 1935 the eye of a huge hurricane struck Islamorada in the Matecumbe Keys. Some people say Matecumbe is a corruption of the Spanish *Mata Hombre,* or 'Kill Man,' and the keys lived up to their name. A big section of the railroad was swept away, and more than five hundred lives were lost. There was never a true count, because so many bodies were never found. It's not a story the real estate people like to tell."

"Couldn't the railroad be repaired?"

"It never really paid off. In fact, it nearly bankrupted Flagler and his partners. So no one had the money—no one wanted to save it. But on its roadbed, and over all those bridges with their Roman arches, the Overseas Highway was built. Here we go, Laurel—the first bridge!"

Listening to Marcus's voice, I'd been able to put my concerns aside for a time, and now I felt a stirring of excitement. This wasn't just a road we traveled—it was part of a fascinating history, and I was glad that Marcus had given me this glimpse.

"In the beginning," he went on, "the road was only two lanes wide all the way. It's still that in places. They used to call it Death Alley because there were no shoulders, no turnoffs. If a car came over from the other side, there was no way to escape a crash, and there were accidents. Now it's being widened and a parallel road built, so each can be one-way. Though there's still not much room, especially on the bridges."

The world seemed to have widened around us, turning into

a far-reaching immensity of seascape and sky that was strange to me—overwhelming and oppressive. The green land areas were tiny by comparison and seemed at the mercy of both water and windy sky.

At first, before the first bridge, a sea of grass washed the banks below the road. Tidal creeks, really, since I could glimpse water shining underneath in the sun. There were mangrove swamps on either hand, with black roots twisting beneath beautiful dark green growth that seemed mysterious—places that would hold no human foot, and never gave up their secrets. The expanse of blue sky, the green and blue shading of the water on both sides, began to seem overpowering. For me, this was a strange, unknown world that both stirred and disturbed me.

On some of the keys little towns had been built, catering to the needs of tourists for lodging and food, for boating and fishing and swimming. The towns seemed nondescript, with the same gas stations, restaurants, motels, and neon signs that covered most of America. I preferred the wild, mysterious stretches in between, even though they made me uneasy.

Marcus must have sensed something of my feeling. "This is the road to an outpost. It's what's waiting at the far end that counts. But you need to get the feeling of its isolation first. There's been a lot of drug running along this road betweeen Key West and the mainland, and a few years ago the U.S. Government set up a blockade. Every car that went through was stopped, and you can imagine what that did to the tourist trade. It's already a long trip, and while the blockade was in effect, many people gave up coming in by car. But Key Westers don't take things like that lying down."

"What could they do?"

He laughed, remembering. I hadn't heard him laugh before,

and the sound made me shiver. *Watch it,* I told myself. *Don't start being attracted to this man!*

"The island declared itself the Conch Republic and seceded from the United States. With celebrations and declarations and pronouncements! Key West loves parties, and they did this to a turn. The blockade was lifted and everything quieted down again. I still have one of the passports to the Republic they issued at the time."

He'd given me a map to follow, and as we drove through, I picked out names: Key Largo (shades of Bogie and Bacall!); Islamorada, where the hurricane had struck; Marathon, a sandy little Florida town. And after that the Seven Mile Bridge. There'd been other bridges carrying us from key to key, some of them quite long, and once we passed a forlorn stretch where arched railroad pilings stood abandoned in the water, by-passed by the modern highway. The bridges were more frequent now, and there was more water—the distance to Key West lessening by the moment.

All my uneasiness swept back. "Tell me what to expect," I said. "How do they feel about my coming? How does my father feel? I won't be put off any longer—I have to know."

He sighed. "All right. I have been putting this off, but now we're nearly there, so let's stop for coffee, and we'll talk awhile. I know how full of questions you must be, but I don't know all the answers you'll want, Laurel. Anyway, there's a place on the next key, and we'll take a break."

I was glad to get out of the car and stretch my legs. At the restaurant we sat at a small table in an airy room with ceiling fans overhead and pots of tropical foliage all around. I asked for tea and a muffin, and waited for Marcus to tell me the worst.

"The only way you can deal with whatever comes is a step at

a time," he warned. "Don't rush in and try to take charge, or fix things up that don't please you."

I sputtered indignantly. "I'm not like that!"

"I hope you're not." His slight smile told me he was trying once more to get under my skin. Then he sobered. "I'd really rather not hand you my ideas and prejudices about the situation at your father's house. At least not in the beginning. I'd rather hear what you think, once you get some idea of what's going on. Something is, I'm afraid, and in some ways perhaps you can do more in the situation than I can. For one thing, you'll be inside the house. And if your father begins to like and trust you, who knows what can happen?"

"What if I don't like or trust him? Perhaps that's even more likely. I may take one look and run. I've had misgivings ever since I left New York."

"The first thing you said to me in Miami was that you don't back out of things."

"I was bragging. I do feel excited and curious—but maybe a little scared too. You haven't helped much when it comes to letting me know what I'm getting into. I'm even wondering why I came."

"You came because your father isn't well, and you'd never forgive yourself if you didn't see him in time. That's reason enough."

"That's part of it, but there's more, isn't there? I wish you wouldn't treat me like an idiot. Even back in New York, I felt there was a lot you weren't telling me. If my father doesn't want to see me, then everything will be even worse than it was before."

"That's a risk you have to take. He hasn't said he didn't want to see you. When I told him I meant to bring you to Key West, there were tears in his eyes."

I didn't want to be reached too quickly. My defenses were still up. "Tears are easy. I've shed a few myself and I don't think they change very much."

I wished that the very thought of my father didn't waken an angry, defensive hope in me. The old contradictions still tore me apart. "What did he say?" I added.

Marcus regarded me over his coffee cup, and again I had that feeling of being looked through too clearly. "What Cliff said was, 'I hope she's as strong as her mother. But softer too.'"

That made me wince. There was still more—something he held back. Something he wanted of me that he wasn't ready to explain.

"I haven't come to fight for anything," I told him.

"In that case, you're going to disappoint me." He studied me again, and I decided that his eyes were not, after all, the gray-blue of the bay at home, but the greenish blue color of the gulf waters on the way to Key West. Why on earth should I think about the color of his eyes, when I didn't really like him —or want to like him?

"Disappointing you doesn't matter to me very much," I said. "I still don't know why I'm here."

He seemed to think about that. "There's something—a sort of angry vitality about you. A quality you may be able to use to help your father. I suspect you're stubborn too, and I suppose that's what I'm hoping for—help for him. I think he needs it pretty desperately, and I don't think his other daughters are of much use to him right now. In fact, they're part of his trouble."

"I suppose it's my sisters who don't want me to come?"

"Feelings of suspicion on their part would be natural enough. After all, you're being thrown at them suddenly, and they're not going to open their arms right away. Though Fern did send you that orchid. Mainly it's Iris who has set herself against your coming. This time Cliff has overruled her."

"Why didn't you tell me before that they didn't want me?"

"Would you have come if I had? Anyway, it doesn't matter. For once, Cliff stood up to Iris as he hasn't done since Poppy died."

"Because you urged him to?"

"Occasionally he listens to me. Of course I still don't know how much of a mistake I may be making. As I told you, Iris plans to marry. It's a marriage that Poppy opposed and Cliff still favors."

"That sounds as though you hope he'll change his mind. Why was Poppy against it?"

"For one thing, Derek Phillips is a lot older than Iris—fifty-two to her twenty-four. Derek runs one of the popular bars in Key West—the Banyan Tree, or Derek's Place, as people call it. He's made a pile of money over the years and spent a lot too. Iris has an inheritance from her mother, as well as what Cliff will leave her, so Derek's money doesn't matter. Since Poppy came from an old Key West family, there was a lot of cigar money there, and in later years it was banking money. Right now Derek's engaged in something Poppy hated—treasure hunting in sunken wrecks."

"He sounds like an adventurer."

"Adventurers are a dime a dozen in Key West. Though I think it was mainly his treasure fever that upset Poppy. At least, that's what she claimed. She didn't want that for Iris."

"What do you mean—what she claimed?"

Marcus seemed to shy away from the question and went on talking about Derek Phillips.

"He's done everything, been everywhere. Africa, the Orient, South America. He even conducted a spectacular rescue mission in Laos, and another one in Africa—along with several mercenaries, ex-Green Berets. Successful but dangerous. He takes big risks and men were killed. He doesn't lose easily or settle for what's conventional. He's powerful—and not all that scrupulous."

"And you don't like him, do you? You don't want him either for Iris?"

"I'm not part of the family," Marcus said stiffly.

"And my father admires this man?"

Marcus hesitated. "Sometimes I think Cliff sees him as a character out of one of his novels—heroic and capable of dangerous, dramatic action. He and Derek have been friends from way back. Derek was away for a long while and returned to Key West only a few years ago. Iris had grown up by that time, and she seemed to fascinate him. She's a fascinating young woman."

I'd begun to pick up something. Whenever Marcus spoke Iris York's name, his voice took on a special concern.

"Tell me about Iris," I said.

"She's beautiful. Intelligent. Very capable too. She deserves better than Derek."

I wondered if there'd been a time when Marcus O'Neill might have wanted to marry Iris himself, but I wasn't going to ask.

"When will the wedding take place?"

"Nothing's been set. Right now Derek's involved in a wild project that may even pay off. For the first time, he may have found an important shipwreck. It's what they call a 'new' wreck, since no one's registered it before. So he'd have salvage rights. Laws have been changing, and I'm not sure where he stands right now."

"Was this a recent wreck?"

"If it's the ship he hopes for, she went down more than three hundred years ago."

"A Spanish galleon!"

"It's possible. He's found two cannons that may identify the ship when he gets them up. The archives in Seville indicate that it might be the *Santa Beatriz.*"

I loved to swim, and I'd done some scuba diving off Long Island, but never in tropical waters. If this was really a seventeenth-century galleon . . . ! I could feel prickles at the back of my neck.

"Watch it! You've got that treasure fever look in your eyes. It can be catching."

"Why not? It sounds exciting. It would be wonderful to dive down and explore an old wreck. Do you suppose I could?"

"The weather hasn't been right for diving, so we haven't done much lately. But the season's opening up and the ocean's a bit quieter now. However, Derek might not want you coming down. Nobody except his own divers is sure what he's found. Treasure hunters are a secretive lot."

"You said 'we.' You're a diver?"

"Amateur. Research for Cliff. He arranged it for me with Derek." Marcus spoke casually, but I had a feeling that he was excited about this wreck too.

"Tell me what it was like. Diving must be completely different down here. What did you find?"

"There wasn't much to see when I've been down—that's the trouble. There's part of a ship's anchor, and the two cannons that have been found so far. Also ballast stones—which are always a good indicator of where a ship went down. Tons of sand have been burying what's there for centuries, and there may be few signs of the ship left."

"Did she sink out in the Gulf Stream?"

"No. The Stream is deep enough to navigate safely. It's when a ship got blown off course that it could be wrecked on a reef."

"How did he find the wreck?"

"A couple of well-known treasure hunters, Mel Fisher, working off Key West, and Kip Wagner, at Vero Beach, have had spectacular success. These days the magnetometer is used. It's an iron detector, so part of the anchor that hadn't corroded away was located by the needle. You tow this contraption back and forth across the water until you get a reading. Unfortunately, it won't detect gold. None of the gold detectors have been sensitive enough to work at any distance. Anyway, Derek found the anchor. If this is the *Santa Beatriz,* the find could be spectacular."

"Historically, you mean?"

"That's what's important. I hope Derek recognizes this. Treasure hunters can do a lot of damage to artifacts if their only concern is gold and silver."

"Why hasn't the wreck been discovered before this?"

"There are thousands of wrecks scattered across the bottom of the ocean. Some will never be found because the water and sand are too deep. Mel Fisher developed a way to blow the sand off and uncover what remains of a shipwreck. A recent storm probably helped to uncover what Derek found. Mel has established the Mel Fisher Maritime Heritage Society—something that may do for underwater archeology what the Cousteau Society has done for sea life."

A new world was opening for me, and I knew I'd have to do some diving to Derek's wreck, if I could.

"Anyway," Marcus went on, "all this treasure hunting is why Derek hasn't time to get married right now."

"You mean treasure hunting comes ahead of love?"

"Iris wants it that way too. It's important to Derek." Marcus didn't sound sorry about the delay.

"Are you going to write about all this?" I asked.

"I want to—if Derek will let me. I'm only an apprentice adventurer. My job's to get the story down on paper."

His voice had quickened with an excitement of its own, though Marcus's "treasure" would be different from Derek's.

"What about Fern? How does she fit into all this?"

He hesitated and I sensed a new reluctance. "You'll understand better when you see her. In a way, she's one of your father's main problems. He worries about her a lot. Fern has always been everyone's pet, but now she's lost her mother, and she'll lose her sister to marriage. She's impulsive and not always sensible, and we're all concerned about her. It's a good thing Poppy had her orchids and taught her daughters to care for them. Fern has that, at least, to keep her busy."

"You said she actually grew that orchid she sent me—do you mean they raise orchids themselves?"

"Not commercially. Poppy had a greenhouse built out behind their home. Her home, really, since she belonged to an old Conch family that owned it from way back." He saw my questioning look and sighed again. "You'd better understand about the Conchs before you set foot in Key West. If you've finished your tea, we can get going, and I'll tell you on the way."

We returned to the car, and during the rest of the journey I learned about Conchs.

"I do know," I told him. "I know about those big shells found in the tropics."

"Sea snails live in the shells," Marcus said, "and they're pretty tough creatures. You'll meet them in every possible manner from now on. You'll eat them ground up in stews and fritters and other Key West dishes. You'll find the shells decorating doorsteps, and you'll hear them blown on at sunset. There's a Conch Train for tourists, and of course Conch houses and Conch people, since that's the name that was given to the tough early settlers. It's still used for those who are born there."

"A lot of them came from the Bahamas, didn't they?"

"Yes. When there was trouble in the islands, some of the settlers moved to Key West. They're from Cuba too, from Virginia, and sometimes after a shipwreck they came from almost anywhere. There were a great many shipwrecked passengers who'd had enough of sea travel and settled on the island to watch it grow. Since Poppy was a Conch for generations back, so are Iris and Fern. There are even 'honorary Conchs.' Tennessee Williams was made one. There's a phrase they use that I like—'beloved stranger.' Your father has lived here long enough to be given that name. Another term, 'Freshwater Conch,' isn't flattering."

This time Marcus had said "here." Without my being aware of it, we'd crossed the last bridge and were in Key West, following a boulevard that ran along the gulf. The island was three and a half miles long, and a mile wide. Only a mile's width of land separated the Gulf of Mexico from the Atlantic Ocean—alarming when one considered hurricanes. The whole place could be wiped out with one big tidal wave, it seemed to me, and it was so small that it would be lost in a corner of Long Island.

The time was late afternoon, and the sun was well down in the sky by this time. My first reaction was one of disappointment. I'd expected something more foreign to America and the rest of Florida, something more exotic. Here were the usual commercial buildings and a jungle of signs, wires, poles, and palm trees, edging the road. Sand. Flatness. That was the thing that had struck me especially about the keys—how flat everything was, how close to sea level. Yet here the island had stood, back into dim history. Except for the Indians, I knew the first settlement was fairly recent—in the 1800s.

The boulevard narrowed into Truman Avenue. President Truman had made Key West his vacation White House during his years in office, and there were many Truman reminders.

The road had narrowed still more. "We're in Old Town now," Marcus said. "Or Conch Town, as some people call it. This is the real Key West. This is where it began."

It was hard to believe what I was seeing. The commercial aspects had vanished. Each side of the street was lined with white clapboard houses and white picket fences. The illusion of New England was startling, but I began to see the differences quickly. Lush tropical growth filled the gardens, and wide southern verandas graced many of the houses—though I was to learn that the word "porch" was used here. Along the sides, louvered shutters were propped open to let in air. Gables and towers abounded, as well as a great deal of Victorian gingerbread. Large rambling houses rubbed elbows with small shabby ones. Some of the structures were topped with captain's walks, and most of them had what Marcus called "scuttles" in the roofs to let out warm air rising from the lower floors. These were houses that could be opened to every breeze that blew in from ocean or gulf. I saw fewer chimneys than at home, which made another difference. Yet the similarities were still striking, and it would be fun to sketch some of these houses and catch both likeness and difference.

"Now I know why my Bellport watercolor caught your eye," I said. "What did you do with it?"

He smiled. "You'll see."

"Tell me about these houses. How do they happen to be here?"

"Most of the old conch houses are wooden. They were built by ship's carpenters who could be as whimsical as they chose. A lot of the architecture was borrowed from the Bahamas, where people knew how to live with tropical heat. But some of the builders were remembering New England too, and the South. Old Town looks like a simple enough, square-set area, but you'll find there are mazes of alleys and tiny lanes that confuse a stranger. And not all of them are pleasant places to wander in. But there's nothing quite like it anywhere else."

His enthuasiasm for his adopted town came through. Now he pointed. "There's your father's house—ahead on the right."

I studied the house we approached, and butterflies started up again. I dreaded all the uncertainty that lay ahead of me.

The house was large, with wide porches and balusters below and above. A tower with a pointed roof rose at one corner, and slim white pillars supported porch ceiling and roof, all edged with still more fanciful gingerbread trim. These steeply pitched roofs, Marcus explained, had once sent rain pouring into cisterns that furnished the only source of water for the islanders until the pipeline came in forty years ago. Above the attic floor a captain's walk with a white railing crowned the roof.

"Captain's walks were useful," Marcus said. "In the beginning the main business of the islands was what they called 'wrecking.' People watched for shipwrecks from housetops, because of the salvage value."

The house he indicated was set farther back from the street than its neighbors, and the front garden was alive with what looked to me like jungle growth. A huge banyan tree spread its roots in one corner, and a breadfruit tree grew in the other. In between, a riot of red, pink, and purple decorated bushes and vines. I was no longer reminded of New England, and both my sense of excitement and my anxiety increased.

When he'd pulled up to the curb, Marcus put a hand lightly on my arm. "Don't expect too much right away."

I must expect nothing, I told myself sternly.

The sun had slipped toward the gulf, and shadows were long when we left the car.

"I'll take you in and stay a few minutes to see how things are going," Marcus told me. "My place isn't far away. You can call me any time."

I hadn't expected to be abandoned so quickly, and my misgivings increased.

"Take it easy," he said, and then spoiled what I thought was concern with his next words. "Don't be upset if things don't go your way."

I was already upset, but the white gate stood open, and Marcus went ahead up the walk, carrying my bags. Since conch houses were raised from the ground on piers to save them from dampness and flood, several steps climbed between white balustrades. A graceful fanlight topped the front door, and long windows with open green shutters fronted on a stretch of porch that ended at the bulge of the tower.

As we reached the steps, a woman came through the door, and Marcus murmured, "Iris," in my ear.

She was tall and dark and cool. The simple lines of her lime green linen set off her figure beautifully. Great dark eyes and a creamy tan with just a hint of rose at the cheekbones—all added up to striking beauty. Her long black hair was drawn back from her forehead and folded close to her head with a severity that only such dramatic beauty could support. I was aware of the contrast with my short, windblown crop that was quickly untidy. Her mouth seemed generous in size—something her lipstick emphasized—but there was no generously welcoming smile lifting its corners. She watched my approach as though she stood apart, remaining remote. If she had any curiosity about me, she was certainly hiding it.

I thought, *my sister*, and felt nothing—nothing at all—which in itself was chilling.

"Hello, Iris," Marcus said, putting my bags down on the porch. "This is Laurel."

She held out a cool hand to me, and as I stood beside her, not quite as tall but just as dark, I felt suddenly hot and dowdy and provincial. A silly and unjustified reaction. My suit was fine for travel, but not for the tropics, and that could be taken care of from my suitcase. No, it wasn't my clothes or my background that made me uncomfortable. I'd probably seen more of New York than she had, and I owned and ran a successful bookstore. So why should she make me feel at such a loss as her dark eyes considered me?

"I'll show you your room," Iris said. "Will you bring up Laurel's bags, please, Marcus."

The central hall was narrow, borrowing no space from the gracious rooms I glimpsed on either side, and a pine staircase rose on the left. Marcus had told me that most of these houses had used pine, brought from the mainland, with some of the mahogany from Honduras.

The halls were bare of rugs—one didn't clutter a house in the tropics—and Iris's heels clicked ahead of us up the stairs and down the upper hall to a door at the rear that stood open.

I looked in to see a charming bedroom, but before I could step in Marcus stopped me in the hall.

"Is this where you mean to put Laurel?" he asked, and I

heard surprise in his voice. An awareness of the way he watched her struck me. There seemed affection in his look, but a questioning as well.

"Why not?" Iris's dark eyebrows lifted. "It's my favorite of our bedrooms."

Now I stepped in and looked around. Two louvered windows along the far side were open, and long, shuttered doors stood ajar upon a rear porch, so that a gentle flow of air stirred through the room. The walls had been left in their natural pine, with a pleasing result. A four-poster bed was covered by a white spread with a flowered border of Chinese poppies. These were not the little poppies of California, but more exotic opium poppies, with their deeper, purplish red.

Suddenly I knew.

"This was my mother's room," Iris said gently. "You won't mind?"

I met her eyes directly—and held them. "Thank you," I said. "It's a lovely room."

"Will you stay for dinner?" Iris asked Marcus. "Angela's in a good humor today, so we should fare well."

He shook his head. "Thanks, but I can't stay now. I've a date for an interview tonight. You'll be all right, Laurel?"

I sensed his hurry to escape, to get away, to leave me to whatever fate awaited me in this unwelcoming house, and I stared at him indignantly. He grinned, and I caught a hint of that challenge once more. He would throw me—to the wolves? —and find out later how I'd managed.

"I'll be fine," I told him stiffly.

"Of course you will. And I'll see you soon." He went off, leaving me in Iris's hands.

"Perhaps you'd like to rest awhile," she said. "The bath is just across the hall, and it will be mostly yours. Only Fern's room is at this end of the house. We're having dinner late tonight. Come downstairs in an hour or so and it will be fine."

"When will I see my father?" I asked quickly, before she could leave.

She widened dark eyes. "I suppose when he decides to see you," she said, and went away.

At least Poppy's belongings had been removed, so that except for the flowered spread the room was impersonal. Nevertheless, I believed that Iris had put me here deliberately to make me feel as uncertain as possible. I wouldn't satisfy her— or Marcus! My mother and I were the injured ones, and Poppy the interloper. Never mind about my sentimental notion of finding a sister. Even though this was her home, I had a prior claim to Clifton York, whether anyone else recognized it or not. Nevertheless, I found myself wondering about the woman who had slept in this room. Apparently apart from my father?

The mahogany bed, the rosewood dressing table, the two Chippendale chairs were all good pieces, though I didn't learn until later that many of the fine furnishings and collectible items in Key West had originally come from wrecked ships. Small rugs—squares of sea grass sewn together—lay across the floor, and gauzy curtains framed the windows.

On one wall hung three silver-framed color photographs of orchids. Two of them were vivid blooms in contrasting shades of yellow and lavender, rose and cream. The center picture was also of orchids, but strange, and not like the two simple flower photographs. A woman's long-fingered hands were clasped about the small pot that held a green and crimson orchid toward the camera. A spot of blue flashed from the sapphire ring on the woman's right hand. She herself was not visible, for a curious reason. Covering her head and face was a large replica of a green and crimson orchid patterned after the one in the pot, and probably made of papier-mâché. She was in some sort of fancy dress, undoubtedly, but as I looked closer I could see her eyes peering from the flower mask, staring eerily from among its petals. Eyes that had the quality of following the viewer. The woman could be Poppy York, I thought, and somehow I didn't like to have her staring at me from that weird disguise here in her room. I turned my head and went through a door onto a rear porch.

The sun had gone down, and night came swiftly. The area immediately below formed a bricked expanse that was now softly lighted. White iron tables and chairs invited one to rest and enjoy the garden. Behind the house, the space was larger and deeper than I'd expected from the street, and again there was the usual lush tropical growth that hid fences and other houses.

Here, however, the trees had been cut back to an outside rim so that the central space was left open to the sky—undoubtedly to give room for the long structure of the orchid greenhouse. Its pitched roof was made of plastic panes that could be propped open. Glass, of course, would have been too hot for Key West. Light glowed softly under the roof of paint-smeared panes, and topping the whole as an awning was stretched a black screen cloth.

I stood at the porch railing where I could look down, and as I watched, the door of the greenhouse opened and a woman stepped outside. She lifted her head at once and saw me. For a moment she seemed startled, and then, mysteriously, she put a finger to her lips and looked around.

"Come down here. Quickly!" Her whisper carried eerily through the quiet evening. "Come down the back stairs. And do hurry before someone sees us!"

I found the stairs and obeyed the urgency in her voice.

When I reached the garden I found her waiting near the door to the greenhouse, and now I could see her more clearly.

Fern was not at all like her sister, but more like a fragile orchid herself. The garment she wore was of some thin, floaty material of pale yellow, and her hair was a light, tawny brown, not dark like her sister's and mine. It curled thickly over her forehead and hung long down her back, caught carelessly at the nape with a gold ribbon that was coming untied. Her eyes that examined me openly were an odd golden brown as well— a shade darker than her hair. Everything about her seemed small and precise—her delicate features, her graceful, tapered hands, the small, sandaled feet on which she ran toward me.

For an instant I thought she would embrace me, but she stopped a foot or so away and peered into my face, as though she might be nearsighted.

"Isn't it strange that we're sisters and we've never met? I've been waiting for you ever since Marcus told me you were coming. I thought I'd feel something when I saw you. Something, oh—sisterly, I suppose. But I don't feel anything at all except curiosity. You're just someone new in the house." She sounded disappointed and much younger than her twenty-two years.

I found myself trying to reassure her. "It's too soon. We need to know each other better before we can feel like sisters." The reassurance was for myself as well, and I added, "Thank you for the lovely orchid you sent me."

"That was a hybrid dwarf I grew myself. I'm pleased if you liked it." She regarded me searchingly for a moment. "I'm really glad you look like Cliff, and not like her " She glanced toward the house, and I knew she meant her sister Iris. So there was rivalry here. "Why haven't you come before?" she added.

"Perhaps I've always wanted to come," I said, and wondered in surprise if this might be true. "Of course I could never come while either your mother or mine was alive."

"I understand." She looked pensive. "Marcus told us about your mother. I hope she died quietly, peacefully."

"She died in her sleep," I said. "And I was thankful when the pain could stop."

Fern gestured toward the greenhouse door, her draperies fluttering. "Poppy died in there, you know. Right in the midst of all her beautiful orchids. But it wasn't peaceful or quiet. It was frightful—terrible!"

Her eyes brimmed with tears, and I could offer nothing in sympathy, when I knew so little. Marcus had remarked that Poppy's death had been senseless, and he'd put me off when I'd asked about it. Nor did I feel I could ask now.

Fern brushed a streak of tears from her cheeks. "I still remember how excited the orchids were that day before she died. I think they knew."

I glanced at her quickly to see if she was serious. She caught the look and laughed lightly.

"Poppy taught me how to understand them. You have to work with orchids all the time and really care, before you can sense their feelings. They never tell Iris anything. She only wants to use them in her ways. But they're my orchids now. Poppy would want it that way. Would you like to see them, Laurel?"

She sounded older now and less childlike, and I wondered how much of her ingenuous quality was used as a pretense— perhaps even as a shield for childish prerogatives she still liked to use.

"I'd love to see your greenhouse," I said.

She corrected me quickly. "We don't call it a greenhouse.

It's our orchid house. Iris said I wasn't to bother you with them right away, but I don't always do what I'm told." Her sudden, sidewise look was impudent, a little wicked. She opened the door and drew me inside. "We try to keep the temperature right for our darlings. They like air circulation, indirect sunlight, and lots of moisture—the way it used to be in the jungle where their ancestors came from."

The walls of the structure were made of more plastic panes that could be opened, all covered on the inside by heavy wire. To keep out raccoons, Fern said.

A gentle stirring of air touched my face and I heard the purr of a fan. Three long rows of orchid plants grew in pots of various sizes set on shelves of open wooden slats, to allow for drainage. Other plants hung everywhere from supports.

Fern moved ahead of me like a yellow moth, lifting her arms as though they were wings, yet careful not to disturb any of the lovely orchids that grew on every hand in a bewildering array of color, shape, and fragrance. I hadn't known that some orchids had a distinctive scent.

"Poppy was especially interested in raising hybrids," she said, "and we've developed some unusual species. She'd register them and send them to shows all over the country. That's the nice thing about orchids—you can grow new types quite easily and have something original and different. These are cattleyas here—there are loads of species in that family, though they're not as popular as they used to be. They were the prom beauties that showed up at dances, and got pinned on guest speakers. I like vandas better—they're more exciting and exotic, and they can bloom all year round. See those deep violets and blues. And those down there that run to yellow and brown. Here's a new little beauty in pink and green—see that spray with eight blooms on it."

I was more interested in this newly discovered half sister than I was in the flowers that so delighted her. Again she seemed to me like one of her own delicately colored orchids as she moved among the plants, stopping here to compliment, to praise, even to chide—as though they could hear her. Perhaps they could, when their caretaker seemed so gentle and kind and was so wholly involved in their well-being.

However, I found that I could grow numb from the sheer extravagance and quantity of the orchids. There was too much to take in all at once.

Fern turned to me, suddenly grave. "Have you seen Cliff yet?"

"I asked Iris when I could see him, and she said when he decided that he wanted to see me."

"That sounds like her!" Fern tilted her head in a quick movement that set wisps of tawny curls dancing about her small gamine's face. "We don't have to listen, though, do we? I have you to help me now. To stand with me. If you like, I'll take you to see him right away."

She was moving too fast for me. I didn't want to be used as a buffer, and this seemed too sudden. He might not be ready to see me, and I didn't want to burst in on my father unannounced, even in the tow of this warmly generous younger sister who so wanted an ally of her own.

"First, I'll shower and change," I told her. "Perhaps later."

"Of course. Iris thinks I'm too impulsive. Anyway, I want to get ready now. Derek Phillips is coming to dinner tonight, and he's eager to meet you. Have you heard about Derek?"

"Marcus told me a little about him. And that he and Iris are going to be married."

Fern pursed her small mouth. "I don't see how he can stand an icicle like Iris! The trouble is, he thinks I'm just a child.

Everyone does. Don't be like that, Laurel—if we're to be sisters."

I smiled at her. "I'll remember."

She looked suddenly troubled. "Iris and I used to be close when Poppy was alive. We loved each other then. Now I can't trust her any more."

She came into the house with me, and up the stairs. At the door to my room she paused, shaking her head.

"They should never have put you in Poppy's room! I told Iris it wasn't fair."

"I don't mind," I said. "It really doesn't matter."

"Doesn't it? Oh, well, I suppose not. If you don't mind, that will put Iris's nose out of joint. Look—my room's right here across the hall. If you want anything, let me know." She opened her door and disappeared inside.

In her quick, light way, Fern had revealed a serious rivalry that existed between the sisters, and my sympathy was inclined toward Fern. But I must not get involved even in defense of this new sister, whom I liked. It was my father I'd come to see —my father I must face—and there was no need for taking sides when it came to the others in this house.

When I went into Poppy's room I knew at once that something had changed. As I looked around, I saw that the center photograph of the woman in the mask was gone from the wall. Only a picture hook remained. In a way, I felt relieved not to have those eyes following me while I moved about the room. Yet at the same time I wondered why that particular picture had been taken away.

For no clear reason the action made me faintly uneasy—so I might as well find out. I returned to the hall to tap on Fern's door.

3

Fern was still wearing her fluttery garment, but she'd pinned her hair into a curly mass on top of her head, so that she looked taller and less childlike. She read my puzzled expression at once.

"What's happened, Laurel?"

"Come and see," I said.

She ran ahead of me into the room and saw the empty place on the wall. "Where has the mask picture gone?"

"That's what I wondered. Someone seems to have moved it, though I don't suppose it matters."

She looked doubtful. "Perhaps it does. Perhaps we should move you to another room right away."

"Whatever for? What do you mean?"

"Maybe Iris is playing games. Don't let that icicle look of hers fool you. She put you in this room to torment you, and now she's moved that picture to upset you even more. She does things like that."

"It doesn't matter. I'm not upset."

Fern seemed to droop a little. "If only Poppy were here! She always knew what to do about Iris. Sometimes I wonder if

Poppy is watching us. Sometimes I think I can catch a glimpse of her. One afternoon in the orchid house I opened the door, and she was there—tending one of her favorite crosses of *Phalaenopsis*. It seemed as though she was there. She looked so sad that it broke my heart. But when I blinked, she was gone—so I couldn't be sure I really saw her. Maybe I only imagined it because I need her so badly."

I felt sad for this younger sister who felt the loss of her mother so deeply. We had that in common, but I didn't know how to deal with what she was telling me.

She fought back tears and went on. "The other time I saw her she was right down there in one of those white chairs where she loved to sit after sundown, when the garden grows shadowy. I just wanted to watch her, to know she was there, but that time she faded away even more quickly. Laurel, do you suppose a person can make something seem real just by imagining it?"

I ought to know, I thought ruefully, remembering my own vivid daydreams.

"I'm sure it's possible," I said. "Perhaps it helps us to drop back for a little while into the sort of make-believe we did as children. Sometimes it can be comforting. Just so we come back to what's real." That was something I was still trying to do.

"You do understand!" Fern's small face brightened. "You really do understand."

Emotion was too close to the surface, and I was afraid of what might happen if I ever let myself go.

Fern went to stand before the two remaining photographs. "Poppy took those pictures a few weeks before she died, and Iris had them framed and hung here. My mother was a very good photographer."

"What about the other picture?"

"That was taken a long time ago. Cliff took it. Poppy had dressed up for a masquerade, and she'd made that paper mask herself. I suppose it's still around somewhere. I was only about six and the mask scared me. It covered all of her head, just leaving her eyes so she could see out. And a place to breathe, of course. When she came to show me, I cried. I didn't think it was really my mother."

Fern broke off and stared at me.

"What if she's here in this room? Sometimes I can almost feel her here. Poppy used to say that I can see what other people can't. A secret gift, she called it. I don't know if I want to believe that. It's too scary. But the anniversary of her death is coming soon—and it makes me afraid."

I remembered Marcus's words about such anniversaries being dangerous. But he surely hadn't meant anything psychic.

Her eyes pleaded with me, and I tried to answer. "Once in a while I have a presentiment myself—perhaps precognition. I suppose most people do at times. But I don't know much about it. Perhaps you can teach me."

It was the right thing to say, and she surprised me with a quick kiss on my cheek, accepting me.

"You're not a bit like Iris," she said, and I knew it was a special compliment.

Both touched and bewildered by this younger sister, I stood watching in the doorway as she ran across the hall.

Just as she reached the door of her room, a sudden roar of laughter came soaring up the far stairs from the front of the house. Fern stopped, her hand on the doorknob. When she turned, I saw her face light with eagerness.

"That's Derek!" she cried. "Oh, good—he's come early!"

She flew along the hallway in her floating gown, once more resembling a yellow moth as she ran down the stairs.

Thoroughly troubled, I turned back to my room—not Poppy's room now. There had been no way to misread the look on Fern's face. My younger sister felt much too strongly about the man who would marry Iris. Perhaps this was a major source of the rivalry between them?

When I'd showered I put on a pleated white silk skirt, with a periwinkle top and a wide white belt that laced in front with blue thongs. As I dressed, I avoided looking at the orchid pictures. If it had really been Iris who'd moved the middle picture . . . But I mustn't jump to conclusions, as Fern seemed ready to do. The answer to why someone had seen fit to remove the picture would eventually turn up, and it probably wouldn't be anything important. People took pictures off the walls all the time.

I was about to go downstairs when someone rapped on my door. I opened it to a tall woman, probably in her mid forties, her gray hair cut close and sleek to her head—like an old John Held drawing from the twenties. Where everyone I'd seen on the streets of Key West had been brightly, casually dressed, this woman wore black. She seemed severely handsome, smooth-complexioned, with a hint of blush at her cheekbones, but no lipstick on her full mouth.

"Good evening, Miss York," she said formally. "I'm Alida Burch, Mr. York's secretary. Your father would like to see you, if you'll come to him. He doesn't plan to join the others for dinner tonight, so he can see you alone now, before you dine."

I wanted to see him—but I still wasn't prepared. Perhaps I never would be, so it was better to face him and get it over with.

Mrs. Burch walked with me to a flight of stairs that led to the attic floor and paused at their foot. "I was sorry to learn about your mother. I met her one time when she came to Key West nearly a year ago. I imagine she told you." Long dark lashes came down discreetly, and I murmured that I knew. Perhaps the time would come when I could ask more about my mother's visit.

The voices from the first floor had grown more subdued, and now I heard another sound. On the floor above, someone had started to play a piano softly, and I caught the light, quick measures of Scott Joplin.

"Your father's workroom is on the top floor," Mrs. Burch told me.

The stairs made a turn upward and opened into an enormous space that ran the width of the house. The pitched ceiling was probably well insulated, for the long room was cool. Portions of it had been broken into islands that simulated rooms in themselves, without being partitioned off. Near the top of the stairs stood a desk with a secretary's chair set before it and the components of a word processor arranged at one side. A handsome Chinese screen painted with pine trees and waterfalls shielded the desk from view of the far end and gave both my father and Alida Burch their private working areas.

It was the distant reaches of this upper room, however, that drew me. Gable windows would allow light and air to come through, and one of the scuttles Marcus had mentioned was propped open in the roof. Two ceiling fans stirred and I felt their pleasant breeze.

Mrs. Burch spoke in my ear. "Please be careful what you say. He isn't well, and this is a disturbing time."

As we started down the long room, my attention was fixed upon the far corner, where a man sat at a small upright piano, his fingers moving lightly on the keys. As we approached, it was as if my whole life until this moment had been reaching toward whatever was about to happen.

He didn't look around or acknowledge us. Behind him stretched a huge mahogany desk strewn with pages of yellow paper and piled with books. This was the heart of the house—the place where Clifton York had written all those wonderful suspense novels on which I'd grown up. I felt both excited and abashed, not only because this was my father, but because of the books as well.

Mrs. Burch stopped beside the piano. "Cliff, I've brought your daughter." The "Mr. York" she'd used with me had been formal, but she was an old friend to my father, as well as his secretary.

As he turned I wondered if he might feel as uncertain as I did. Perhaps that was why he'd continued to play, postponing the moment of our confrontation.

Now he stared at me in silence, his expression guarded. His dress was casual—a T-shirt and jeans. He seemed as handsome as his photographs, but he looked worn and considerably older. His hair, still dark and thick, showed only a streak or two of gray, and his eyes were dark as well—like Iris's, though the lids drooped, so that he'd lost the wide look of his younger pictures. At least the dramatic eyebrows were the same—heavily marked, with an upward curve at the outer edge. Rather dashing eyebrows, I'd always thought them. After all, they were my own as well!

When he'd stared long enough, while I tried not to blink, he left the piano and came toward me. I didn't know what to expect, but he merely gestured toward his desk, where a visitor's chair of red morocco stood near his own chair. When he'd seated me, he went to stand at one of the gable windows that looked out at the dark sky, his back to me.

All my early eagerness, even my doubts, had disappeared. I felt only a blank emptiness. What was happening was like none of the young fantasies I'd played out about meeting my father. Some had been angry fantasies, but all had been dramatic and not like this numbing reality.

Mrs. Burch went quietly away, and after a moment I heard the chatter of the word processor from behind the oriental screen at the far end of the room. The silence grew oppressive, embarrassing, but I wouldn't be the one to break it. He had asked me to come upstairs—so let him lead the way!

Pretending casual interest, I looked around this end of the big room and saw that it was lined with packed bookcases and shelves of art objects he must have collected in his research for many books. I recognized a vicious-looking spiked shell from the Caribbean that he'd chosen for a murder weapon in one novel, and a grinning little Chinese god from another. This would be a room to explore, if I ever were permitted—which didn't seem likely right now.

Among several framed pictures on the walls I was surprised to find the watercolor I'd painted of a white clapboard house in Bellport. Behind its picket fence the yard was orderly, and I'd painted the scene at azalea time, so red and pink blossoms flowered among the neatly trimmed green shrubs. Very different from the lush and tangled overgrowth of the tropics. I felt a twinge of homesickness that I shrugged away. I was here. This was the "elsewhere" I'd wanted, and I didn't mean to turn and run because this meeting with my father disappointed me. There were accounts to settle before I left, and I was relieved to find that his very silence could strengthen my resentment of everything he stood for in my life.

After a moment at the window, he returned to the chair behind his desk, moving as though he'd come to a decision.

Three white envelopes lay beside an old-fashioned typewriter, and he picked them up and handed them to me.

This was becoming a bit weird—his silence and odd actions —so that I took the envelopes reluctantly, not knowing what to expect. They had been postmarked and were still sealed. As I examined them my heart fell in dismay. The return address on each was Key West, and they were all addressed to me, the postmarks old. Across the face of each was written neatly in my mother's hand: *Return to sender.*

"You wrote to me?" I said, and my words sounded like a challenge.

"I tried. There were other letters I didn't keep. You can see what happened."

My hand shook as I set the envelopes on his desk. I didn't want to read his letters—it was too late. And far too late to be angry with my mother, though what she'd done made me feel a little sick.

"You know that she has died?" I managed.

He bent his head in assent. "Yes, I know. Were you very close? It's always hard to lose someone you love."

Sympathy? But I suspected that he was thinking of Poppy, not Janet, and I found myself resisting.

"I still have a few snapshots of you," he went on. "Taken when you were little—before I went away."

I had looked at those same pictures recently, and it hurt me to see them. How harsh and cruel divorce could be to the children suddenly left behind. Both parents had removed so much from my life—so what was left for him to give back to me now?

He went on, almost as if to himself. "We weren't right for each other—your mother and I. It was one of those young things that happened too fast. We were only the beginnings of people then. I knew sooner than she did that we'd made a mistake."

At least there was one question I could hint at. "I've never heard how you met."

His smile was for something in the past. "I expect that always embarrassed Janet, so she'd never tell you. She was rather a proper young lady when I knew her. We met on a train —the Twentieth Century out of Chicago. I was going to New York and so was she. It was wartime, and the dining car was crowded when I went in for dinner. We both had to wait in line —at opposite ends of the car. When our turn came, the head-waiter saw we were two singles and he put us at the same table. It was as fortuitous as that. Six months later we were married. Totally out of character for your mother. You were born the next year."

I couldn't imagine my mother being that young and impulsive. The man before me had no connection with the imaginary father I'd made up to fit the pictures on the book jackets —sometimes more villain than hero, but always exciting, always part of an enchanted world. Now all these bits and pieces of make-believe that I'd patched together since childhood were flying around and settling into new patterns like a kaleidoscope—patterns not recognizable to me.

He mused aloud, half to himself. "It's strange—one of the strangest things about life. I mean the way reverberations go on and on. I've been thinking about this in the book I'm writing now. We take some casual step, almost on the spur of the moment, and destiny's changed forever—down into future generations. If I hadn't met your mother on a train, my life might have been very different."

"And I wouldn't be here at all," I said.

His smile was warmer, and for the first time I glimpsed the

man on the jackets. "So destiny isn't all bad? The problem of the catalyst always fascinated me. I mean the person whose fate is so carelessly established, and who in turn changes everything all around. Are you a catalyst, Laurel?"

"I haven't come here to change anything," I said. "Besides, a catalyst doesn't change himself, and perhaps I'm already changing." That might even be true in ways I wouldn't invite.

"Right. You are the one who may be most changed by taking this step."

"Perhaps that's something I don't want."

"I'm afraid events don't wait for us or give us much choice." He sounded sad, lost, and when he went on there was a tightening in his voice, a tension. "Laurel, have you felt the undercurrents in this house? Perhaps threatening undercurrents?"

His words startled me. "How can I tell? I've just come, and I don't know yet what's normal or what isn't."

I thought of the orchid photograph that had been moved, but I wouldn't worry him about that now.

"Of course you don't," he said. "Never mind. Forget what I said."

Something worried him, but he wasn't ready to tell me what it was, and he changed the subject abruptly again.

"I understand you own a bookstore."

That gave me an opening. "I know the truth now, though I didn't before. I know that you helped buy my store. Mother left me a letter that explained things she'd never told me. If I'd known where the money came from at the time, I wouldn't have taken it."

"Then I'm glad she didn't tell you." He spoke dryly. "Do you enjoy the work?"

"I like to be involved with books—yes. Yours sell very well, you know." I was beginning to hate this chitchat. Nothing was going as I'd imagined or hoped.

"So you do allow them in your shop?" He was mocking me now.

"We're fencing, aren't we?" I said impatiently.

"So you can cut through the superficial? I like that. If we're going to duel, let's take the buttons off the foils."

He had come to life as he hadn't done before, and I saw how he could use those dramatic eyebrows to good effect.

"Must we duel?" I asked.

"What else can we do until each finds out if the other can be trusted?"

Trusted with what? I began to wish I hadn't come. Better to leave dreams alone than to have them destroyed in the space of moments.

"Have you met your half sisters yet?" he asked.

"Iris welcomed me when I arrived." "Welcomed" wasn't the word, but it would have to do. "And I met Fern when I went downstairs to see the orchid house."

At the mention of orchids, he closed his eyes. When he opened them I glimpsed the grief he tried to hold away. Not the sort of sorrow I felt over my mother's death, but something infinitely more destructive and desolate. But then Janet hadn't died in some shocking way. Her death had been a release, while Poppy's had cut off a life in full course.

"Do you know what happened?" he asked. "I mean, do you know how my wife died?"

"No one has told me."

"If you are to visit here, you'd better know. How she died has placed a burden on all of us." He spoke with quiet tension, and the momentary light that had sparked him was gone. "Poppy was an expert in raising hybrid orchids from seeds. It's a special process. The method is to plant seeds in nutrient agar placed in a sterile flask. When the seedlings grow large enough to fill the flask, it's broken and the plants are moved to something larger."

He paused, making an effort to control his pain. After a moment he went on.

"Somehow, when she broke the flask that last time, glass cut her wrist—an artery. She must have tried to get help, but there's only one wire-screened door to the greenhouse—heavy chicken wire. The plastic windows are small, and they're protected with the same heavy wire. Without cutting through, there's no way to get out except through the door. But sometimes that door jams, and in her fright she couldn't open it. We know she must have screamed, called, pounded. But Alida and I were up here and we never heard her. I was playing the piano and Alida was at her typewriter. Poppy couldn't stop the bleeding, or break through solid wire, and no one else was at home. She bled to death there among her orchids. So they were more beautiful with color than ever, and still alive—when she was gone."

His words poured out, stark and terrible in themselves. Yet it seemed a release for him to talk about these things. He must look into a deep and dreadful horror and self-reproach that would live with him forever.

I wanted to touch him, to offer some gesture of human feeling. But I didn't dare. We were strangers, and I could only blink back the tears that came into my eyes.

He saw and spoke to me more gently. "Sometime we'll talk about this again, Laurel. And about other things. For now we'll let it go. Where have they put you?"

I hesitated. "Iris has given me her mother's room."

He seemed to stiffen, but he also seemed to have no more

emotion to spend, and he moved a hand in dismissal. "If you don't mind, perhaps it doesn't matter. Nothing matters to me very much right now."

He had two other daughters who ought to matter a great deal, but that wasn't for me to point out.

I was suddenly aware of Mrs. Burch's exotic perfume, which seemed to go with her amber beads, and looked up to find her beside me.

"It's nearly time for dinner," she said. "Would you like to go downstairs now, Miss York?" I sensed that she wanted him free of my presence and that my being here at all disturbed her. How much she'd heard of our talk I couldn't tell, but her machine had been quiet for a time.

My father spoke quickly. "Yes, of course you must go down, Laurel. Angela doesn't like people to be late for meals. We'll talk again soon."

He had already returned to his own typewriter, and I followed Alida Burch toward the stairs. When I looked back I saw that he was staring at the sheet of paper in the roller as though it threatened him. A sense of something hidden had been present throughout our meeting. He hadn't told me everything, any more than Marcus O'Neill had done.

"What is my father frightened of?" I asked Mrs. Burch as we reached the stairs.

A hint of alarm showed in her eyes, before dark lashes came down. "I'm sure I don't know what you're talking about, Miss York. Are you feeling all right?"

"I'm fine. It's just that—that he told me how his wife died— so terribly."

"He told you that? We all try never to talk to him about what happened."

"Perhaps he needs to talk about it," I said.

She rejected this at once. "His heart isn't strong. He mustn't put emotional strains upon it. He must not be upset. I've been concerned about your coming here, Miss York, and I'm not sure Marcus did the right thing in bringing you to Key West."

"I'm not sure either," I told her. "But I'm here now."

"Then you'll try not to upset him?"

"I can't promise, but I'll try." I'd had the strong feeling that my father was already in a state of anxiety, for all that it surfaced only now and then.

When we reached the second floor level, I stopped with my hand on the banister. "Mrs. Burch, you know the room I've been given—Mrs. York's room?"

"Yes, of course. I didn't think it a good idea to put you there, but Iris made the choice."

"Do you know of any reason why someone would come in while I was out for a few minutes and remove one of those orchid photographs from the wall?"

She stared up at me from the step below. "Remove a photograph? What do you mean?"

"The one in which a mask was shown is gone."

She shook her head soberly. "It might be a prank. The sort of thing Fern might do, if the whim took her."

"It happened while I was in the orchid house with Fern. So it must have been someone else."

"Then you should be careful, Miss York. Be very careful."

"What do you mean? Careful about what?"

She shook her head, closing the discussion. A warning had been given. To help me, or frighten me away?

So far I'd met three people who obviously held some secret they were unwilling to share with me. Even my mother had written that something was wrong in this house. If there was a role I was intended to play, I needed to know what it was. And whether I wanted to play it.

We'd reached the lower hall, and Alida indicated a wide doorway. "I'll leave you now. Just go on in."

I had time to pause on the threshold and note both the attractive living room and the three who waited for me there. The room had been furnished with an eye to hot weather comfort. Pale Turkestan rugs were scattered across the floor spaces, leaving bare, polished wood between. Two small sofas, covered with printed cotton in leaf scrolls and rosy blooms, stood opposite each other, occupied now by the two sisters and the man who had laughed so resoundingly—who must be Derek Phillips.

Small tables here and there bore fascinating objects that Clifton York would have collected in his travels. I glimpsed brass pieces, ivory figurines, bronzes, lacquered boxes, cinnabar carvings. A series of colorful oils decorated the wall between porch doors, all of bright tropical scenes.

The man sitting next to Iris rose—a big man, with a large, well-shaped head of thick white hair and a dark tan. He looked vigorous, healthy, fifty-plus, and the fact that his nose appeared to have been broken at one time only added to his rather fiercely arresting quality. I noticed his eyes particularly because they seemed lighted by an inner brilliance—the sign of someone permanently excited by the possibilities of life and probably confident of his own ability to meet whatever came. I had the immediate sense that winning would be all-important to this man, even in casual encounters. His hard intensity seemed intended to conquer even me.

When I gave him my hand, he smiled and held me away, studying me with disconcerting frankness.

"You do look a lot like Cliff," he said, as though agreeing

with someone. "The same cheekbones and strong chin. Though it's all pleasantly gentled in you. Deep blue eyes and that black hair—stunning! Marcus was right. Welcome to Key West, Laurel. I'm Derek Phillips."

I wasn't used to being summed up to my face, and as he bent with a flourish to kiss my hand, I wondered what on earth Marcus had told him. No one moved while this performance was going on, but now Iris spoke smoothly from her place on the sofa.

"Derek, do stop playing pirate from some old Sabatini movie. You're not capturing Laurel! Just ask her what she'd like to drink."

There was amusement in his booming laughter, and though he appeared to take no offense, his wide mouth tightened, giving his face a suddenly harsh look. He didn't like being put down.

"What would you like, Laurel?"

They were through with their drinks, and I shook my head. "Nothing, thanks."

"Then we'll go in," Iris said.

She had changed to a simply cut frock of pongee silk with a fitted bodice and thin straps over the shoulders that left her arms bare. The skirt swirled to just below her knees, and her bronze legs were beautiful. Fern sat curled up on the opposite sofa, her yellow moth wings folded about her, tawny hair pinned high, eyes bright, as though she watched a play. Now she unwound herself and came to take my arm in a friendly fashion.

The dining room opened off the far end of the living room, both running along one side of the house, with doors open onto the circling veranda. I had a feeling that Poppy had left her stamp on this room. It flashed with tropical colors that were never strident, and its furnishings were anything but traditional. The dining table was large and round, its top a great cartwheel of shining wood set with woven place mats and silver. The chair backs were of woven cane, right for warm weather, their linen seats a delicate wisteria print. Again the walls were pine, as they were all through the house, and on one side a large, lighted oil portrait dominated the room. The woman was of course Poppy York, and the two small girls were her daughters. I could hardly take my eyes from the portrait as I sat down at the table. Somehow I'd expected Poppy to be dark like Iris, but her golden hair swirled on top of her head in a style that Fern had imitated, and she had the fairness of some north country beauty. Her blue gown, strewn with delicate white flowers, flowed from shoulder to sandaled toe in a graceful line that suggested the sensuous body beneath. Perhaps her face was a little long for true beauty, but one sensed in it a state of arrested excitement that gave it life. The artist had suggested a woman to whom movement was natural. Her pose wasn't that of someone relaxed and resting, and one almost expected her to laugh or speak or turn her head—perhaps even spring from the chair at any moment. There was that sort of suspended animation about her. The two small girls leaned against their mother, and they were as different then as they were now.

Fern must have been no more than four, and her dress was the lavender color of an orchid, with its ruffles like petals about her. Iris wore a simple pale blue frock, and her dark hair was brushed back severely, even then. Her gaze was not upon her mother, but on her younger sister. Again the artist had touched in character—Fern's joyousness, her sister's—what? Jealousy, envy? Misplaced, certainly, for even at that age Iris was the beauty.

It was the woman, however, who drew my eyes all through the meal. I thought sadly of how little defense my mother would have had against her, and old anger against my father stirred in me once more.

A ceiling fan above the table swept air through the room—far more pleasant than air conditioning at this time of year. This was a table without head or foot, and I sat with Derek Phillips on one side, Fern on the other, and Iris across. Angela, the Cuban woman who ruled the kitchen, looked in now and then to see that all went well, while her young assistant—a boy not yet twenty—served us with what seemed more like an engaging performance than the skill of a waiter.

"Pedro wants to be in movies," Fern whispered to me when he went out of the room.

While we ate a delectable cucumber salad, decorated with sliced banana, green bits of kiwi fruit, and coconut shreds, Fern was the one who chattered. Now that I'd seen Poppy's portrait, I realized how much Fern looked like her mother, even though her hair was a shade or two darker and she lacked Poppy's sensual quality. Fern was pretty in her own sparkling way, and the animation the portrait suggested had found an echo in her quick, graceful movements.

"You've been upstairs to Cliff's study, haven't you, Laurel?" she asked eagerly. "How did it go?"

She seemed to bear me none of the resentment I sensed in her sister. Iris had hardly spoken to me, but I knew she was listening intently.

"We didn't have much to say to each other," I admitted, with no intention of talking about what had been said. "We're strangers and there are years to catch up with."

Fern looked disappointed, as though she had expected some

emotional account, but before she could rush on with more questions, Iris spoke coolly to Derek, changing the subject.

"How is your search going?"

"It's day-to-day slugging right now. Blowing tons of sand out of the way, and mostly finding nothing underneath. We've located the ship's anchor—the iron part. Of course the wooden crosspiece is long gone. If the wreck is there, it could be scattered for miles and buried under centuries of silt. At least we've found cannons and ballast stones."

"It's all so exciting!" Fern cried. Her eyes glowed almost as brightly as Derek's when she talked about sunken treasure. "Those stones must mean a Spanish galleon!"

"Perhaps. When they're found in one place they can even still retain the shape of a ship, but that's not the case here. This ship could have hit the reef, which ripped out some of its bottom so that it dropped part of its cargo right there. But that didn't necessarily release all of it, or empty the cabin of passengers. A ship can go bouncing on and off the reefs for a long stretch, scattering treasure—and people. It may take years to locate where the rest of the ship finally sank."

I thought of passengers going home to Spain and drowning in those stormy depths, sinking to the seafloor, along with their jewels and rich possessions, to become whitening bones in a sandy grave.

"Will there be gold bars?" Fern asked eagerly.

"There could be, if it's the *Santa Beatriz*. Not all these galleons that sailed home from Havana carried gold. There were guard ships as well, loaded with arms—muskets, arquebuses, cannons—and those ships didn't carry gold. We know the *Santa Beatriz* was lost somewhere in that vicinity, but other ships went down in the same storm. Spanish archives have told us that. A search for the *Santa Beatriz* has gone on for years without success. The Spanish even tried to salvage her the same year she went down. There were a couple of survivors, so the general area of the wreck was known. But they lacked the equipment for diving that we have now, and they couldn't bring up what might have been there. Some of it would be tumbled along the sea bottom in storms, and then buried in sand. We were lucky with our first find of the anchor only because a storm had shifted what lay over it. We've claimed the wreck because of what we've found—but we aren't certain what it is."

"Aren't there sharks?" I asked uneasily.

"We keep a lookout. Mostly they don't bother us unless there's blood in the water, or garbage thrown overboard." Derek spoke matter-of-factly, but I could sense the fever that burned in him—treasure fever. And there was an echo of it in Fern—or perhaps only hero worship for Derek. Iris watched her sister, and they both made me uncomfortable.

Iris's reactions were cooler, more intellectual. "What sort of cargo do you hope to find?"

Fern answered quickly, not waiting for Derek. "If it's the *Santa Beatriz* there'll be silver bars and gold bullion! Doubloons—pieces of eight too!"

"That's why we slog along with the search," Derek said. "The archives, cargo records back in Spain, tell us what the ship was carrying. But look, Fern, while none of this can be kept secret, don't feed the rumors and spread what I say all over Key West."

She shook her head vigorously. "I haven't told anyone! Not a single person. I know there are always pirates ready to move in on someone else's find. Treasure hunters watch each other like sharks. But I haven't spread anything—you know I wouldn't."

"Good. Then let's leave it that way until I know what we have."

"I suppose the value could be enormous," Iris said. "But it could also waste your whole life in the searching."

Derek's eyes shone with their strange brilliance. "Money's not the point. That will be split in a good many ways. There's a lot of litigation that's gone on in the courts. Mel Fisher won the right to the *Atocha*'s treasure, but somebody's always trying to get new laws accepted. To say nothing of the historians and archeologists, who want to see everything preserved. So who knows what will happen? I'm in debt already, and the costs are enormous. Treasure hunting doesn't make many people rich. We do it because it gets into the blood. I suppose it's like gambling—a disease, once it takes hold. We can't stop when we're on the track of something."

Iris shook her head. "I hate all this. It's horribly dangerous. Someone always dies in these expeditions."

"The curse of the gold!" Fern cried dramatically, as if it were a blessing.

Iris ignored her. "You don't need this, Derek."

His smile humored her, though there was a hard edge to it. Sometimes he looked at her as though she were treasure, but he didn't give her objections an inch.

Pedro came in to take away dishes, and Angela emerged from the kitchen with a savory platter of pompano. No one mentioned sunken wrecks for a while. When we'd begun to eat, Fern picked up Iris's last words. "Of course Derek needs it! You just don't understand. He's a throwback to the old wrecking days. Aren't you, Derek?"

I picked up the term that I'd heard before from Marcus. "Tell me about the wreckers," I said.

Iris answered me, deliberately calm, as though she tried to

counterbalance both Derek and her excited sister. "Wrecking was Key West's first industry. Before the lighthouse, ships were constantly wrecked off the reefs. It was a major business here in the keys to watch for wrecks, since whoever reached a ship first had the right to everything on her. The laws of salvage were quite exact. That's why we have a captain's walk on the roof of this house. So someone in the family could always keep a watch out for ships aground when there was a storm. It was such a big business that warehouses were built in Key West to store salvaged goods, and buyers came from all over to purchase what was sold at auction. The men who risked their lives for salvage were called wreckers. There are a good many things in this house that came from wrecked ships."

"Sometimes," Fern put in, "they say wrecks were deliberately caused, ships led onto the reefs by false signals. You know, lanterns—so the ships could be robbed of whatever they carried."

Once more Iris changed the subject smoothly to more current matters, and for a little while I hardly listened. My own questions were tugging at me, and while we were eating cheese and fruit, I asked the thing that had been troubling me ever since I'd seen Clifton York.

"Is my father afraid of something?"

I'd meant to startle them and I'd succeeded. All three stared at me, and Iris set down her paring knife. "Why do you ask that?"

"It's a feeling I had when I saw him. As though something is worrying him to a degree that has made him afraid."

Derek smiled reassuringly. "I know what you mean, Laurel. But I think it's just Cliff's manner these days. He's been in a state of anxiety ever since Poppy's death. He feels guilty because if he'd known, he might have saved her that day. We've all talked to him about it and tried to make him feel less to blame, but I'm sure this will haunt him for a long time. Perhaps your coming will give him something new to think about."

The explanation didn't satisfy me. "Does Mrs. Burch live in this house?" I asked.

Again I sensed surprise. Perhaps even a guarded surprise. "Of course not!" Fern cried. "I love her dearly, but we couldn't stand all that gloom around every minute."

Iris said smoothly, "Alida is a splendid secretary. And she was Poppy's friend. That's how she came to work for Cliff ten years ago. But she has a house of her own on the south side of the island away from Old Town. She doesn't live here."

"Is there a Mr. Burch?" I asked.

"She's divorced," Iris said. "It was a young marriage that didn't work. And now, if we've finished, perhaps we might sit outside for a while. Usually we prefer the privacy of the garden, but tonight, Laurel, you might like to watch from the porch as a bit of Key West goes by."

For me, nothing had come out of the dinner hour with these three except a sense of further concealment. But to what purpose, I had no idea. What could anyone fear from me? Their discretion was carried to an unnatural degree.

We sat outside on the wide white porch in the tropic evening, and I was aware of an open window in the tower room at the far end. I wondered if my father was there listening, and if he cared what we said.

No mosquitoes came to pester us, though I'd seen screens on all windows and doors, and I commented on the fact that we could sit outside so pleasantly.

Iris explained. "We have inspectors who come around to check our yards for any standing water—in flower pots, bottles, even discarded tires. Old, unused cisterns all have fish, to eat the larvae, or have a top layer of kerosene on the water. And of course there's spraying—by trucks in the evening, or sometimes even by planes that fly low over the keys in the early morning. Scary, because you can think they're going to crash. Mosquitoes can be bad after a heavy rain, or if a rare high wind drives them from the Everglades down the keys. Mostly, thanks to good control, we can sit outside comfortably."

Fern seemed restless now and unable to be still. In contrast, her sister sat quietly, poised and controlled.

Derek stayed only a little while longer. "Thanks for dinner," he told Iris. "I want to stop in at the Banyan bar before I go home. I'll see you tomorrow sometime."

"A room will be ready if you'd like to come back and stay here tonight," she said.

"A boat's coming for me, so I'll go out to the island as soon as I can get away."

Fern broke in, explaining to me, "Derek owns his own island —Doubloon Key! You'll love it out there, Laurel. Wait till you see his house! Invite us out soon, Derek."

His smile was easy, but I knew he was perfectly aware of Fern's crush. "You're already invited, remember? And of course Laurel must come too."

When he'd gone, Iris spoke in her cool, light voice. "I'll never understand treasure fever. Derek's been hunting the oceans for years. There've been other times when he thought he'd found something big—and nothing happened. I hope it's really true this time, for his sake."

"You don't understand anything about him!" Fern cried. "He really has found something. If it's the *Beatriz* he'll bring up fabulous treasure. That's why he keeps the workboat on guard all night, with the men sleeping on board and taking watches. He can't risk having pirates move in."

I had the feeling that I'd been plunged into a foreign country—perhaps even into an older time. This talk about sunken treasure and pirates was almost casual, taken for granted. As Iris had suggested, Derek was a bit like a buccaneer himself. You'd only need to put him into costume with a black patch over one eye, and he'd pass on any movie set. Perhaps it was this very aura of excitement and adventure that appealed to Iris, being so far removed from her own reserve. I wondered for the first time how Clifton York's novels had affected his other two daughters. Had they grown up immersed in his adventurous tales, as I had?

The day had been a long one, and when I could excuse myself I went inside and started upstairs. I was no more than halfway to the floor above, when a door opened at the foot of the stairs and my father spoke to me.

"Will you join me for a moment, Laurel?"

He stood waiting in the door of the tower room, and I saw a sadness in him, an uncertainty that hadn't been there before—as though he'd not be surprised if I simply went on up the stairs and refused to talk with him.

But here was another chance to know him a little. I went down again and walked through the door of the tower room, into Clifton York's private quarters.

4

Tonight he looked different—rather distinguished in his blue silk dressing gown, with a maroon ascot at his throat.

"I wanted to talk to you alone for a few moments," he said.

By "alone" he undoubtedly meant when Alida wasn't around. That was understandable, from what I'd seen of her managing ways.

I stood in the doorway trying to see Clifton York in his own space—as a man apart from his work. The man I wanted to find. Yet I could never forget what he had done to my mother, and to me. The fact that he'd helped with money, and had even written to me, wasn't enough. Sooner or later there must be some resolution between us—whatever direction it might take. Only then could I go home in peace.

The room I stepped into was large, filling the circular tower and opening from it. It had been furnished as a sitting room, as well as bedroom. Poppy's colorful taste hadn't prevailed here, though it wasn't a somber room. Sisal rugs and beige curtains had been used, and there was no heavy mahogany, or even rosewood. The furniture had a look of the tropics about it, and my eye was caught by a tall wicker chair, its flaring peacock back beautifully woven.

He saw my look. "That was Poppy's favorite chair. Sometimes I can still imagine her sitting there. It set off her perfection. Come over here by the window, Laurel, where there's a breeze."

Mention of Poppy made me stiffen again—a reaction I couldn't help. I skirted the chair with its unseen ghost and sat down in a plain wooden chair with wide, flat arms. Outside it was dark, but I could see streetlights, and lamps in houses across the way. The front windows were open, and a smell of the sea came through. A warm smell, a spicy scent, as if from more exotic shores. Not the sharp smell of northern waters. I was glad to be aware of these contrasts. They kept me from forgetting who I was and where I belonged.

My father finished lighting his pipe and waved it at me. "Author's prerogative. Or anyway, it used to be." Tonight he seemed more at ease, less tensely watchful. It was I who felt more tense than ever since I'd seen something of Iris and Fern.

"Tell me about Janet," he said.

"What do you want to know?"

"What was she like in her later years? Was she happy?"

"How could she be? How can you ask that?"

"A person who is determined to be unhappy will manage to be. But perhaps I'd like salve for my own conscience. What I did wasn't easy, you know."

"I don't know! How could I know anything about you, or why you behaved as you did?" Earlier restraint was gone, and I was ready to attack now, to tell him how I felt.

He answered me quietly. "I suppose I deserve your anger—though not all of it. Never mind about Janet. I think she had very little talent for life. I hope you have more. It's a rare gift and not to be lightly dismissed. What were your growing-up years like? Were *you* happy?"

I didn't know how to answer that. There'd always been that dark unease in me, that feeling of waiting for something, without knowing what it was. I'd thrown myself fervently into various activities, and at college I'd gotten myself into an escapade or two. Mother had been terrified, seeing my father in me. Perhaps there were times when I'd struck out at her in my pain over not having what other girls had—blaming her. Sometimes I turned furiously to my painting—and had been dissatisfied with the results. I'd worked all hours to make my bookstore a success, and there I'd done well. But all the while there'd been a rage deep inside me—a hunger that had never been fulfilled. I wasn't even sure what it was I was hungry for. I couldn't tell Clifton York any of this. But I resented his saying that my mother had no talent for life.

In the face of my silence, he sighed. "It takes a long time to be rid of resentment. Perhaps I've never let go of my own. I wish there could be some sort of peace between you and me. But first that means facing a few truths. Both yours and mine. I'm not sure either of us can do that yet."

I was silent and he went on, musing out loud.

"You're attractive, spirited. You had the gumption to come down here and beard me in my den. But I still don't know anything about what motivates you, and I'd like to know. For instance, is there a man back home you care about?"

He'd touched a sore spot. Of course I'd had men friends. Once or twice I'd been quite passionately involved. But nothing ever worked out. Now there was only Stan, whom I didn't really want, for all that Mother had approved of him so thoroughly. Probably because he was what she regarded as "safe." But I wasn't ready yet to settle for safety.

"There's no one right now," I said, sounding grim.

He smiled without amusement. "I seem to have a knack for asking questions that ruffle you. And of course I have no right to ask."

That was true—he didn't have. "I don't know you," I said. "How can I talk to you about my life?"

He closed his eyes for a moment, and I saw his sadness. I didn't want to be disarmed—and weakened. At the moment all I had between me and wild tears was the anger I needed to hold on to.

"All right," he said. "We'll let all the questions go, and I'll begin again. You have a talent for painting, Laurel. Key West is a wonderful place for an artist. Go sketching tomorrow and find out. I like the Bellport watercolor Marcus brought me. I remember those houses from the time when I lived there."

I was always self-conscious about my painting, since I didn't think it was all that great. Mainly it was a hobby I enjoyed. To fend off any more probing, I asked a question of my own.

"I don't even know where you grew up," I said. "Mother told me once that you were born in New York City, but she would never really open up about you."

"We lived in Greenwich Village for a while. For a long time I was footloose. A writer can work anywhere he can hang his hat. After I met your mother, I followed her to Bellport, and we lived there for a time."

A time—yes. Until Poppy crossed his path. But I wouldn't ask about that. All conversational roads seemed to have barriers across them—danger points past which I didn't want to go. Nevertheless, I had to say some of what was troubling me.

"You needn't have kept the pact you made with my mother! Giving your word on something that was so unfair to me—and then holding to it for all those years!"

"I didn't keep it," he said gently. "As you've seen by those letters I wrote you. And if we'd corresponded, perhaps I'd have been able to see you. Janet might even have relented. In the face of her opposition it was hard to get through."

"I think you could have, if you'd wanted to! Less than a year ago my mother came to Key West—and you refused to see her. She was only able to talk to Mrs. Burch."

He took the pipe from his mouth. "Janet came here?"

"Mrs. Burch didn't tell you?"

"Exactly when was this?"

"I think it was soon after your wife died. It's hard to believe that your secretary would keep my mother from seeing you. How could she dare?"

His laugh didn't sound amused. "Alida would dare, all right, if she saw it that way. She was Poppy's friend long before she worked for me, and she's been more a member of the family than a secretary. She might have thought she should protect me from something else disturbing at a very bad time. Perhaps she was right, though I would have talked to Janet, if I'd known she was here."

Now I had something to settle with Mrs. Burch as well.

"What do you think of your sisters?" he asked.

"I haven't been here long enough to have an opinion."

"I don't know you, either, but I suspect you develop strong opinions rather quickly. Isn't that so?"

He was all too right, but I didn't want to tell him my uneasy reactions to Iris and Fern. "I don't want to leap to wrong conclusions," I said lamely.

"First impressions are often true, even if we revise them a bit later. So tell me."

"All right then. Derek Phillips can't take his eyes off Iris. He's certainly in love with her. It's harder to tell how she feels about him. Mostly she watches Fern, who watches Derek with her heart in her eyes."

"I know." He spoke sadly. "Fern will break her heart over this if she can't be turned in another direction. She was frail when she was little, and we all spoiled and protected her. Fern attracts affection, as Iris seldom does."

There was a special warmth in his voice when he spoke of his youngest daughter that I hadn't heard before.

"Yet it's Iris Derek wants to marry," I said.

"Of course. She's remote and beautiful and tantalizing. He could have Fern's love easily, and he probably knows it. She's out there in the open, to be read in a moment. Perhaps for Derek, Iris is the ultimate treasure ship in deep water, never to be fully explored—always just eluding him."

I had thought something of the sort myself. "Are you for this marriage?"

"Poppy was terribly against it because she thought him too old for Iris—and something of a wild man."

"That isn't what I asked," I said.

"Derek's an old friend. I admire him. Maybe because he's always done the things I only play at and write about. I think he'll be good for Iris."

"I have the feeling that Iris doesn't want me here."

"It's possible. Your coming may seem like a threat to both girls. You have to recognize that."

"Why should I be a threat to anyone?"

He didn't answer, and his look made me uneasy again. He was like deep water too, and never easily read. There could be reefs around Clifton York. If he were a conniving man would he try to use his oldest daughter—me—against the two younger ones? If there were something he wanted from them?

"Remember," I said, "I'm not a catalyst. And I'm not a pawn either, in any game you're playing. Are you playing a game?"

He wasn't smiling now. "If I am, it could be a deadly one. Perhaps a life or death game—just as Poppy may have been playing."

"What do you mean by that?"

"I can't explain, Laurel. Not now. But perhaps you can do something for me while you're here."

I waited, promising nothing. I needed answers myself.

With an effort he seemed to summon inner resources and went on. "Poppy was worried in the days before she died. Frightened. I tried to find out what was the matter, but she wouldn't tell me. Yet what happened in the orchid house couldn't have been anything but a terrible accident. So why do I keep feeling that she was terrified about something, and that there might have been a connection between her terror and her death?"

"What do you want me to do?"

"Just watch, Laurel. And listen to all of them. Pick up anything you can, even if it's something you don't understand. Find me something to go on. But don't tell anyone I asked you."

This was a course I'd already chosen to follow, so nothing had changed, and as father and daughter we were no closer than before.

"I suppose I can try," I said doubtfully.

I didn't believe this was all he wanted of me. There was something more. And until what he held back came clear, I could side with no one. Of one thing I was certain. The fear I'd sensed in him earlier was still there, though I had no idea whether it was for himself or someone else. He was a far more troubled man than I'd expected to find. And more real than all my fantasies.

The telephone rang just then, and he picked it up. "Yes, Marcus . . . she's here. Do you want to talk to her?" He held out the phone and I took it.

"Hello, Marcus."

"Hello, Laurel." I knew the deep tones of his voice, and I liked the sound. Marcus wasn't to be easily read either, but at least there was no miasma around him of the sort I'd sensed in this house.

"I won't ask how things are going," he went on. "That's probably too complicated to answer. Are you willing to get up early tomorrow morning—to see the sunrise?"

I didn't hesitate. "I'd like that."

"Fine. We won't wake the others. Just come downstairs at six o'clock and open the door for me. I'll be on the porch." He rang off in his usual abrupt way, and I replaced the phone.

"We're going to look at the sunrise tomorrow morning," I said.

My father seemed oddly uncertain, and I studied him for a moment. "Is there any reason why I shouldn't? Marcus is your friend, isn't he? Why can't you turn to him about whatever's worrying you?"

He shook his head vehemently. "Marcus is too close, too involved with all of us. You're the newcomer who can see us more objectively. Marcus's view may be different from mine, so hold off and don't let him influence you too much."

"It seems to me that I am becoming involved, whether I like it or not," I said.

"But in a different way." Again his sigh came from some unhappy depth. "When Poppy died . . ." He broke off and closed his eyes for a moment.

I could sense his pain. It wasn't fair—when he was hurting other people.

"What am I supposed to call you?" I asked. " 'Father' doesn't come easily, and I expect you have to grow up with 'Dad.' "

"The girls call me Cliff. It was Poppy's notion that we should all be chummy and good friends, so they grew up that way. I'm not sure it worked."

"I'll call you what they do," I said. "Good night, Cliff."

He was standing at the window again, and he said, "Good night," over his shoulder, not looking at me.

I closed the door softly and once more started upstairs. My meeting with him had been thoroughly disquieting, and it had put a burden on me that I didn't want to accept. At least I'd made him no promises.

As I walked down the hall to my room, I heard someone on the attic stairs behind me, and when I turned Alida Burch came running down. Without noticing me in the shadows of the hall, she hurried to the lower stairs and disappeared from view. Working late, I supposed, and wondered why the woman disturbed me so.

The moment I opened the door of my room I saw that someone had intruded again. The photograph with the orchid mask had been returned to its hook on the wall, and I could only wonder why someone had borrowed it in the first place. The row of flowers seemed to stare brightly, mocking me, and I saw at once what had been done to the missing picture. A narrow piece of black tape had been pasted on the glass in such a way that the eyes behind the mask were hidden.

What sort of trick was this? Certainly, it seemed malicious. I had noticed no one around, except for Alida on the attic stairs. But I'd been with my father long enough so that the picture could easily have been rehung in that time. What I wanted to know was who had done this, and why.

I rapped on Fern's door, and when I had no answer I went out on the rear porch and looked into the garden. The panels of the orchid house glowed with light, so someone was there.

I ran down the back stairs and crossed the lighted area of the garden. The night air was gentle on my face—still a surprise. I tapped on the door, and when there was no answer, I opened it and walked in. Lights burned in the work area, and Iris sat on a high stool at the potting bench, absorbed in an orchid that resembled a white moth.

"May I come in?" I asked.

"Oh—Laurel? Yes, of course. I just need to finish this."

She had changed to jeans and a light sweater—no longer the elegant figure I'd seen earlier, though these jeans would wear a designer's name, I was sure.

"I don't suppose you know much about orchids?" The question required no answer. "Most people don't, though you'd be amazed how many orchid fanciers there are. Right now I'm gathering pollen to fertilize another flower," she added, instructing me.

What I had to say could wait, and I watched as she used a toothpick to transfer a sticky bit of pollen from the anther of the plant to the stigma of another. Then she drew out more pollen and placed it delicately in a gelatin capsule.

"I'm doing the job insects and bees do in nature," she explained. "Orchid pollen's too solid to be carried by the wind. Most orchids are bisexual, but they can't be fertilized by their own pollen."

I hadn't heard Iris talk this much since I'd met her, and I wondered if she were trying to distract me, perhaps less sure than she looked under that cool exterior.

"I'll refrigerate this and finish tomorrow," she went on. "Poppy used to do all of this herself. It made her happy when she could breed beautiful new hybrids. Fern and I helped her even when we were small. So now we have to take over altogether."

I was still marking time, waiting for the right moment. "What do you do with all these orchids?"

"That's the trouble. We just enjoy them and give them to friends. But I'd like to see this turned into a real business. That's what I'm working toward now. Of course we don't have a big enough place here. We'd need an orchid range somewhere else, with more shade houses and a big greenhouse. It will mean hiring a full-time grower—and that will upset Fern. She'd like everything to stay just as it was when Poppy was alive."

Her voice seemed to grow colder as she spoke. Because she suppressed her own feelings? Because she disliked her sister so much? Iris had everything going for her, yet her bitterness was clear. Against what—whom? At least for the moment she seemed less antagonistic toward me, and I realized that orchids were a good part of her world too, just as they were of Fern's, but with a different perspective.

"I saw the lights on, so I came down to find someone to talk to," I told her.

Iris carried several capsules to a small refrigerator and placed them in a dish inside. "All right—what about?"

There was no warmth in her, no interest, but I continued. "This afternoon when I was out, someone came into my room and took one of those orchid photographs from the wall. The one with the mask."

"Fern may have wanted the picture for some reason," Iris

said. "Perhaps she meant to tell you later. What's troubling you, Laurel?"

"It wasn't Fern. At least, she didn't take it down. The photograph was removed when I was in here talking with Fern this afternoon. Then a few minutes ago, when I came upstairs, I found that it had been returned to the wall just as it was before —except that a strip of black tape had been pasted on the glass to cover the eyes in the mask."

Iris had begun to work with a splendid tiger orchid—a creamy bloom with garnet striping—preparing to move it to a larger pot. "Perhaps someone wanted to upset you. Perhaps whoever it was has succeeded."

"Why should anyone want to upset me?"

Iris didn't look at me, her hands busy with the transplanting. "We're none of us sure just why you've come here, or what you want."

I had no answer for her, and I moved on along the walkway, stopping to look at a row of orchids that were entirely blue or violet shades.

Iris seemed indifferent to what I'd told her, and she went on informing me. "Those are some of our current breeders. Especially fine studs we're using to cross with other species."

Impatience swept through me. I didn't really care about some silly trick with the picture. It wasn't this lush world of orchids that interested me most, either. What I wanted to know was what might be troubling my father, and what I might learn that could help him—and help me. Perhaps, whether I liked it or not, I was already committed.

"When I saw Cliff a little while ago," I said, "he told me about how your mother died. I'm terribly sorry."

Still holding the pot with its tiger-striped orchid, Iris stared at me, the veneer of coolness gone, her hostility palpable.

"Poppy was found right there where you're standing. Look at those boards under your feet, Laurel—you can still see the stain of my mother's blood."

It was as though I'd opened some chink in the armor Iris wore, so that emotion had suddenly spewed out at me with words intended to shock.

I felt forced to look down. Some effort had been made to scrub away the brown stain on the walk, but I could see the dark, spreading mark as though it flowed freshly. I could almost see blood on the orchids as Cliff had described them. In that instant Poppy was more real to me in the visualization of her death than she'd seemed in that idealized portrait with her two small daughters. A life had seeped away on these boards beneath my feet, and now I could feel the shock and pain my father must have suffered, and the full horror for Poppy's daughters. More than ever, this seemed a haunted place.

Iris went on as if compelled. "By the time Alida found her, it was all over. If only I'd been home, she might have been saved!"

"Please," I said, "I didn't mean to distress you. It's just that Cliff seems so—so worried about something, and I'd like to understand."

She went on as though she hadn't heard me. "Marcus drove me to a flower show at the Garden Club that afternoon, and Fern was checking information for Cliff at the library. When Alida came downstairs to look for Poppy, she found the door jammed and had no answer to her calls. So she forced the door and came in. Poppy was already dead. They couldn't revive her. Derek had just stopped by the house, and they sent him to the library to bring Fern home. Alida lost her friend, Cliff lost his wife, and Fern and I our mother." Tears welled in her eyes, and she blinked them away furiously. "Now you walk in and think you can take Cliff over! When we'd never even heard of your existence for all these years!"

This was another count against my father—that he'd never told his daughters about their older half sister.

Iris's explosive anger alarmed me, and I moved toward the door. "I'm sorry," I said again. "I wouldn't have come to Key West if I'd understood—"

She made an effort to control herself, though the orchid trembled in her hands. "You're not wanted here. If someone moved a picture in your room, perhaps that's what they were trying to tell you. Just go away and don't interfere with us. Not even Cliff really wants you here. It was Marcus's crazy idea."

There was no answer I could give her, but as I moved toward the door, she stopped me.

"Of course Cliff is upset and suffering! He could have saved Poppy. Her death was needless. He should have saved her! Do you think there's anything you can do about that? He doesn't need another daughter. Half the time he doesn't know that Fern and I exist. Most of his emotions go into his novels! That's where his heart lies! He's never had anything left over for us. Any more than he had for our mother. It was worst of all for her. And then—" Iris broke off abruptly, staring past me at the door, and the pot slipped from her shaking hands to shatter and spill its contents on the slate walk.

We'd neither of us heard Fern come in, but when I looked around and saw her standing in the doorway, her white face framed in tawny hair no longer pinned on top of her head, I knew she had frightened her sister. She clutched a wide scarf of primrose lace about her shoulders as she rushed to the orchid, which was lying bruised in the midst of the pot shards and planting material.

Iris put one hand on a shelf to steady herself. "Oh, God!"

she said. "For just a second I thought you were Poppy. That's her scarf you're wearing."

Fern gave her attention to the broken pot. "Look what you've done, Iris! Oh, my poor darling!" Kneeling on the walk, she scooped up the plant, nestling its roots in her hands. "Give me another pot, will you? Quickly, Iris!"

Iris handed her an earthenware pot from a stack nearby and then brought a bucket of fresh potting material. Without a word she helped Fern replant the orchid in pulverized bark. When Fern was satisfied, she stood up, brushing earth from her yellow dress. Her hair fell about her shoulders in a shining mass—hair as golden in this light as the pollen of the orchids.

"They're really very strong, you know," Fern said, as if to reassure me as she placed the pot on a shelf. "They can recuperate quickly, and they're surprisingly resistant to all sorts of pests and diseases. They look fragile, but they're stronger than most plants. And they live a long time too. Just the same, they have feelings and they shouldn't be treated like this. You're not careful enough, Iris. Maybe you should stay out of the orchid house and leave it to me!"

"The orchids don't belong to you, so don't talk nonsense." Iris was her cool self again. "You do look a mess, Fern. You'd better go upstairs and take a bath."

"So you can upset Laurel some more?" Fern demanded. "Oh, I heard all the things you were saying. Cruel things. Come along, Laurel honey—she doesn't want us here. But my orchids will wait for me. They won't even grow for her."

She grasped my hand and pulled me toward the door. I looked back apologetically at Iris. She was studying the replanted orchid, but I doubt if she saw it just then. Outside in the garden, Fern linked an arm in mine, and we moved across the bricked area together.

"Don't mind Iris," she said. "She's not like me. She holds her feelings back too much. Then when she lets go everything bursts out. Afterwards, she's sorry and ashamed. You'll see. We'll just let her alone for a while to recover. She's not a happy person, my sister. What would you like to do now, Laurel?"

"Just go to bed," I said wearily. Iris's outburst had been frightening in its ferocity, and Fern's words didn't reassure me. When I was small, I'd wished for a sister. Now I'd found two— and could take no joy in either relationship. Iris disliked me and Fern worried me. The only event I'd begun to look forward to was seeing Marcus in the morning. He might be the one person who could help me. This time I hoped he would open up.

Fern came with me upstairs and glanced into my room as I opened the door. She saw the mask photograph in its place on the wall, saw the black tape, and ran quickly to stand before the picture.

"Who did this?" she cried.

"I haven't any idea."

She stood for a moment studying the row of orchid faces thoughtfully. Then she reached up and peeled the tape off the middle picture.

"There! That's better. Now she can see you again. Just don't dream about them tonight, Laurel. Sometimes I do. Dream of orchids, I mean. Awful dreams. In the daytime I love orchids, but at night they can turn carnivorous. Sometimes I think they're going to destroy me, the way they did Poppy." Her eyes were enormous—haunted.

I knew about dreams. I'd had terrible ones sometimes myself. It didn't do to dismiss them as having no meaning, but I wouldn't give in to the fear they prompted either.

"It wasn't the orchids that killed your mother," I told Fern gently. "She broke the glass flask herself and cut her wrist."

"She didn't have to die! I want her back so much. I'd cut my own wrists if I could bring her back."

This time I ventured to touch her—a light touch on the shoulder where Poppy's yellow lace scarf had slipped down. She turned to me almost fiercely, and in a moment she was sobbing in my arms, weeping brokenly against my shoulder.

I held her, more deeply moved than I'd felt since I was a little girl and my mother had once wept with her cheek against mine.

Fern's outburst didn't last long. She pushed me away and dashed quick fingers over her cheeks, brushing off the tears. "I mustn't do that—I have to be strong. I'm glad you've come, Laurel. I'm glad we're friends."

"So am I," I said, and walked with her to the door.

In the hallway she turned to face me again. "You'll help me, won't you? We need to stop this marriage, Laurel. Poppy didn't want Derek to marry Iris, and she was right. Marcus is the one Iris ought to marry. She was engaged to him once, you know—before Derek came back to Key West. He's still in love with her, so we've got to stop her from what she means to do."

I couldn't help thinking with renewed amusement that Fern might have her own designs on Derek, however childish they might be.

"What about Iris? What does she want?"

Fern's look was frantic, a little wild, and she ran from me across the hall and closed her door with a bang. Obviously, I'd said the wrong thing.

I shut my own door and began to get ready for bed, keeping my eyes carefully averted from Poppy's orchids watching me from the walls. I didn't want to remember they were there, or think of Fern's word "carnivorous."

Marcus in love with Iris? I had caught the way he looked at her and wondered. But clearly Iris would have no one but Derek, and I didn't think Fern or anyone else could stop her. Perhaps no one should try anyhow. Yet I wondered how much Marcus had been hurt by her fascination with Derek.

I was no longer an outsider, observing. There was no way I could remain uninvolved—or wanted to. I was in the middle now, yet still not knowing enough to take any sort of sensible action. I could only continue to play it by ear until there was some handle I could take hold of. Tomorrow I would begin with Marcus. It was his turn to answer questions.

I was glad to turn off the light, grateful for the luminous dark that misted the room with faint moonlight and hid the orchids from view.

Whatever my dreams that night, they were only mildly disquieting, and I couldn't recall them in the morning. At least they had nothing to do with orchids.

5

I was awake at five, and I lay drowsily quiet, running through a make-believe dialogue in my head. I would tell Marcus everything that had happened, and I would enlist his help and support for whatever course it seemed wise for me to follow. Perhaps this time he would tell me whatever it was he'd been holding back. Perhaps we could begin to be friends. I felt quite peaceful thinking that was all I really wanted.

At five-thirty I rose and put on beige slacks and a candy-striped shirt. When I'd slipped into a light jacket, I went downstairs and unlocked the front door. Marcus sat on the steps, waiting for me. He looked comfortable in jeans and a crewneck pullover, but I found myself watching him warily—not quite as much at peace with myself as I'd been. I didn't like the surge of response that had rushed up in me at the sight of him. If I couldn't trust myself—!

I'd expected that we'd drive somewhere in his car, but he came inside and pulled me toward the stairs.

"Let's hurry—the sun won't wait. The best view is from the captain's walk on the roof. Come on!"

We ran up two flights to my father's study and stepped

around the oriental screen that shielded Alida's desk from Cliff's. We both heard a sound and looked toward the far end of the room. Alida sat at Cliff's desk, her head on her arms.

For a moment we hesitated, and then Marcus moved toward her. "Alida, what's wrong?"

She looked up in dismay, her cheeks streaked with tears. Her close-cropped gray hair was rumpled from its usual neat combing, and her face looked pale, with no touch of blush this morning. As she stood up abruptly I caught the faint, exotic scent she wore.

When she chose, she could summon her own rescuing dignity. "I didn't expect anyone up here this early. I wanted to transcribe some pages that I fell behind with yesterday. Is there something I can do for you?" All quite haughty and remote, not explaining her collapse into tears at my father's desk.

Marcus didn't push the matter. "We're going up to see the sunrise," he told her. "I'm sorry if we startled you."

He drew me toward the narrow upper flight that led to a trapdoor in the roof. When he'd raised it with both hands he climbed out upon the platform and pulled me after him into the wind.

We were just in time. Out of the eastern Atlantic a bubble of gold was rising against streaks of orange and gray. Above, the sky brightened as the sun slowly took command of the morning. The view was immense in all directions, and I savored it a bit at a time.

There were more tiny keys—coral islands scattered southeast across the ocean. Clear to the Marquesas, Marcus said. The green water of the Gulf of Mexico was cut across by the islands that made up the Florida Keys. Key West would be caught between Atlantic storms that crossed into the gulf—a tiny wedge of land to stand against great forces of wind and water.

Marcus pointed out nearer landmarks in Old Town—the naval base on the southern rim of the island; the fashionable Pier House, long and white, near the foot of Duval Street.

"That's Mallory Square down there to the left of where Duval Street ends," he said. "The busy heart of Conch Town. Do you see that big red brick building—the old customs house? Walk down there this morning, Laurel, and get a feeling of the town."

"I will," I promised. Now, looking out across pitched roofs and other captain's walks, with the wind whipping my hair, I could glimpse the intricacies of this older Key West. There were indeed a myriad of lanes and little alleys cutting in from the orderly checkerboard of the streets. Mostly the pavements were empty at this hour, with only a few pedestrians stirring. The town would begin to wake up soon, along with the rest of the more distant East Coast.

What I had seen downstairs worried me, however, and I found myself thinking of Alida's weeping. This might be one of the undercurrents I should be aware of.

"Why do you suppose Mrs. Burch was crying?" I asked. "And what is Cliff so worried about? I know now how Poppy died, and everything seems to be connected with that. You're still holding out on me, Marcus."

He gestured toward a bench set against one white railing. When we sat down, he began to talk. "I'm sure Alida blames herself for Poppy's death—perhaps for not hearing when her friend must have called for help. When Cliff is playing the piano, he can be so absorbed in his own imagination that he doesn't see or hear anything around him. But Alida feels she should somehow have known that Poppy needed her. Useless regrets, of course, since they make her suffer and can't change anything. Who knows what Cliff blames, besides himself?"

"But this is nearly a year later. Isn't it time to try to accept? Time for healing to at least start? Maybe we all need to try to forgive ourselves first?"

"The anniversary of Poppy's death is haunting all of them. If they can get past this safely—"

"What do you mean, *safely*? You told me before that anniversaries can be dangerous. Just what do you mean?"

"Emotionally dangerous, that's all. Hard to get through psychologically. What happened still bothers everyone. If Alida could open the door to the orchid house when it jammed, why couldn't Poppy?"

"What did the police think at the time? They must have been called."

"That door really can swell and become damned hard to open. They accepted that, and also the fact of Poppy's frightened, weakened state that made her even more helpless. Panic always makes things worse. There were cuts and bruises on her knuckles where she'd pounded on the door."

And blood as well, Cliff had said.

Marcus looked out over long shadows cast by the early morning sun, and his hair seemed more fiery than ever. I mustn't wonder how it would feel springing under my fingers, or what its texture would be like.

I went on. "I've begun to make friends with Fern—I think."

"Making friends with Fern can be tricky, fond of her as I am."

"Because of her crush on Derek?"

"That's part of it, poor kid. She doesn't adapt well to the real world, and it's hard to deal with someone who sees everything through a colored mist of fantasy."

"Yes, I've glimpsed some of that."

"What about Iris? Have you made friends with her?" He spoke her name more gently.

"Iris doesn't want me here. Nor does Mrs. Burch. They've both made that plain."

"I'd like you to stay," Marcus said.

I looked at him quickly—into grave, unsmiling eyes. Iris or not, he was looking at me, and for just an instant there seemed a current between us that I'd felt once before—a touching that was almost physical.

Then he went on as though nothing had happened. "I want you to stay because Cliff needs you here. And maybe Fern does too. So don't go into all that defensive stuff about how your father wasn't there when you needed him. That hasn't anything to do with now."

This real conversation was nothing like the one I'd imagined earlier this morning. The hint of electricity in the air was gone at once, and I was relieved to find that Marcus could still irritate me.

"You're the one with tunnel vision!" I told him, and felt it was true. He saw clearly in the one direction of his own intent, his own indebtedness to Clifton York, and he wouldn't hesitate to bend everything else to that purpose. I suspected that he might even be as ruthless a character as Derek Phillips if he chose. So I mustn't let him compel and manipulate me—as he'd already done to some extent.

He took no offense at my words—which in itself was disarming, if I allowed it to be. "That's possible. I expect most of us keep our heads in tunnels part of the time. Though I do try to look outside once in a while. What's really troubling you, Laurel? You're edgy this morning."

I still needed to talk to him. Whether he understood or not, he would at least listen, so I began with the orchid photographs and went on to the episode with Iris in the orchid house, when Fern had overheard us. Marcus seemed concerned about Iris's outburst, but he let me finish.

I didn't tell him about the request my father had made, since that was between Cliff and me.

"Who do you suppose is playing tricks with the orchid picture?" I asked.

"I haven't a clue. It doesn't seem too serious."

"That depends on how I react, doesn't it?"

He irritated me further by laughing. "I already know the answer to that. You'll set that chin you got from your father, and you'll refuse to budge."

"How can you say that? I told you I didn't come down here to fight for anything."

"Battles don't always ask the consent of the participants. I think you're caught and you'll stay. Maybe that's what I've counted on. You do have an inside edge that I don't. I want to know why Poppy was against Derek's marriage to Iris. Once I know that . . ."

He didn't finish, and I wondered if he would try to stop the marriage because of his own interest in Iris.

"I thought you'd already explained the reason," I pointed out. "Derek's age, his reckless past."

"Those are the obvious reasons. I think Poppy knew something more about him. Something that might even be dangerous to Derek if it were known. But she died too soon to use it."

"You can't possibly think that—that anyone had a hand in her death? Surely that doesn't seem possible."

He was silent and I knew he wouldn't answer. I stood up, and wind whipped around me as I started for the stairs. Marcus had only pretended to open up. There was more he hadn't told, and didn't mean to tell me.

He stayed where he was, and his next words stopped me. "Would you like to go out to Derek's wreck this afternoon and watch some treasure diving? I think I could arrange it."

I turned and saw that his expression had changed. The challenge was there again—as though he dared me.

"That might be fun," I said.

His smile was the same brief flash I'd seen before. He was much too attractive a man, and if I had any sense I'd resist.

"It's amazing what the word 'treasure' can do to the imagination," he went on. "Not that I'm the real thing in a treasure hunter. I don't have the fever for the search the way Derek and some of the others who work for him do. I can get caught up in that crazy exhilaration—especially when there's a find. Or even the promise of one. But then I can leave and come home, to set it down on my typewriter. I can feel just as excited living it over again in my head." Even his voice quickened as he spoke.

"You're writing about treasure diving?"

"It's Cliff's subject right now, for his new novel, and I'm helping on the research. He's especially interested in piracy and hijacking in the Caribbean, since this will come into the story. Of course I may use some of this material eventually for a nonfiction book of my own. Recently I did a piece for a sports magazine about the danger these days of hijacking for cruisers and yachts."

"I've read about piracy in Caribbean waters. Is much of that going on?"

"It happens. Most of the expensive craft go out with firearms aboard. Derek keeps a constant guard on his workboat—and guns on his cruiser. Word gets around in a seaport town like

Key West, and usually that's enough to keep off marauders. They like easy targets—not ones that can defend themselves forcefully. If you want to go out this afternoon I can come back for you around one o'clock. Wear old clothes, if you've brought any along."

"Do you suppose I could go down? Diving, I mean?"

"Since you've done some scuba diving, I'm sure it can be arranged. Providing Derek says it's all right."

"Would you have equipment I could use?"

"Sure—I'll manage that."

I went to the rail and stood for a moment longer, held by the view. It was like looking at a colored relief map of Key West. Everywhere there were exotic tropical greens splashed with red and purple, where royal poincianas bloomed and bougainvillea climbed the walls. Trees and plants I'd never heard of all thrived lushly in this tropical climate.

North Roosevelt Boulevard, on which we'd come into Key West, looped around the island and became South Roosevelt on the southern shore. Marcus said the commercialism vanished on that side, where there were expensive modern homes. The sun was growing warm, the sky cloudless. Even in winter the sun down here could burn the skin quickly because of the nearness of the equator.

"Key West," I sounded the words aloud. "When did it get its name?"

"There are stories about that. Some people say it was given the obvious name of *Cayo Oeste*. But others claim that it's a corruption of *Cayo Hueso*, for 'Bone Island'—because of the Indian bones found here in early days. Anyway, you can see why the wreckers liked to have these platforms on their houses, so they could watch—scan the reef for vessels foundering in a storm. Key West is the end of the line, Laurel. The end of a continent, really—the southernmost part. Nobody goes on by land to anywhere else from here. You can only go back. So unless you're going to cut and run, you might as well relax and let it get to you. I promise you it will."

It was already doing that, and so was this man beside me. I could remember all those warnings my mother was full of—beginning with *always distrust first attraction*. Had she been right —or very wrong?

When we went downstairs, Alida was busy at her word processor, and she merely nodded as we passed her desk. Undoubtedly she resented our catching her in tears.

I saw Marcus to the front door and then wandered toward the back of the house. In spite of my continued questions and doubts, I had a sense of freedom that I'd never felt before. In the past whenever I'd met a new man, old training had made me see him through my mother's eyes. She had doubted most men as she doubted life itself and warned me to be on guard, lest I be hurt as she had been. Few boys I'd brought home in my teens had met with her approval. So I'd grown up more wary than I wanted to be. Now restraint was gone and all the old advice was fading. For the first time I could admit to myself that I didn't really like the sort of man my mother would approve of. Perhaps I didn't know yet what manner of man I could fall deeply in love with, but I was beginning to have a sense of him.

He would probably be exciting, puzzling, irritating—because he'd always do the unexpected. Nor would he be fatuous about me. Maybe I'd never be quite sure where I stood with a man like that, but he would stir my imagination, fire my emotions. He might very well be a man like Marcus O'Neill.

A mirror near the end of the hall caught my expression and startled me. The woman in the glass was a stranger who looked enormously alive—as though she'd begun to reach out for life. A woman who would make something happen and never run away. She was the secret woman who had lived only in my fantasies. Now it was time for us to blend into one. I remembered when Marcus had said I was afraid of my shadow. He was wrong. I was only afraid that someone would find out what the real woman inside me was like. Or that I wouldn't be able to cope with her myself. Now it was beginning not to matter.

The big, modern kitchen at the back of the house was empty. Without paying much attention to what I was doing, I dropped bread into a toaster, found butter and marmalade, sliced a banana, and made a pot of coffee. Then I put everything on a tray and carried it to a small white table outside. The garden was still in shade this early, but the morning air smelled fresh, and birds were singing.

I felt curiously excited, and yet more peaceful with myself than I'd been in a long while. As though some troublesome problem had been resolved—which was hardly the case. My problems had only just begun. At least I could now enjoy these moments away from the cold and blowy North and even enjoy exploring the unexpected stranger I'd glimpsed inside me.

At home the glorious colors of spring would fade quickly, but here flowers bloomed the year round. I was a little like a plant myself, putting out new tendrils, exploring new territory.

I must have been smiling to myself, when a sound made me look around. A man I'd never seen before stood at one side of the garden, watching me. I had a feeling that he'd been trying to slip past without attracting my attention, but when I turned with a smile that wasn't intended for him, he came a step or two toward me.

He was middle-aged, with sandy hair rimming his balding head, and a tanned, weathered face. He looked sinewy in khaki shorts that revealed knobby knees and a pair of hairy legs. And he was returning my smile with one of his own that seemed cherubic and incongruous in a face that was less than innocent.

I stopped smiling and stared in surprise.

"Hey," he said, "you must be the big sister from up North. The one who's got everything stirred up? Right?"

I didn't like his easy, familiar tone, or anything else about him, but I felt no alarm. Not then.

"Who are you?" I asked.

His eyes were pale blue, and he had a trick of seeming to look far beyond me into the distance.

"Nobody you'll be meeting around," he said slyly. "But don't worry—I got a right to come in here if I want. They all know me."

"Would you like me to call someone to talk to you?"

"Nope. I can look out for myself. But you, now—do you know what you're getting into coming down here where you ain't wanted?"

"That's hardly your business, Mr.—?"

He was shaking his head with its sparse circle of hair. "My name's not your business. Thought maybe I can give you a tip. Just go easy while you're here and stay out of trouble. Key West can be a rough place for anybody who gets in wrong. Maybe you better think about that."

He strode off around the side of the house, and I noticed that he held one shoulder stiffly. My brief spell of calm had been disrupted, and I couldn't recover the feeling of peace. His unpleasant words echoed in my mind—as if I'd been subtly threatened, though I had no idea why.

As I sat finishing my breakfast, the door of the orchid house opened and Alida Burch came out carrying a single white orchid in one hand. When she saw me, she walked toward my table.

"Good morning, Miss York." As though she hadn't seen me earlier. "May I sit down for a moment?"

"I wish you would. Did you see that man who was here just now?"

"What man?"

While I explained, she fetched another cup, poured coffee from the pot I offered, and sat stirring it thoughtfully, the white orchid resting on the table beside her.

"I know who you mean. Don't worry. Sometimes he does odd jobs around here. But never mind him. I need to talk to you."

This morning she had changed her amber beads and black dress for a navy skirt and white blouse. She wore coral around her th   and managed a certain dated elegance. Her short gray hair had again been brushed close to her head in the twenties style she affected, and any tear stains were gone from her cheeks.

"Yes?" I said, and waited.

"Not here." She glanced uneasily around, as though expecting to find listeners in the shadows. "We need to talk away from the house."

"All right. Shall we go for a walk in a little while?"

"Not together. Wait an hour and then walk down Duval Street to Mallory Square. You'll find the Conch Train depot and benches where you can sit. I'll find you there." She picked up the white blossom, not waiting for my agreement. "I like to keep an orchid on my desk," she added pensively. "To remind me of Poppy. Iris lets me help myself."

She carried her cup inside, and I looked after her thoughtfully. Alida Burch was apt to be extravagantly mysterious, but I was willing to hear anything she had to tell me, and I would certainly meet her in Mallory Square.

"Hi, Laurel." That was Fern, floating out of the kitchen in green muslin. "I'll join you for a minute, though I never eat breakfast." She dropped into the empty chair. "I must get to my orchids soon. My poor Tiger was injured last night. What was Mata Hari after just now?"

I smiled. That seemed a good name for Alida, but I wouldn't tell anyone my plans. Until I knew what was up, I'd follow Alida's directions and meet her quietly.

"She just came to get an orchid. Fern, I climbed to the roof with Marcus this morning. To see the sunrise. That's why I'm up so early."

"That's a good beginning," Fern said. "But Sunset is the real experience here. It's a *happening,* and we always spell it with a capital S. When there's going to be a fine one, I'll take you to watch. What did you see from the roof—anything special?"

"It was all special to me. It's a marvelous view to match a gorgeous morning. Marcus has invited me to go out to Derek's wreck site this afternoon. You've been there, I suppose?"

This caught her attention, and Fern's small face glowed. "Yes, of course I have. It's very exciting. Derek's going to be famous and rich, if things work out as he hopes. Not that he isn't already rich, but treasure diving can eat up millions. Only this time he's onto something pretty big."

"Does he dive himself?"

"Sometimes—when there's a real strike. Mostly he sends down divers he hires. Mostly men who have been with him for a long time. He's taken me down in scuba gear a couple of times, and I loved it. Iris won't go down. She's not very brave, and deep water scares her. How brave are you, Laurel?"

The sudden question seemed less a challenge than an appeal, though I couldn't tell what lay behind it.

"I've never had a chance to find out," I told her.

This morning Fern's tawny shock of hair was again caught decorously back with a green ribbon, though a few locks always escaped to dance around her cheeks with the quick movements of her head. Once more she studied me, and when she spoke her voice was low, all its sparkle gone.

"Sometimes I get the feeling that I'm living all alone in this house. As though there were only ghosts around me. I used to be close to my father—but not any more. Not since Poppy died. All he wants is to have her back, and that can't be. Not for any of us. Even I know that, though sometimes I pretend."

There seemed a need in this younger sister that made her terribly vulnerable. With her guard down, she looked forlorn and defenseless.

"We are sisters," I reminded her gently. "And I hope we can be friends."

Tears welled into her eyes, but she wouldn't accept this self-betrayal—perhaps she didn't trust me yet—and she ran across the garden and through the door of the orchid house.

I'd forgotten to ask her about the peculiar intruder whom Alida had dismissed so casually.

Had Cliff any idea, I wondered, of the hunger that existed in his younger daughter? Resentment against my father had a tendency to renew itself too easily.

When I'd carried my tray into the kitchen, I went upstairs for my handbag and sketch pad. Then I let myself out the front door. Having studied the town from the roof, I knew where Duval Street was and I walked toward it slowly, taking an irregular course down one street and up another. I had nearly an hour in which to explore before it was time to meet Alida in

Mallory Square. I could move as slowly as I liked, looking at each house, while a sense of new adventuring came to life in me. Now and then I stopped to sketch a scene that caught my eye.

Behind similar white picket fences, each house was different from its neighbors. Touches of the Bahamas showed everywhere in scuttles and louvered shutters, and there were hints of New England, the Creole, and the Victorian. Slim white columns were a reminder of the classic revival style in the South. On most of the houses wooden filigree offered its delicate, fanciful lace. I penciled an intricate bit of corner carving, pleased with the richness for an artist that I found on every hand.

Often there were fanlights over the front doors, some of which might still hold their original stained or frosted glass at the entranceways. Here and there an outside staircase slanted up from lower to upper veranda. Yet for all this imaginative construction, these houses had been set sturdily into coral rock, built to withstand hurricanes that blew in from ocean and gulf. They had stood for a long time.

One huge house—a perfect Queen Anne fantasy—was so fascinating in its complexity that I stopped to study its surfeit of gables, balconies, and turrets. This I must sketch! As I paused near a yellow elder that overhung the fence, a woman appeared in the doorway, and I stepped instinctively into deeper shade so she wouldn't see me. Iris York emerged on the porch, speaking over her shoulder to someone out of sight.

"You've got to talk to him!" she cried. "He won't listen to any of us, now that *she's* here. If he goes ahead with this—" She broke off, and I could see that she was as agitated as she'd been last night in the orchid house.

Now the man she spoke to came through the door, and they

descended the steps together. It was Marcus O'Neill. They stopped only a little way from where I stood, though neither saw me. I didn't dare to move. This concerned me, and I had to know the meaning of Iris's words.

6

Iris caught her breath and went on. "He's using Laurel against us. We don't think he's quite sane any more—he's so filled with these weird notions. He's convinced himself that Poppy was murdered and that now there is some threat to him. And of course Fern has picked this up and is singing the same tune— only the threat is supposed to be against her!"

"Could what Cliff believes be true?" Marcus asked.

"Of course not!" She sounded furious. "It's not like him. Not the way he used to be. Fern's another matter—she's always been off in another world. Poppy could keep her whimsies in line, but I can't. And Cliff doesn't even try."

Marcus put his hand on her arm, and I could hear the tenderness in his voice. "Don't mind so much, Iris. He'll come out of this. Fern is well cared for, and you'll escape when you marry Derek. If you marry Derek."

"Of course I'll marry him, but I won't ever escape. You haven't even begun to understand, Marcus. It's the orchids— the orchids most of all! Oh, how can he do anything so wicked? Poppy's orchids! You've got to talk to him, Marcus."

"All right, I'll try. But don't count on anything."

She whirled away and ran down the walk and through the gate. Marcus stood looking after her for a moment, and I saw the sadness in his face. Neither one had glimpsed me standing there, and by this time I didn't dare to reveal myself. I'd heard too much—yet not enough.

When he'd gone back into the house and Iris was out of sight, I retraced my steps along the block, walking soberly toward Duval Street by another route. I could find very little meaning in what I'd heard, but the blight that even my mother had sensed lay heavily upon everyone in Cliff's house. What was more, it seemed likely that Marcus was still in love with Iris.

My sense of adventure had evaporated, and I no longer wanted to sketch, though I kept up my pretense of being a curious tourist. At least this was a way of focusing my distracted thoughts.

On Duval Street renovation was still under way, and I moved from the shabby to the spruced-up. Restoration had brought about remarkable improvement in a town that only a few years ago had been run down and seedy. Yet in the coming days I would hear arguments both for and against the changes. There were those who preferred Key West in its own colorfully decayed state as an old seaport town. Individualism was what mattered most, and for the privilege of being oneself, people had been settling here for a long time. Influences that brought the pressure of change could be resisted and resented. When Key West called itself the Conch Republic, its tongue wasn't always in its cheek.

Tolerance for others who lived here was something of a creed. Gays had been coming to the island for years, to become part of a community that accepted them for their worth as individuals and to which they could contribute their own notable gifts of imagination and creativity. All these things I would learn in bits and pieces in the days to come.

After the early business of "wrecking" died out, due to changes in the laws and with better lighthouse protection, cigar making had taken over, with tobacco shipped from nearby Havana. Then sponging had its turn until the sponge field died. Now even the fish and the fishermen had vanished, and shrimping—pink gold—had moved to Stock Island. For better or worse, the real business of Key West was now tourism.

Even early in the morning, this was evident as I walked past the shops on Duval Street and reached Mallory Square at its foot. Eager visitors with cameras slung around their necks were already about, their dress apt to be even more colorful and informal than that of Key Westers. Around Mallory Square architecture became a jumble of styles, ranging from the modest to the more dignified and distinguished. One old building of red brick displayed a handsome wrought-iron balcony right out of New Orleans or Savannah. A tiny eating place presented two or three tables outside, where the breakfast rendezvous appeared to be common.

I found the Conch Train depot easily—a long, roofed wooden structure, open on all sides, with the benches Alida had mentioned—and I sat down to watch the first loading of the train that wasn't a train, but a jeep masquerading as an engine and pulling a string of cars behind. It would tour the island, offering visitors a way of getting an overall picture.

Mostly, though, my thoughts were on the disturbing snatch of conversation I'd heard between Iris and Marcus. Perhaps I should have confronted them and demanded to know what it was that concerned me. Most of all, I kept hearing Iris's voice when she'd said that Cliff believed Poppy had been murdered.

She'd dismissed the idea so fervently, yet I'd had the feeling earlier that Marcus too was worried.

When Alida came into sight she was a block away, and I noticed the restraint of her walk. Here was a woman who used no swinging stride, but moved with short steps that constantly hesitated. An uneasy walk, as though each step was unsure—as if it might plunge her into some treacherous abyss.

She didn't speak, but nodded for me to follow as she walked by. We crossed a narrow, busy street, and Alida led the way past the walls of what looked like an old ruin. An iron gate closed an opening to the space beyond, and we went around to another gate, where we could enter an enclosed area of mottled sunshine and shade. High brick walls surrounded what looked like a small one-room fort. Trees had entangled great roots in the crumbling walls, their branches overhanging to cast patches of shadow across bricks that made a patio of the enclosure. In one corner red hibiscus brightened the shade.

"What is this place?" I asked.

"It's been turned into a garden, but originally it was a cistern. All the water Key West had in the days before the pipeline was collected in cisterns all over the island. When it's raining you can stand outside and hear the sound of water clattering into this old receptacle. Though of course the water's not held here anymore."

The island was full of memories of a long gone time. Away from narrow, busy streets, the little garden was so quiet that I could hear Alida's deep-drawn breath. A small greenish lizard clung to brick, flicking its tongue at an insect now and then.

"Why are we here?" I asked with intentional directness.

"I wonder if I can trust you, Miss York?"

There was that word "trust" again—with a question behind it.

"Call me Laurel, to start with. Perhaps that will help. Though how can I tell if you can trust me until I know what you mean by trust?"

She clasped her hands nervously and then as quickly unclasped them. "I don't know what to do! I think I must tell you. Even though you won't thank me for it."

"I'm listening," I said.

"It's about the day Poppy died. Perhaps you know that I found her?"

I nodded, thinking again of what Iris had said.

"When I went to the orchid house to look for her, I couldn't open the door at first because it was jammed shut."

"Yes—my father told me that."

"It was jammed because a metal wedge had been pounded in between frame and door, so it couldn't be opened from the inside. I managed to pull out the wedge, and when I went in I found Poppy lying there, white as paper in her own blood."

Alida covered her face with her hands, and I waited, too shocked to say anything.

After a moment she went on. "I was too late. She was already dead. I ran inside the house calling for Cliff. He had come downstairs and heard me. Thank God he could handle everything. What was happening—what *had* happened—didn't hit him until later. When he'd called the hospital and the police, I told him about the door and showed him the metal wedge. He said not to tell anyone what I'd found. I should simply say the door had jammed—as it sometimes did."

"Why didn't he want you to tell the truth?"

"He said the wedge must have been put in the door to annoy Poppy. Anyone might have done that. But if the police knew about it, there might even be a murder charge when they found the person who did it. So Cliff didn't even tell Derek

Phillips when he came around the side of the house to find us there. He'd been ringing the doorbell, with no answer because Angela and Pedro had gone home. So no one else knows about this—except you."

"Why are you telling me?"

"Because—oh, I don't know! I'm not sure your father even wants to take care of himself any more. Though he thinks about that wedge and he's afraid. I know he's afraid. Whoever jammed that door is sure that I pulled out the wedge to get in, and that I would have told Cliff. Someone may be getting worried."

"Has anyone threatened you?"

She looked suddenly confused. "I don't know. I hid that dreadful wedge in a drawer of my desk—and it's disappeared. But I can't be sure I didn't misplace it. Sometimes I can forget. There's been so much to distract me lately."

"But this could only have been a way to tease Poppy. No one could have known what would happen to her. No one could have intended her death."

Alida was silent for a moment. "Anyone at all could have come back to the orchid house that day. The outside gate is always open, and it's easy to walk along either side of the house to the back garden without being noticed." She seemed to be reassuring herself.

"You mean someone outside the family?"

"I don't mean anything. I don't know. But you should know this, so you can be on guard and help your father."

"Why haven't you at least told Iris and Fern?"

"Your father ordered me not to. He didn't want me to worry them about this."

"But if you haven't talked about this for a whole year, why should someone worry now?"

"I'm not sure." Long lashes came down, hiding her haunted look.

"Can't you consult Marcus? I should think he could be trusted."

"I wanted to, but your father wouldn't let me. He said Marcus shouldn't be drawn into this. It's different with you—you're part of the family now."

Was I? "I doubt if he'd want you to tell me either."

"That's why we've come here—so no one will know."

"But what can I do?" The implications of what she'd told me were so murky that I'd begun to catch her uneasiness, even though she hadn't told me what she feared.

She threw out her hands in a despairing gesture and began to walk about the enclosure, her low-heeled shoes clicking on the bricks.

"Poppy had a terrible quarrel with Iris the very day she died. It was about Derek, and Iris wouldn't listen."

"Do you mean Iris might have wedged the door?"

"No—no! I don't mean anything. Only now I'm afraid for your father. What if he's to be next?"

"Mata Hari," Fern had called Alida. Perhaps Alida had lived too long with Clifton York's stories. Her wide, dark eyes looked a little wild, and I spoke soothingly.

"Let's go back to the house. I'll think about what you've told me and see if there's anything sensible I can do."

She knew I was putting her off, and she gave up and started toward the gate, the very set of her shoulders rejecting me as useless.

"Why wouldn't you let my mother see Cliff when she came here nearly a year ago?"

Alida stopped with her back to me, and she spoke without

turning. "Cliff was sick with grief over Poppy's death. I couldn't let her see him. It would have upset him even more."

"You had no right to make such a decision! You had no right to keep her away from a man she'd been married to. You could have at least told my father she was here."

"Then he'd have seen her, and he couldn't take any more. I told her I'd arrange something if she'd come back another time."

"You should never have refused her," I repeated. "My mother was dying. She knew she'd never come again."

Alida had no space left for outside emotions. She was a mixture of cold rage and hot, driving determination, all of it held back by the lid she'd placed on her own feelings, and all of it circling in a protective barrier around my father.

"How long have you loved him?" I asked softly.

She walked out the gate, and I had to hurry to catch up with her. As we went back through the square, her resistance to me was like some icy encasing that I would never be able to chip through. Whatever she felt for my father was inadmissible by her standards, and she would never forgive me for asking that question.

As we turned toward Duval Street, she stopped suddenly, and I followed the direction of her stare. Across from the Conch Train depot was a small restaurant with three tables set in a row outdoors. Derek Phillips sat at one of them, breakfasting with another man.

At once Alida seemed agitated. "I can't stand Derek Phillips! I hope you'll never go out to that wreck he's exploring."

"Marcus O'Neill is taking me there this afternoon. Why shouldn't I go?"

Her dismay was clear, but she explained nothing. "We mustn't be seen together," she said, and walked quickly away. I watched as she lost herself among some tourists crossing the street and disappeared up the block. Mystification was her stock in trade, and I suspected that she had a genius for confusing everyone. But how much belief could be put in anything she said, I didn't know, and I didn't dare dismiss any of it.

I sat down again on the bench in the open-air depot and watched early morning Key West go by. There were at least two Key Wests that I'd glimpsed. The tourists who gathered in Mallory Square and roamed the town formed the transients of the island, plus a few lingering hippie types who drifted in and out—both of these groups were served by the other world of residents, who came in all categories and whose home lives went on quite separately from the visitors. This second world lived behind the facades of Old Town, or in the newer sections, and it could be social, intellectual, artistic—even political— though existing side by side with the sightseers who brought the island its life's blood.

This second world belonged. It concerned itself with the past and made an effort to preserve the island's historic heritage for the present and the future. Because of Cliff (and even more because of Poppy) I'd been permitted to step behind the tourist scene. Whether I might ever win myself a place—in fact, whether that was what I really wanted—I still didn't know.

As I watched idly, I glanced now and then at the two men breakfasting across the street. Derek Phillips looked vigorous, tanned, healthy, with his handsomely shaped head of white hair and strong features. A dominating sort of man, with a natural command of any situation. The other man was even bigger, but with none of Derek's polished manner. Younger and rougher looking, unshaven, he seemed to be arguing rather than eating.

Prompted by some impulse, I took out my pad and set down

a quick sketch of the scene, concentrating on the two men. Both made good subjects in their individuality—Derek calm, strong, in full charge of himself, the other man's face set and fierce as he confronted Derek.

As I watched, the second man stood up suddenly and strode away. Derek seemed undisturbed by his leaving and continued to eat his ham and eggs calmly.

Presently he felt my eyes upon him, for he glanced across the street and saw me sitting there. At once he smiled and waved a beckoning arm.

"Come on over, Laurel."

I put away the sketch that I didn't want him to see, and, since there was no reason not to join him and I wanted to know more about this man who was going to marry Iris, I went across.

By the time I reached his table, a waitress had cleared a place for me, and Derek stood up to seat me with a flourish that seemed half-mocking and very typical. I asked only for coffee, and when the waitress had gone, Derek looked at me with obvious satisfaction.

"This is a break for me. I've wanted to talk with you. Why didn't you come over when you saw me?"

"You had someone with you."

A hint of irritation crossed his face. "Oh, that! If you'd come, I'd have been rid of him sooner. Not an especially savory character, I'm afraid. I saw Alida just now crossing the street. Was she with you?"

"She was showing me Mallory Square."

"What do you think of her? Sometimes I wonder why Cliff keeps her on."

"She seems devoted to him, and I expect she works with him better than anyone else. Besides, she was Mrs. York's close friend, wasn't she?"

"I never understood that either. Sometimes the woman seems demented, if you ask me. Unbalanced. Iris would like to get rid of her and find her father someone else more suitable."

"She must have suffered a terrible shock—finding Mrs. York dead that day."

He studied me for a moment. "All this must seem pretty weird to you—plunging into a household like Cliff's. Not exactly reassuring. I'll be glad when I can take Iris out of it. At least you don't need to stay a minute longer than you want to."

There seemed to be several people urging me to leave, and I could feel my resistance growing. I sipped coffee and waited for whatever might develop. I'd never lost my streak of obstinacy—if there were Mata Haris around, I belonged to the same club.

Derek warmed to his favorite topic. "I understand you're going out to the wreck this afternoon with Marcus. I've loaned him one of my powerboats. Marcus believes in sailboats, but this will get you there faster. We're finding a few more things. We brought up a clump of silver coins embedded in coral recently. There're still two bronze cannons down there that will be a job to bring up. Though these may be what identify the *Santa Beatriz.*"

"How will the cannons give you identification?"

"Only early seventeenth-century cannons were bronze, as these are, and they were marked with numbers. We have a copy of the manifest from that vessel—right from the Archives of the Indies in Seville. There can be absolute identification, if we're right. Of course that doesn't mean that we've located the main treasure of the ship. It's down there somewhere at bedrock, with tons of sand burying it. And an ocean to search."

His face lighted, and I saw the same hard brilliance glowing in his eyes that I'd glimpsed at dinner last night. He spoke with enthusiasm about some of his previous adventures with wrecks in the Caribbean, and I could see why Iris must think him an exciting man. Though I suspected he would never lose sight of the millions of dollars involved in what he was doing. Once more, I wondered at the unlikely combination of Derek Phillips as adventurer with the cool, distant Iris. Though of course I knew by now that Iris had her own smoldering depths.

It was difficult to distract Derek from his diving adventures, but I managed to bring him around to another subject. "This morning Alida told me more about finding Poppy. I don't think she's convinced that what happened was an accident. Do you think anyone hated Poppy enough to . . ." I let my voice trail off, so he could supply any words he chose.

He stared at me with no great approval. "If you mean do I think that someone went into the greenhouse and cut Poppy's wrist with broken glass—no, I certainly don't. I doubt if anyone hated her, though she probably made a few enemies, as people do if they've any character at all. She could be high-handed when she chose, and I'm sure she stepped on a few toes. Including those of her friends and family. What do you have in mind, Laurel?"

I hadn't anything in mind. I was merely throwing out bait to see what I might pull in. So far the hook was empty.

When I didn't answer, he went on. "With the anniversary of Poppy's death coming up, I think the important thing is to put on a show of busyness that will get Cliff through a depressing time. I'm planning to throw a small party on board the *Aurora* at the site of the wreck. We'll bring up some treasure that day —even if I have to send down things we've already salvaged! I hope the weather will cooperate. Cliff hasn't gone out there yet, and we'll put on a real bash for him. With dinner afterwards at my house on Doubloon Key."

Giving any sort of party on the anniversary of Poppy's death seemed inappropriate, even if it was intended as a distraction for Cliff.

"I hope you'll still be here for the party, Laurel," he added.

"I expect I will be," I told him, feeling increasingly uncomfortable. I even wondered if he might have some other motive than the one he claimed for giving this party. When I saw Marcus this afternoon, I'd ask him about this affair—and whether Cliff really ought to go. Or—I might see Marcus sooner. A new idea was stirring in my mind.

"You don't look enthusiastic about my plans," Derek said.

I hesitated. "With everyone so troubled, I wonder . . ."

"But that's the whole idea! Cliff's been hiding away up in that workroom of his for months. He needs a change to wake him up. Gold fever—treasure fever!—can be catching. Once he's out there he won't resist it. And of course it will be good for his writing. He's slowed down lately."

I let the matter of the party go and asked the question I was considering. "Where does Marcus O'Neill live?"

"In a big old Queen Anne house not far from your father's. Key West's full of guest houses these days. Most of them are old, and they're being well cared for. This place is on Eaton Street, and you can recognize the turrets and gingerbread extravagance."

"I may have seen it," I said.

In a few minutes we left the table, and he went off toward the docks with a casual wave of his hand.

If I waited till this afternoon, there were still several hours ahead before I could talk to Marcus. But there was another way to see him immediately, and I decided not to wait.

I began to retrace my steps, looking for Eaton Street and

one particular house. I found it easily, and this time I entered the gate.

As I came up the walk, a man on the front porch looked up from his newspaper and smiled in greeting when I told him I was looking for Marcus O'Neill.

"He's in—you can hear his typewriter. Up on the second floor. At the back."

The house was larger than my father's, with a huge downstairs living area running the width of the house. The floor had been painted in fanciful colors, but the furnishings were old and elegant. At the back, doors opened on an enclosed garden built into the heart of the house.

I walked up the flight of wide, dark stairs and followed the sound of Marcus's typewriter. He didn't hear me until the second time I rapped on the door. Then he came to open it, dressed in duck shorts and a short-sleeved shirt, his legs bare and his feet slipped into comfortable zori sandals.

"I'm interrupting," I said, "but I couldn't wait until this afternoon to talk to you."

"Sure—come on in."

He seemed matter-of-fact and unsurprised. If his red hair had been combed recently, it was only with his fingers, and as he gestured toward the sofa, I sat down with a greater awareness of him than I wanted to feel. Not only because of his physical effect on me, but because of the rising questions about him that I wanted to have answered. Questions of who he was, what he thought, how he felt. He was still a huge puzzle to me, and I was increasingly drawn and curious—as well as a little wary. My mother's voice hadn't wholly stilled in me, and I wasn't at ease.

The apartment was made up of one large room, and Marcus's desk had been placed near a window that overlooked the inner garden. A door opened on a rear porch. It seemed a comfortable room, where books overflowed on the floor and a large wastebasket invited crumpled yellow sheets. I wondered what was on them, what he chose to throw away.

The couch sagged a bit at one end when I sat down. Now that I was here, it was difficult to begin. Easier perhaps to blurt everything out—which I started to do, sounding more defiant than I intended.

"I went for a walk early this morning," I told him, "and happened along Eaton Street in time to see Iris and you come out of this house. You were talking about something that concerned me, so I stopped, though I didn't set out to listen."

He smiled. "I saw you lurking behind the yellow elder, but I thought I'd better not say anything. Iris would have been upset. And you might have too."

"I'm not apologizing," I told him quickly. "I wish I'd heard more. That's why I've come back. What is it that Iris doesn't want my father to do? What does it have to do with me?"

He pulled a captain's chair away from a table in the adjoining kitchen area and sat down, studying me.

"Believe me, I didn't know what Cliff would have in mind when I brought you here. If I had, maybe I'd never have gone after you. He means to change his will. Fern is to have the house, which is what he always intended. Poppy's house. Iris will move away when she marries, so that won't bother her. The money will be divided, and you'll get a share. That doesn't matter either. Poppy left both her daughters well off. The thing that's eating Iris is that Cliff means to leave the orchid house to you."

I stared at him blankly. "But that's awful! I don't know anything about orchids, and I don't want that burden. The orchid house belongs to Fern and Iris."

"Cliff is looking ahead. If anything happened to him and the orchids were left to both, or either, of his younger daughters, a war would start. They both love orchids, but Iris wants to commercialize and Fern doesn't. They'd tear each other apart. You're neutral. He thinks you might be able to bring them together. Or at least arbitrate."

"So they can tear me apart? No, thank you. I could see how bitter Iris was this morning."

"Cliff believes you can handle it. He thinks you are capable and sensible—smart enough to run a successful bookshop at home."

"He doesn't know me! Nobody knows what I'm like. I'm only just beginning to find out myself."

Marcus had stopped smiling, but his expression still seemed amused and quizzical. An amusement that ruffled me. How could he attract and aggravate me in the same moment?

"Look—I won't have my life rearranged like this," I told him. "If anything happened to my father and those orchids came to me, I'd just give them back to Fern and Iris and escape as fast as I could."

"Would you really? Another clause he'll put in the new will gives you the right to live in his house for as long as you like, if you choose. If Fern or Iris should try to put you out, their own inheritance might be in jeopardy."

"I wouldn't stay under those circumstances! I don't belong here anyway," I finished with a crack in my voice that I hated to hear.

He came to sit beside me. His arm around my shoulders steadied me, though I turned rigid at his touch. I wasn't going to be comforted and persuaded and have my mind changed. He'd done this sort of thing to me before, and this time I would be on guard. He could be altogether too compelling, and I didn't trust him—or myself.

"Does Fern know about this?" I demanded.

"Not yet. Cliff has only told Iris. He hopes that you'll have made friends with Fern by the time she knows. In fact, I think he also hopes that you may eventually support Fern against Iris, since he doesn't think Fern can manage this by herself. God knows, we all hope he'll live for a good many years and that everything may resolve itself gracefully long before he dies."

I pulled away from Marcus's arm because of my own treacherous desire to lean into it and walked to the door that opened on the rear porch. Bougainvillea burgeoned over the rail, and I experienced a sudden longing for orderly shrubbery that wouldn't fight flamboyantly to take over all outdoor space.

When I turned back I was under better control. "Why am I here, Marcus? Please tell me."

"All right. I wanted you to get the picture first. Otherwise you might turn and run. As you may think you want to do now. You're here because of the way Poppy died. Because of that jammed door, and what happened earlier that same day."

I returned to my place on the couch and sat down, clasping my fingers around my knees tightly, so my hands wouldn't shake. "You'd better explain," I said.

"Just by chance, I was in on the whole beastly scene that morning. I'd stopped at Derek's Place before the bar was open. He knew I was coming and had promised to answer a few questions for a piece I was going to write. So I was sitting at the far end of the bar making notes when Poppy came in. There was no bartender on duty yet, and Derek was alone on a stool behind the counter, talking to me. We could both see how excited she was, how angry. She was wearing one of those colorful caftan affairs she used to affect, so she looked like a violet cloud."

I could visualize the picture he was painting, and I was already afraid of the outcome.

Marcus went on. "She paid no attention to me but came straight to the bar and confronted Derek. She said, 'You're not going to marry Iris. I won't have it!' He didn't turn a hair, but he picked up the phone and called Cliff. He told him he'd better come right over and get his wife.

"I'd never seen Poppy in such a frantic state, but as she listened to Derek on the phone, she turned icy—like snow poured over fire. She set her hands on the bar and spread her fingers, and I can still remember the sparkle of the rings she liked to wear—that big sapphire Cliff had given her and that Iris sometimes wears now. When she spoke again, her words sounded as brittle as though they might splinter in the air. She said, 'If you try to marry Iris I'll kill you.' Both Derek and I knew she meant it, and he didn't even try to bluff. He just poured himself some Scotch and drank it down straight. And nobody said anything more until Cliff walked in. Then Poppy went right over to him and said, 'I've just told Derek I'll kill him before I'll let him marry Iris.'

"Cliff always liked Derek a lot better than I do, and he really does care about how Iris feels. But he knew better than anyone how emotional Poppy could be, and he just held her and soothed her and didn't argue. Over her shoulder he nodded at Derek and told him he would take his wife home. While he was worried about Poppy, I don't think he was taking any of this seriously then. She went with him meekly enough, and just before Cliff went out the door he asked Derek a question.

"He said, 'Do you mind telling me why my wife doesn't want you to marry Iris?'"

" 'You wouldn't want to know,' Derek told him. 'It might spoil a beautiful friendship.'

"Cliff didn't say another word. He just walked out with Poppy leaning on his arm and looking as though she was ready to fall apart. When they'd gone, Derek had nothing more to say to me. He just got busy on some ledgers. I knew I'd better hold any further questions, so I went home. Poppy had a bang-up fight with Iris later that same morning, and I took Iris off to the Garden Club and left her there. I guess Poppy shut herself in the orchid house after that. She always used the orchids to calm herself down when she was upset. That's where she died the same afternoon."

"Someone put a wedge in the door so Poppy couldn't get out," I said softly.

Marcus looked startled. "Who told you that?"

"Alida Burch. Just a little while ago. She made a point of telling me. She said she told me so that I would go away and leave them all alone. It was as though she was threatening me, trying to frighten me."

"Alida was Poppy's friend, and she's like an aunt to Poppy's daughters. You're the outsider who might diminish her influence on both girls, and even more on Cliff."

Beyond the porch, the morning seemed to be growing warmer, and Marcus turned a switch so the ceiling fan came on. I was no longer cold, and I raised my face to the breeze and tried to quiet my confused thoughts.

"I still don't understand how I can have any part to play now. Everything happened without me, and it will go on happening when I leave."

"Only you won't leave for a while." He sounded convinced, though he had no right to be.

"Is that what you're counting on?"

"Maybe."

"But why?"

For the first time since I'd met Marcus O'Neill, he seemed at a loss. He slapped across the Indian rug in his zori and threw himself disjointedly into a big armchair.

"Snatching at straws, I suppose. Any straws I could find. Laurel, I care a lot about Cliff and what happens to him. In a way, he's my family, and so are Iris and Fern. Look at this for a minute from where I sit. First, Poppy dead under unexplained circumstances. Cliff giving up, not caring about life. The marriage to Derek still set for Iris, with her father making no attempt to stop it. And Fern in love with the man her sister is going to marry. Yet apparently nothing at all is to be done. I'm really on the outside—a helpless friend. Helpless unless I could inject a whole new element into what is happening— you. Cliff's eldest daughter—with a right to be in his house, if he chose to have you there. A right to watch over him as no one else is doing right now, except maybe Alida—who isn't much help. Iris and Fern are centered on themselves, and Derek is going to get what he wants, because Cliff has given up and doesn't care. He's never shown in his treatment of Derek that he has any memory of what was said in the bar that morning. And maybe he hasn't. With Poppy dead, maybe he had to forget what Derek said—whatever it meant. Now that you're here, Cliff's coming to life and even taking some steps of his own. Just the idea of your coming made him start thinking about life again. You've already managed that."

"Enough to be frightened about something. He is afraid."

"Maybe of the truth—whatever it is."

"There was the wedge in the door. Alida said only she and Cliff know about that."

"Cliff only told me that it was jammed. One thing that worries me is that he's not a fearful man. He's always had plenty of courage—so why should he become afraid now? Maybe it's not really himself he's worried about."

"Then what?"

"That's something you can discover. Try to find out."

"I doubt if he'll talk to me, but I'll try. Thanks for seeing me, Marcus." I stood up, still feeling confused. Now I had two assignments to snoop!

He came with me to the door. "Our trip's still on for this afternoon, isn't it? I'll pick you up at one o'clock, and I'll bring some lunch along that we can eat later on the boat."

He waited in the doorway of his room, watching as I went down the stairs.

I found my way blindly back to Cliff's house, taking a few wrong turns. The front door stood open, but except for Angela in the kitchen, no one seemed to be about. I stopped to tell her I wouldn't be in for lunch and went outside to the orchid house. The sun was higher now, and the air felt humid and warm—the jungle climate tropical orchids liked best.

The door opened easily, and when I closed it behind me, it showed no signs of sticking. Probably it had been planed down since that fatal "jamming." The existence of the wedge had been kept from police and reporters.

The orchid house had become a shivery place for me, and I wasn't sure why I'd felt an urge to come here now. Perhaps it was to find Poppy—something of her spirit. I remembered Fern's tales about seeing her mother, but I wasn't looking for visions—just some sort of understanding.

I walked slowly down the central aisle to the place where she'd been found and stared around at the dozens of bright blooms, growing in sprays or individually in all their pots. One orchid near where I stood looked as though drops of blood had been scattered across its face, but this was, I assured myself, only a natural coloration.

I closed my eyes and listened with an inner ear. Perhaps if I concentrated, I might hear the orchids whispering among themselves, as Fern claimed they did. If only I knew how to listen, perhaps they would tell me the answers I sought. But the only sounds I heard were of the fan and the watering system.

Then someone came through the door at the far end of the greenhouse, and I looked around to see Cliff walking toward me down the center aisle.

My father was a tall man, but now his shoulders rounded, making him seem shorter. When he saw me there, he stopped in surprise, and his dramatic eyebrows questioned my presence.

"I'm communing," I told him lightly. "Fern says the orchids whisper to her, and I wondered if I could hear them too."

"Do you like orchids?"

I thought of his ominous will. "Not very much. Of course I don't know anything about them, and I'm not especially interested. I like the company of books better."

He looked about with a vague air of bewilderment and pain that touched me. I'd never expected to find Clifton York so vulnerable. This was not the moment to express my feelings about the changes he planned in his will. I'd have to speak to him, but not now. I wondered if he came here sometimes to try to find the wife he'd lost.

He moved past me among the flowers, stopping now and then to study individual orchids, almost as though he'd never seen them before.

"She used to spend so much time here," he mused. "Hours of painstaking care. It must have been far more creative work than I ever realized. I wasn't interested in orchids either—and I didn't share this with her as I might have. I suppose I treated the orchid house like a pleasant hobby. I indulged her, but I didn't take any part."

When it was too late we always blamed ourselves for what we hadn't done. If I wasn't careful now, I might make the same mistake with my father.

He went on, still half to himself. "I remember how excited Poppy always was when she developed some new species that turned out to be as beautiful as she'd hoped. And she always took an interest in my writing and read my manuscripts—while I didn't bother enough about her orchids. Lately I've been listening to Fern, and I'm just beginning to understand the wonder of a newly created variety that can surprise and delight everyone. But it was Poppy I should have listened to in the first place."

"Can't you let her go?" I asked gently. "Isn't it time?"

He bent his head, and I saw his grief again. "I don't want to let her go. As long as I can feel pain, she'll stay alive for me."

The old, old paradox. When the hurting stops, death becomes final, so we cling to pain.

He stood close enough for me to touch him, and I wanted to put my hand on his arm—to comfort him in some way. My ambivalence toward him was dying, and all my old resentments with it. In some strange way, my new, reluctant feeling toward Marcus had made me more aware of my own emotions. Who had been fair or unfair in the past, or even who was being so now, didn't matter as much as it had. It was time for this man, who was my father, and me—his eldest daughter—to begin something new between us, no matter how tentative and fragile. And the time to begin was now.

"Cliff," I said, "would you let me take you to dinner to-night?"

That startled him into an awareness of me, and his look softened. "No, Laurel, but I would like to take you to dinner, if you'll let me."

"I'd love that," I said, and heard a new warmth in my voice. "This afternoon I'm going out to Derek's wreck with Marcus, and I hope to do some diving. So I'm not sure when I'll be home."

"You're going down yourself?"

"Marcus said he could arrange it, though he didn't sound enthusiastic about having me dive."

"I think you'll prevail. I haven't been out to this new site yet myself."

I wondered how much he knew about Derek's plans for a party, and how he felt about them.

"We'll go to Casa Marina," he decided. "It's a marvelous old hotel—practically prehistoric and still thriving. Let's say seven-thirty, if you're back in time."

I thanked him and slipped away, knowing that he wanted to be alone with Poppy's orchids. I could feel better now about leaving him there. Tonight I would see him away from this house and all its undercurrents, and perhaps we could begin to find each other. Perhaps he might even tell me what was troubling him.

As I crossed the garden I remembered again the handyman whom I'd seen early this morning. Alida hadn't been disturbed about his presence, but I still didn't like the way the fellow had spoken to me. If I saw him again, I'd ask him a few questions.

The morning was gone, and I went up to my room to change for the boat trip. Poppy's two orchid photographs regarded me serenely, and her eyes watched me from the orchid mask in the same eerie way. I'd have felt happier with all those pictures out of my room, though not because of the woman herself. If Poppy's was a troubled spirit, as Fern believed, I didn't think she would bother with me. Nevertheless, the words Marcus had heard Derek speak to my father haunted me . . . *you wouldn't want to know.* Words Cliff must have thrust away after her death, since he appeared to hold nothing against Derek and had probably never confronted him with any demand for an explanation. If he could wipe the whole incident out, he was lucky.

I couldn't. More than ever, I wanted to know what sort of woman Poppy had been. Or even if Derek had been lying in whatever insinuation he might have intended. He was a man who would like to play with fire.

But most of all, I wanted to know my father—to feel more than curiosity and resentment toward him. A sense of warmth stirred in me again—the beginning of affection? Love of one sort for my father, and another, more disturbing feeling toward Marcus O'Neill? At least a melting had begun, a dissolving of protective ice that had held me for much too long. To feel was to be hurt, as my mother had so often warned me— and now I didn't care. Like my father, I might even welcome pain. At least it would mean that I was alive. That was what mattered. This afternoon perhaps I could let everything else go and simply enjoy being with Marcus.

For a time, that was what happened.

7

The afternoon sun was high and warm, and the sea moved in a gentle swell as Marcus headed Derek's outboard motor cruiser toward a portion of distant reef. He sat behind the white wheel of the *Snapdragon*, with me in the opposite seat behind the slanting glass screen.

I watched water sweeping past, lace-trimmed with froth. In places where the depth was greater, the color was a deeper blue, or where it covered sandy patches, blue-green.

"Is the Gulf Stream visible out here?" I asked above the roar of the motor.

Marcus shook his head. "The only way you can really tell where it is is by temperature change."

"You will take me down, won't you?"

"I suppose I'll have to." He smiled. "I've brought gear for us both." He made a wide gesture with one arm. "The *Santa Beatriz* would have been sailing somewhere off to the south, following the Carrera de Indias, the Highway of the Indies. That was the trade route connecting Spain with the New World. She'd have been sailing home, loaded with treasure, probably hoping she could make it before the hurricane season. She waited too long, and a storm blew her off course and smashed her on a reef. Derek is convinced that he's found the right stretch of coral rock to locate her. What's left of her.''

As I listened, feeling comfortably lazy yet warming to the hint of excitement in his voice, I grew more eager than ever to swim down to whatever waited for us on the sea bottom.

I'd worn my shorts and shirt over my bathing suit and had borrowed sneakers for my feet. With my skin well oiled against the sun, I felt comfortable and keenly aware of water, wind, and fresh salt air, and all too sharply aware of Marcus. He was brown enough not to burn, though his billed cap had left a white mark across his forehead. He too seemed relaxed this afternoon, with tension between us eased for once. The feeling of peace—however deceptive—soothed me. Perhaps this was only a sea spell, since I'd felt much less comfortable with him on land.

We were an hour out of Key West when Marcus pointed and swung the wheel to bring the boat about. Our speed lessened, and I saw Derek's workboat, an oversized, battered tug named *Dolphin*, which had been anchored close enough for divers to go down to the wreck site. *Dolphin* seemed an incongruous name for a boat so lacking in grace and elegance, but she moved in the water with her own competence—she was a survivor.

As we neared the site, the sense of excitement in Marcus seemed to increase. I could see why he would be a good writer —he responded with all his senses and emotions to everything around him, and he would later convey his own exhilaration to his readers.

''The cannons Derek has found are near the first reef,'' he said. ''Reefs can go on and on in rows, and the inner ridges can be hard to reach—dangerous. A single surge in the water can smash a boat into them, so we have to anchor far enough away."

I was already getting out of my shorts and peeling off my shirt, eager to be underwater.

He watched me doubtfully. "Are you sure you want to do this?"

"Of course I do. I'm not a beginner."

"In these waters you are. Once we're under, stay close to me, and don't go wandering off because something attracts your attention. If I give you a signal, follow it. The anchor line's our way back to the boat, but we'll have to leave it to get closer to the reef. Just don't go putting your hand into any crevices or caves. Moray eels have nasty little teeth, and they lurk around rocks."

"What about sharks?" That was a question I'd asked before. I had seen the movie, and we had them off Long Island.

"Sometimes they come around, but if you don't make any sudden movements, you're probably all right. It's usually blood or jerky motions that attract predators. Even something shiny like a ring can catch the attention of a barracuda or a shark. I'm glad you're not wearing any today. A barracuda can be pretty big, and they're curious fish, but they aren't likely to attack—or sharks either—unless you make them think you're prey."

He was making me thoroughly nervous, but it was necessary to be forewarned when, as he said, I was a novice in these waters.

"I'll take you over to the *Dolphin* later," he went on. "First, we'll go down and look around. Stay away from the divers— especially if an airlift is being used. If there's any sudden silting that clouds the water, we'll go straight up."

"How deep is it out here?"

"Not very deep—perhaps thirty feet. The water's fairly warm, so we can go down for a while without a wet suit. Derek's divers wear wet suits that look like long red underwear. One special warning, Laurel—stay away from coral, no matter how pretty it looks. It can cut deeply, and sting, and even cause infection if you touch the wrong kind."

"I'll be careful," I promised. I meant to be careful about a lot of things.

"Maybe you'll even have beginner's luck and find something. I'll take down a mesh bag on my belt, just in case."

"If Derek's crew has been searching, won't they have everything up by now that's there to be found?"

"They haven't touched the main treasure—if it's still in this location. The bottom of the ocean's alive, and currents shift from day to day, so the sea bottom changes all the time. It can bury what you uncovered yesterday, and uncover something you never saw before. If you find anything, of course it goes over to the *Dolphin*. Finders aren't keepers in treasure hunting, when somebody else was there first."

Marcus helped me with the tank harness and face mask. Not easy in a bouncing boat, but we managed. I tried the regulator in my mouth and breathed good air from the tank. Except for the fins, my weight belt went on last. Marcus warned me against a roll backwards from the deck, or a stride-off, so I went meekly down the boarding ladder and put my fins on in the water. Until he could trust me, I'd have to behave.

Marcus had stripped to swim shorts, and I'd helped with his gear, so he followed me into the water. We would swim against the current going toward the wreck site, he had said, since that would make it easier swimming back to the boat—less energy involved. Our own air bubbles would give us the direction of the water current.

The first liquid shock seemed cool, but I grew used to it quickly and it felt delicious. The sensation of gentle support was always exhilarating. Following Marcus, I flutter-kicked just under the surface, not heading down till we neared the reef.

This underwater world seemed marvelously different from the waters off Long Island. Bands of sunlight cut through a bluish translucence. Schools of fish darted away from us in unison, but as we went deeper, I experienced the wonderful sense of flying that was a release from earthbound heaviness. When I reached the bottom, I finger-walked along the sand, my body equalizing the pressure, so I felt nothing of the weight of water around me. Sand stirred under my fingertips, and tiny clouds of it rose and settled again. The water was so clear that I could see for a hundred feet or more. It was reassuring to glimpse the bottom of the *Snapdragon* and locate the anchor line we had followed down.

A strange sense of joy filled me. The last time I'd experienced anything like this was in the opposite element, when I'd stood on a mountaintop in Vermont looking out over a great panorama of forest and ranges. I felt the same joyful wonder then, but though this was different, the surge of emotion was the same—an awareness of boundaries removed, of reaching into the limitless.

At the same time I was, as always, sharply aware of Marcus, now swimming beside me. His thick hair stirred in the water, and at this depth it seemed brown instead of red, as though with a life of its own. We were so close at times that we touched, and without all this gear it would be very easy to swim into his arms.

I wondered how all this felt to him. The use of words for communication between us was lost, but I made a circle with thumb and forefinger and waved it at him. His eyes seemed to shine through his face mask, and he returned the gesture. I felt closer to him in sharing this adventure than I'd done on land, where he seemed ready to aggravate me.

When he pointed ahead I saw small scarlet buoys floating in the water, anchored to something in the sand. Divers from the *Dolphin* were working farther along with hand blowers, and apparently earlier finds had been marked to keep them visible. As I swam between the buoys, I saw that yellow lines had been laced back and forth in a grid that marked the area for divers. We were able to swim above the pattern, and as I looked down through my face mask I saw what seemed at first to be a long rock, half-buried in sand. When Marcus pointed, I realized that it was one of the bronze cannons. Underwater it looked greenish, and when I swam closer I saw two bronze lifting rings cast in the shape of dolphins.

The water around me seemed suddenly charged with electricity. This cannon had ridden the deck of a Spanish galleon, and the hands of men lost in the sea had touched it more than three hundred years ago!

I swam on and saw how close I'd come to the coral reef. Here sea fans waved, and over there was a forest of golden staghorn. It seemed a fantasy world out of dreams—yet as real as it was beautiful.

Another buoy marked an irregular shape that might be a ship's anchor, and beyond it coral rose massively. I resisted the push of the current while I studied the irregular bank. There in the rock, encased in coral, was the great form of a ship—a ship with broken spars, masts, and timbers, all outlined in living rock. I forgot to breathe for a moment, and then sucked in air.

Marcus was a little way off, and I kicked my way over to nudge him. When he looked around I pointed. He must have sensed my excitement, but he only shook his head, and I knew that whatever I was seeing had been noted before and meant nothing. To treasure hunters, coral growth must often look like old timbers or metal—even to the extent of seeming to take on the shape of a ship.

We swam on, and when he pointed at a section of the grid, I saw stones lying on the bottom. Ballast stones, undoubtedly, that had been packed into holds that would sail empty to the ports Spain had opened in the Caribbean, and from which her ships would sail back filled with treasure from the New World. On the return voyage some of the ballast would be used again if needed, so these stones didn't mean a ship empty of treasure.

As I swam close, a tiny spot of light caught my eye, and I swam over and poked it with one finger. Silt rose at once, burying the yellow gleam. I fanned sand away gently with my hand and closed my fingers about the drop of light. Something hard pressed into my palm. Holding it up tightly, I showed it to Marcus. He took the bit of metal from me and put it into the mesh bag that floated from his weight belt. His nod of approval told me I'd found something.

Dreamily I swam on, aware of all around me. Sea growth on the bottom swayed gently in the current—like a row of slow-motion dancers in grass skirts. The little fish seemed almost friendly and for the moment unafraid as I watched the marvel of their coordinated movements. They had their own secret signals, just as birds could fly geometrically in a flock.

Lost in this world of new sensation, I didn't notice when Marcus went on ahead, probably expecting me to follow. When I looked around again, silting had risen in the water, blurring my vision, and I could no longer see him. In a moment he would miss me and return, so I needn't worry, but I wished I'd paid attention to where he'd gone, as he'd told me to do. If the silt didn't settle, I would go straight up, and the dive boat would orient me. But the sandy fog brought a curious confusion, so that I wasn't sure which way was up, and which down.

Before I could strike out toward the surface, another diver came into view, kicking toward me. His head was encased in a yellow helmet that was part of his double-tank outfit and breathing apparatus, so I couldn't see his hair. Black gloves hid his hands, and somehow the loss of human identity seemed unsettling. From behind his mask, his eyes were intent and unblinking in their watchfulness, so I felt that a threat was being directed toward me.

My inability to speak or shout for help was suddenly terrifying. Why a diver from the *Dolphin* should seem menacing, I didn't know, but as he swam around me, circling me again and again, deliberately kicking up more silt with his fins so that the water grew more opaque, my sense of danger increased. He was trying to frighten me, and when he came straight at me, bumping me hard, I kicked furiously upward—I hoped it was upward—and felt enormous relief when my head broke the surface.

The *Dolphin* floated nearby, with Marcus waiting for me at the diving platform. The other diver had disappeared. At the ladder I removed my fins and looped them over my wrist so I could climb aboard more easily. Marcus boosted me up, and one of the men gave me a hand. When I was out of my gear, I looked back over the water, but I could see no sign of the other diver. Had I exaggerated the threat? I didn't really think so.

The aft deck of the *Dolphin* was cluttered with objects salvaged from the sea bottom, and to me mostly unidentifiable and not very valuable-looking. Marcus introduced me to Captain Curtin, who was in charge, and took out the bit of metal

I'd given him. In a moment, crew and divers grouped around us, and I sensed their excitement.

"Is it a piece of eight?" I asked.

Marcus shook his head. "Pieces of eight are silver. It's not a gold doubloon either, is it, Captain?"

"It's gold all right," Captain Curtin said. "Looks like a medallion of the Madonna." He was a big man with a full beard and faded blue eyes almost lost against his ruddy tan. "Gold never changes underwater. It's about the only metal that never gives anything up and doesn't collect coral growth or tarnish."

I felt pleasantly dazed and a little giddy. I'd gone down to the sea bottom and picked up a gold medallion lost three hundred years before—probably from the *Santa Beatriz*.

Marcus smiled at me. "I told you—beginner's luck!"

I took the medallion and turned it about in my fingers. Perhaps some nobleman had worn this sailing back to a Spain he would never see again because a hurricane would blow his ship off course and smash it against the line of reefs. I wondered if his bones lay somewhere beneath the sand where I'd found this medal.

"Derek will be pleased," Captain Curtin said. "It's one more bit of evidence that we've only touched the edge of what's down there. Thanks, Miss York—we'd better send you down again."

I found the air cool now, and someone saw me shiver and brought a terry robe to wrap around me. Marcus borrowed a jacket, and we stayed on deck so he could show me some of the objects that had been brought up from the sea bottom. There were cannon balls by the score, some encrusted forms that were thought to be arquebuses, shards of broken vessels, and the sulphide impression of a silver coin in coral.

"Coral's crazy stuff," Marcus said. "It has to grow on something, so it attaches to anything it can find—sometimes even itself. But it can bury one area and leave another close by untouched. It needs oxygen to multiply, so it picks the crevices and angles of anything that sinks to the bottom."

Captain Curtin nodded. "In the Red Sea coral growths are massive. They turn into huge trees. Here the formations are smaller, but nuisance enough if you have to carve into every coral lump to see what it's concealing."

A diver had just come up over the platform, and someone went to help with his tank and harness. I watched closely, to see if this was the man who had circled me under the water. When he stood on deck in his red wet suit and looked around, he spotted me and grinned mockingly. He was the diver I'd met below, and with a shock I recognized him as the unpleasant fellow I'd seen in the garden at Cliff's house—the man who'd given me an odd, veiled threat about my not being wanted there.

As he went off toward the crew's cabin area, I grabbed Marcus's arm. "Who is that man who just came aboard?"

Marcus looked after him. "Eddie? Why—what's up? That's Eddie Burch."

"Eddie—*Burch?*"

"Sure. The skeleton in Alida's closet. She was married to him way back when. He works for Derek now."

My teeth were chattering, not just from cold, and Captain Curtin noticed. "Come along to my cabin. Coffee will warm you up. Besides, there's someone who'll be interested to see what you've found."

The captain's cabin was up a companionway. I followed, slapping along wetly in bare feet, with Marcus behind me. I wanted to tell him what had happened, but there was no chance. When I stepped over a sill into the compact cabin, I saw the woman who sat at a table that had been anchored to the floor. It was Iris York. She greeted me coolly as I came in.

Marcus seated me, poured coffee for us both, and then took the gold medal I still clutched and slid it across to Iris. Captain Curtin stayed near the door, watching.

"Look what Laurel picked up on the bottom just now," Marcus said.

Iris took the bit of gold and examined it, looking like something carved out of gold herself, with her well-oiled tan, her back and shoulders, arms and legs bare in a white halter and shorts. She sat sideways at the table, her legs crossed—long and golden from thighs to ankles. Her black hair had been released from its pinned-up swirl and hung forward in a thick mass over one shoulder. Around her upper left arm was clasped a band of wide, antique gold. Rather an Egyptian touch, I thought, and yet it suited her. When I glanced at Marcus, I saw that he could hardly take his eyes from Iris. Any woman who looked as she did could have any man she wanted.

The medal seemed not to please her, and she pushed it back to Marcus. New finds probably meant further postponement of her marriage to Derek, since they would intensify his search.

"How did you like diving?" she asked me, though I doubted that she cared in the least. I remembered that Fern had said her sister would be sorry and ashamed of the way she'd behaved in the orchid house, but she showed no evidence of regret to me.

"It was wonderful," I told her. "Exhilarating. Fern says you don't care for diving."

"I don't even like to swim." She changed the subject as though it bored her. "I hear you're going to Casa Marina tonight with Cliff?" She spoke lazily, long lashes half veiling her eyes.

I came to a quick decision, disliking her half-hidden malice.

"Yes, I am. I invited him to dinner, but he said he wanted to take me. Perhaps I can talk to him more freely away from the house. I need to tell him that I know about his plans for a new will, and I want none of that for me. I don't want him to leave me anything. Certainly not the greenhouse."

Dark lashes fluttered down as Iris closed her eyes for a moment. When she opened them, I saw her disbelief. Nothing I said would convince her that I hadn't come here for whatever I could get from my father. It didn't matter. I only needed to convince him, and I let the matter of the will go.

"I'd like to know about something that happened while I was in the water," I said. "A few minutes ago, a diver from this boat tried to frighten me. He swam around, stirring up silt, and then he came straight at me and bumped me hard enough to hurt. I broke away and swam up. I couldn't see him anywhere then, but while I was on deck, the same man came up from the bottom, and when he took off his helmet, I knew I'd seen him before. He spoke to me yesterday out behind Cliff's house. Marcus says he's Eddie Burch. What was he trying to do? Why on earth should he try to scare me?"

As I spoke I wondered if Iris might even have sent him down to torment me. However, she only looked displeased as she spoke to Captain Curtin.

"Ask Eddie to come down here for a moment, will you?" When the captain had gone, Iris turned to me again. "He shouldn't come to the house at all. Cliff doesn't want him around, since he disturbs Alida. I wish Derek hadn't hired him."

The captain didn't return, and Eddie came up the companionway alone. Again he wore khaki shorts, his upper body bare and his chest as hairy as his legs. Curving from front to back over one shoulder was a conspicuous white scar—where he must once have been cruelly sliced with some sharp instrument that had gone deep. On land he moved as though the shoulder was stiff, but he overcame this in the water, swimming easily, as I'd had reason to discover.

While he had stared at me deliberately underwater, now his pale blue eyes seemed to shift beyond me evasively, just as they'd done yesterday morning in the garden.

"Why did you try to frighten my sister a little while ago?" Iris asked directly. I noted her use of "sister" in surprise.

Eddie blinked and examined a blistered stain on the ceiling of the cabin. "Scare her? I didn't scare her. I just gave her a pat on the shoulder. I'm sorry if she got scared." His look dropped suddenly, disconcertingly, to me, and there seemed a warning in his eyes that contradicted his apologetic words.

"All right, Eddie," Iris said. "I suppose we'll have to accept that. But don't try anything else. And don't show up around the house again. My father doesn't want you bothering Alida."

An angry flush came into the man's face. "If you want to know—it was Alida who asked me to come," he said. "God knows, I don't want to have any truck with her!"

Eddie returned to the deck and his job as a diver. I felt queasier than ever as a roll of the boat slid my coffee cup away.

"I'd like to go outside, please," I said.

Marcus got me out of the cabin quickly, and fresh air revived me. We picked our way across the cluttered deck to where we could get into our diving gear again. It was a relief to be away from the *Dolphin*, pushing through the water swiftly with the aid of our flippers. By the time I was on board the *Snapdragon* again, I felt fine. It was the cabin, and Iris and Eddie, even the smell of the *Dolphin*, that had been unsettling.

Now when Marcus brought out a lunch hamper we unwrapped chicken sandwiches, cold juice, and slices of apple pie, and I could eat with a good appetite.

"How could Alida ever have married a man like Eddie?" I asked Marcus.

"Who ever knows why anybody marries anybody? Maybe she didn't have much other choice, and maybe he was a lot more attractive twenty years or more ago. It didn't last long, anyway. Alida was better off without him."

"Then why would she ask him to come to see her now?"

"We don't really know that he was telling the truth. Maybe it's better not to ask too many questions and stir things up."

"You're being mysterious again."

He grinned at me. "Maybe that's my attraction—the man with a terrible secret. Why quarrel with it?"

But I felt so much less comfortable with him now than I had when we were in the water. I didn't like my own contradictory responses—sometimes easy and half affectionate, sometimes uncertain and resentful. Besides, there was always Iris. I had never felt like this toward a man before, and I wasn't sure that I wanted to wake up suddenly and discover that I was in love. But how did you stop the feeling, once it started and you were on the way?

"I'm glad you came out with me, Laurel," he said. "It's been a good day. Go easy with your father tonight. You fly into things sometimes, and right now he's pretty vulnerable."

"I don't want to hurt him—not any more. But neither do I want to be used for some end of his own against Iris and Fern."

Marcus started the motor, and we sped back toward Key West.

"What will Derek do with that stuff he's found?" I asked when we were on our way. "It didn't look especially valuable—except for the medal I picked up."

"History can't be valued. A musket ball could be important. No matter what he finds, it shouldn't be sold. But then—that's always the argument between historians and treasure hunters."

"It's the treasure hunters who find things, isn't it?"

"Sometimes. That's a quarrel that hasn't been settled yet, and maybe it never will be. Arguments can get pretty fierce on both sides."

I didn't try to talk again until we'd docked at the Landsend Marina at the foot of Margaret Street.

"It's Alida who worries me most," I told him when we were on our way in the car. "I keep feeling that she's involved in something—well, perilous, that may shake everyone up."

"Then leave it alone, Laurel," Marcus said quietly. "You'd better stay out of the way if you see a tidal wave coming! I don't know exactly what Alida has on her mind, but you may be right. Unless she wants to talk, let it go."

"I don't think she'd use Eddie for something little. Not the way she probably feels about him."

"Right. Anyway, I don't think Eddie will bother you again."

"What about this boat party of Derek's?"

"It's coming up soon, and I don't like the idea. I wish your father would refuse to go. But Derek usually gets his way."

I had one more question to ask before we reached Cliff's. "Why do you suppose Iris went out to the *Dolphin* on her own today?"

"I've been wondering about that ever since we found her in the cabin. Mostly she only goes out there with Derek, and then reluctantly. She's not the little fish Fern is, in spite of growing up in Key West. Funny thing—Poppy wasn't crazy about the water either. She used to say she'd probably drowned in a former lifetime."

"And this time she was murdered by orchids," I said softly.

Marcus pulled up to the curb in front of the house. "Neither Iris nor Fern would ever have hurt Poppy. They both adored their mother. In spite of Poppy's opposition to Iris marrying Derek, there was never anything Poppy could do to stop that, and they both knew it. So Iris didn't need to fight back seriously."

"But she and Poppy did quarrel."

"And probably about Derek, but that's not for you to worry about now."

"All right," I said. "Thank you for the day, Marcus—it was glorious."

I started to get out of the car, but he pulled me back and leaned over to kiss me on the cheek. I felt more pleased than I liked. The gesture had been casual, and I didn't look back as I went up the walk to the house.

When I reached the steps I found Fern on the porch, watching me quizzically. I said, "Hi," and moved past her into the house, in no mood for any of her whimsies just then.

She bounced up from her chair and came after me. "Iris went out to the *Dolphin* this afternoon, didn't she? All on her own, though she hates boats. And without Derek! How come?"

"You'd better ask her," I said, starting up the stairs.

"We aren't speaking right now. Look, Laurel, I like you, and I don't want to see you get hurt. Marcus and Iris belong together. They always have. So you'd better not get too interested in him. He'll never look at anyone else."

Leaving Derek for Fern? I wondered. When I didn't answer, her fair skin pinkened and tears came into her eyes.

"I know what you think—that I'm crazy about Derek. And it's true!"

"I'm sorry," I said. "We seem to be a pretty mixed-up family, don't we?"

Fern touched my arm as we reached the door of my room, and came in with me. "It's not your fault things are so mixed up. Have fun tonight with Cliff."

The grapevine certainly worked around here, I thought as I went into my room, glancing automatically toward the row of orchid photographs. And then I looked again—shocked.

Glass had been broken from the frame of the center picture, so that only jagged teeth remained around the edges, and bits of glass lay on the floor. The photo of the masked woman had been slashed into strips that hung askew in the frame.

Fern backed into the hall, her eyes wide and frightened, and I turned to catch her by the arm. "Did you do this?" I demanded.

She shook her head wildly. "It must have been Poppy! I've felt it all along. She doesn't want you in her room, Laurel. Oh, I can't bear this any more!"

"Stop it!" I told her. "It wasn't Poppy. A spirit couldn't use a knife so vigorously! Besides, she must have liked that picture."

Fern stared at me for a moment and then pulled her arm free and rushed off. I heard her bedroom door slam, and the sound left me utterly drained. An afternoon of wind and sun, the experience of diving to the wreck, plus all these wild emotions was too much. All I wanted was to get under a shower and then throw myself on the bed to rest until it was time to dress for dinner with my father. But there would be no peace for me while the two remaining orchids stared at me reproachfully from the wall—as though they blamed me for the destruction of their sister photograph.

I took the smashed picture from its place, shook broken glass into a wastebasket, and cleaned up the floor. Then I piled the framed photographs, with the slashed one on top, and carried them into the hall.

No one appeared to be around as I climbed the stairs to my father's study. There I placed the frames on Alida's desk, found paper and a felt pen, and wrote *Please put these away*.

As I was about to leave, I noticed that the trapdoor to the captain's walk was open. Late afternoon sun glowed at the top of the stairs, and there was someone up there. When I stepped close, I saw that Alida sat huddled on the top step, her hands clasped about her knees. For a moment she stared at me without moving.

I said, "I want to show you something, Alida."

Reluctantly she came down the steps, clinging to the rail, and I gestured toward the photographs I'd piled on her desk. "Will you put these away somewhere, please? So that whoever is playing these tricks will stop. You can see what's been done to the top photograph."

Almost as if she feared to touch it, she picked up one of the slashed strips and stared at it. But now it was Alida herself who held my attention. She looked awful—her skin mottled, and with deep shadows under her eyes.

"Something's terribly wrong, isn't it?" I said. "Isn't there someone you can talk to? Someone you can trust?"

She dropped the colored strip as though it burned her and shook her head. "There's no one I'd dare to trust. Fern and Iris are like my own daughters, but I can't talk to either of them."

I drew her toward her desk. "Sit down for a minute. This afternoon Marcus took me in Derek's boat out to the *Dolphin*. Eddie Burch turned up in the water near me when I was diving, and he tried to frighten me again."

She moved in her swivel chair, turning from me.

"Look," I said, "if you're concerned about the change my father may make in his will, I mean to ask him not to do what he plans. Iris doesn't believe me, but I really don't want anything from him."

"What you want is—everything," she said. "What you want is his love."

I left her there staring at the orchid photographs and went away. I knew that she was right.

8

What you want is his love.

Alida's words haunted me as I showered and dressed for dinner. Was this the deep reason, the true reason that had brought me here? Had this always been the hidden longing I'd fought against? Longing for a father who would love and care for me? But even if this were true, why should anyone else mind? The giving of love took nothing from others. If Cliff ever came to love me, it wouldn't affect his love for Fern and Iris. Would it?

I put on my lemon shantung and slipped a comb backed with beaten gold into my hair. Mother had given me the small gold earrings I put on as a last touch—so that I would have a bit of her with me as a mascot through what might be a difficult evening.

Cliff was waiting when I went downstairs. His eyes seemed to approve the way I looked, but I didn't know him well enough to gauge his mood. I seemed to want approval these days, not only my father's but Marcus's as well.

Everything in Key West was nearby, so it took only a few minutes to drive to Casa Marina on the Atlantic shore. On the way Cliff told me about the hotel's history, avoiding personal topics.

"You know, when Henry Flagler brought his railroad to Key West, he promised to build a fine resort hotel on the island. But he died before he could keep that promise, so construction on Casa Marina didn't begin until 1918."

The building was a huge, far-flung Spanish creation built from poured concrete, with a straight central portion, two wings on either side slanting toward the front, and arched windows on the lower level decorating most of the building. Restoration by a well-known hotel chain had brought it back to its original splendor of Spanish Renaissance.

The lounge, with its vaulted black cypress ceilings and great fireplace, was as spacious as a ballroom, its dark floor gleaming with a high gloss and left bare where people would walk. A sitting area offered oriental rugs, handsome wicker furniture, and small glass-topped tables. Again there were arched windows opening on a rear piazza and swimming pool. Green plants abounded everywhere, and wrought-iron lamps were set in the wall at intervals, shedding agreeable light.

This was a more elegant Key West than one saw around Mallory Square, and dress was somewhat more decorous. At least in the evening.

My father looked handsome in a light suit and brown shirt, and at every turn he was recognized and greeted. I was proud to be introduced as his oldest daughter. If some people looked puzzled, he didn't explain, and once he gave me a sly wink.

Since we were early for dinner, he found a place where we could sit on the long brick piazza overlooking the pool. The hotel rooms would have wonderful views of Key West, the Atlantic Ocean, and the Gulf of Mexico. Below where we sat, the pool waters shone blue in soft, reflected lighting.

More than anything, I wanted to relax and not think about Marcus, not think about the way I wanted him here tonight. I wanted to forget those beastly orchids and get better acquainted with my father. But first there were matters I needed to talk to him about. Alida was wrong when she said that all I wanted was his love. I needed his concern, his advice. I wanted him to be my friend as well as my father. He gave me an opening by asking how I'd enjoyed the trip out to the *Dolphin*.

I told him about my underwater encounter with Eddie Burch and about the way he'd spoken to me at the house as well.

"Iris told him to stay away," I finished. "She said you didn't want him to come around bothering Alida."

"That's right. And I don't like this behavior toward you."

"Has he worked for Derek long?"

Cliff looked over green shrubbery toward the pool. "Derek and Eddie started out as enemies," he said after a moment. "Years ago, before he married Alida, Eddie got mixed up in some sort of illegal escapade. He was a pretty wild buccaneer type when he was young. Maybe that was the unlikely quality that appealed to Alida. I've never been clear about the story, and I don't know what part Derek may have played. Key West builds its own legends, you know, and you can't believe everything that's told. Anyway, there was a nasty fight, and Derek sliced Eddie's shoulder open with an old army sword. Then he turned right around and saved Eddie's life by getting him to a doctor and paying all the hospital bills. In some strange way, Eddie's been attached to him on and off ever since. When Derek located evidence of a wrecked galleon, he hired Eddie to work for him. He's a good diver. But he was certainly no husband for Alida."

"He gives me the creeps," I said. "Another thing—Iris went out to the *Dolphin* on her own, and everyone seems to think that was strange. Perhaps that's something she's never done on her own before?"

"It could be she just wants to involve herself more in Derek's interests. I've even suggested that. She's been frowning on treasure diving all along. Perhaps an older man will be good for Iris. She's more mature than Fern will ever be, but she still needs someone to take hold."

That was what women had been taught for centuries, but I wondered if it was really what Iris needed.

"What about Fern?" I asked. "I mean about this feeling she has for Derek?"

His voice softened as he spoke of his youngest daughter. "Fern is a lot like her mother. Emotional, impulsive. She has crushes because she's still so young—younger than her years. I don't want to see her hurt, but I think she'll get over this obsession and fix her attention on someone else as soon as her sister is married."

Once more I asked the question to which I'd never had a full answer. Perhaps it was a dangerous question, after what Marcus had told me, but I had to ask it.

"Why was your wife so against this marriage to Derek?"

He answered easily enough. "Poppy was always governed by her emotions. She didn't like Derek."

That was a comfortable explanation for him, and I didn't push it any further.

Cliff went on speaking of Fern. "Unfortunately, Fern's crush on Derek came before Iris was interested in him. I think he was amused by Fern and foolishly played along, teasing her for a while. He was never serious, and I don't think he ever understood for a minute how she felt. When Iris turned her attention on Derek, he woke up to the fact that Iris was a woman, and not the little girl he remembered."

He sighed deeply, and I waited for him to go on.

"Fern, of course, didn't stand a chance with him in the first place. She has always needed more than I could give her. Help her, if you can, Laurel. She likes you."

His appeal touched me. "I hope she likes me, but I'm not always sure. Sometimes she bewilders me."

"That's her delight, her special charm," Cliff said. "Her mother was dazzling, unpredictable, and sometimes Fern has those qualities too."

For a moment he lost himself in some memory, and I had to bring him back to what was, for me, the most important question of all.

"Cliff, I've been told about the changes you might make in your will."

He was instantly alert, on guard. I sensed a wall being raised between us, but I had to persist.

"Please don't do this, Cliff. I don't want to get into the middle of a fight with my sisters. And I didn't come here for any sort of gain."

"Why did you come?"

I tried to answer him honestly. "At first I thought it was because I was angry with you, because I wanted to pay you off for leaving us when I was a child. I don't feel that way any more."

He lowered his guard just a little. "I wish I had more to give you, Laurel. Of myself, I mean. There's no feeling left in me. Everything died when Poppy left me."

He made a slight, sad gesture of dismissal and glanced at his watch. Nothing had been resolved, and now something of his own depression had touched me.

"Come along," he said, rousing himself. "It's time to go in for dinner. I've made a reservation for us at Henry's."

I knew he would listen to nothing more I might say about his will, and I had to give in to him for now. There would be another time, and I'd return to this.

We walked through the hotel to the restaurant that had been named for Henry Flagler and were led to a table on the lower level. The room was large, with soft lighting, dark woodwork, and a feeling of elegance about it. Arched Spanish windows looked out at the evening, and there was air conditioning, instead of the usual ceiling fans.

When we'd ordered, with a wine of my father's choice, he surprised me by reopening the subject of the will.

"Who told you about my plans, Laurel?"

"Marcus told me this morning. You mustn't do this, Cliff! It would be awful for Fern and Iris if you gave me the greenhouse."

"You're not in a position to judge," he said curtly.

Once more, the topic had been sharply closed. He was a stubborn man, my father, but sometimes I could be stubborn too. I wouldn't give up meekly on this, even if I had to drop it again for now.

Having been sharp with me, he now chose to exert himself to be entertaining and charming. As we ate our green turtle soup and tossed salads, he told me enchanting stories—funny stories about Key West, about his searches for book backgrounds, about some of the local characters he knew so well. There were even "characters" among the cats that abounded in Key West.

None of this touched on the personal, however, until the waiter brought the swordfish we'd both ordered. As he picked up his fork, Cliff began to talk about Poppy. Tonight his memories must seem so close that he had to put them into words.

"I never eat fish without thinking of her. Not that I don't

think of her all the time. But I remember how strange it always seemed that she could be a Key West girl and dislike fish. She loathed it. Somehow, she was a land child, perhaps even a mountain child, born in the wrong place. Whenever we traveled to mountain country she was happy, and she wanted nothing to do with the sea. Whereas I love the sea. Fern is practically a mermaid, of course, and that used to upset Poppy."

The swordfish was perfectly broiled, and I was quiet as I ate, wanting him to go on with whatever he chose to tell me, pleased with his confidences and valuing this rare time alone with him.

Unexpectedly, he began to talk about the love between a man and a woman.

"It's a subject I write about often in my books. How my characters feel is as important as what they do. But love can't be written about in general terms. Granted the affinity that can grow between two people, it's still the small details that fill it in. Perhaps the way a lock of hair falls across a woman's cheek, or a breathless break that comes into her voice. Even a scattering of freckles across a nose can break your heart. Or the way a woman looks at a child, and the different way she looks at a man. Always the endearing detail that adds up to make a whole. Sometimes it can become an annoying detail when you're falling out of love. A tapping foot that seemed attractive in the beginning turns to maddening monotony."

I wondered how many times this stranger who was my father had fallen out of love, and what details had maddened him about my own mother. Though of course he'd never stopped loving Poppy.

He went on, talking half to himself. "It's always the bits and pieces that add up inexplicably to the state of loving someone.

When that person vanishes from your life, you go right on remembering details, hundreds of those details you were still adding up to make the whole person you loved."

He was doing this now with Poppy, but he'd also struck a chord of recognition in me. Just such an adding up of details had begun for me—Marcus's red hair that I sometimes wanted to touch, his eyes that were like a changing sea, sometimes with storms in them and an excitement that stirred a response in me. The sense of his physical presence—always that. And behind all the details my eagerness to find out all about him.

"Are you in love?" my father asked.

I looked past lighted candles into his eyes. "I'm not sure I want to be." That wasn't true. If I were honest, I wanted to love with all my heart—and was still afraid.

"That sounds like your mother's caution," he said. "In her purposeful way, Janet could be a destructive woman. But you're my daughter too, and you won't let your head influence your heart too much. Is it someone back home?"

I gave up. "It's Marcus O'Neill," I said bluntly.

He looked troubled, and suddenly I felt irritated. "Oh, I know it's too soon. And more than one person has told me that Marcus is in love with Iris. So maybe it's time he got over that!"

For a moment my father stared at me. Then he laughed. I had never heard him laugh before—a ringing laughter that held nothing back and that made a head or two turn at other tables. I liked him all the more for not being decorous.

"I'll bet on you, Laurel," he said.

I wasn't so sure I could bet on myself. I had no idea whether Marcus had begun to add up any endearing details about me—or even what they might be. It was so easy to put on a bold face of confidence when inside one was nothing but a quivering uncertainty.

For a time we both stayed away from thin ice. It had been skated on just long enough, and I think neither of us wanted to break through into deeper water. Yet it was a reassuring time for me. The beginning of new feeling had sprung up between my father and me—a seed from which some stronger emotion might grow. I could never recapture the trust and adoration I'd had for him as a child—that I knew I'd had, even though I couldn't remember. Everything between us was tentative now, and tenuous. The wrong word might set it back forever. We were still strangers reaching out just a little—father to daughter, and daughter to father. For the moment, I told myself, this was enough.

But it wasn't enough.

I longed to put more of my new feeling about him into words—before it was too late. Always the ominous knowledge of his mortality hung over me. Though I hated to think about it, I knew I could lose him at any time.

Without really expecting to, I reached my hand out to him across the table. He took it so quickly that I knew he'd been waiting too. We needed no words. In that moment he was truly my father, and I would remember this always.

We were finishing our cherries jubilee when the headwaiter brought Iris and Derek to our table. Iris looked distraught as she dropped into the chair pulled out for her. Derek stood by, clearly impatient over whatever was happening.

"What is it?" Cliff asked. "Has anything happened to Fern?"

Iris tried to speak, choked, and began to cry, so that Derek took over bluntly.

"It's Alida. That idiot woman's swallowed a bottle of sleeping pills—tried to kill herself. Iris found her upstairs in your study, Cliff, and called me. She's been taken to the hospital, and Iris thinks you'd better be there when she comes around. *If* she comes around."

Cliff rose at once. "I'll drive over right away. I'm sorry, Laurel. Derek, can you and Iris take Laurel home?"

"I'll go with you to the hospital, Cliff," Iris said quickly. "Laurel, when Derek drives you home will you look in on Fern? She was upset when I left, and she shouldn't be alone."

Outside, I went with Derek to his gunmetal sports car, while Iris and Cliff drove off together.

"What do you suppose got into that fool woman?" Derek said impatiently when we were on our way.

I liked neither his tone nor his words. I didn't like him.

"I don't know," I said. "I saw her late this afternoon, and she seemed awfully depressed." I wondered if the orchid photograph that had been destroyed could have proved the last straw.

Derek drove too fast, and with considerable skill. "Funny thing," he said, "the way events turn out. It was Alida who introduced Poppy to Cliff way back when. Alida was probably carrying a torch for him even then, though she didn't come to work for him until much later. But she's never had the real gumption to go out after anything in her life. She'd rather run away."

His words told me that he would never run away from anything. Yet I couldn't admire the sort of "courage" that would be likely to mow down anything in its path.

"Of course Alida was never Cliff's type anyway," he added.

"She doesn't seem like Eddie Burch's type either."

Derek threw me a quick look. "What do you know about Eddie Burch?"

I told him of my underwater encounter, and he scowled. "I

don't like that—I'll look into it. How did you like diving down to the wreck this afternoon?"

"It was wonderful. Though all I really saw was a cannon half buried in sand. I did make a beginner's luck find—a gold medal."

"Yes, I heard about that. I'm glad you didn't start bringing up gold bars."

I wondered why he'd say that, but my real attention was still on Eddie Burch and Alida.

"It's a wonder Eddie's willing to work for you," I said. "Marcus told me how he got that scar on his shoulder."

"He had that coming." Derek sounded grim. "He tried to kill me. But there's more than one way to tame a guy like Eddie. He'll listen to me now if I talk to him. So don't worry. Alida may have put him up to something with you. She's always scheming."

"I don't think so. He sounded as though he hates her."

"Here we are," Derek said, pulling up to the curb. "Want me to come in with you?"

"Thanks, no," I told him, and he went off, glad to be away. Iris had given me a key, and I let myself in without ringing the bell. The house was fragrant with some sweet night-blooming flower—jasmine, probably. I went straight upstairs to Fern's room and knocked on the door.

When there was no answer, I opened it and looked in. It was the first time I'd seen past her door. The whole room was as flowery a place as the orchid house—with bright blooms painted in great sprays across the walls. Poppy's work? I wondered. They were flowers of the imagination, rather than replicas of anything real. Some had faces peering eerily from between leaves, while others reached out with thin fingers like the tendrils of a vine. It was not a room I'd have liked to sleep in.

In any case, Fern wasn't here, and I crossed to my room to change from high-heeled sandals before I went looking for her. However, I needed to search no further.

Every lamp in my room had been turned on, so that it glowed with light. Windows and porch door stood open, and a breeze blew through the screens, carrying the sweet night scent from the garden. Pillows had been piled high at the head of the bed, and Fern sat curled up against them on top of the poppy-bordered spread. I saw with a sense of dismay that she was wearing the same long blue gown sprinkled with white blossoms that Poppy had worn for the portrait downstairs.

She had been crying, for there were stains on her cheeks, and she'd fallen asleep sitting up, her lips parted with the puffing of her breath, her tawny hair spread across the pillows, and gold eyelashes touching her cheeks.

Almost at once, she opened her eyes, sensing me there. "Alida? How is she?"

I sat on the edge of the bed. "I don't know yet. Iris and Cliff have gone to see her. Your sister asked me to come home to stay with you. We can call the hospital, if you like."

"Everyone dies!" Fern wailed, covering her face with her hands. "I can't stand it any more. Poppy—and now Alida. Even my orchids die!"

"I don't think Alida is going to die. They must have taken her to the hospital very quickly. Fern, have you any idea why she did this?"

Fern's eyes widened, more amber than brown. "Maybe Poppy wanted her to. Wherever Poppy is, she must be very lonesome. And Alida was her friend."

She sounded like a child, with a child's simplicity. But Fern was neither a child nor simple.

When she saw that I didn't mean to follow her down that road, she sat up, crossing her knees beneath the blue gown. "Alida left a letter for you. It's over there on the dressing table. I saw it when I came in, and it wasn't sealed, so I read it. I thought there might be something we ought to know quickly. Maybe it will make you feel better about what's been happening."

I snatched up the envelope and took out the single sheet. Though my name was on the outside, the handwritten note began without salutation.

> I've been wrong about you, and I'm sorry. I wanted you to feel so uncomfortable that you would leave quickly. I didn't want you to fit in and take Cliff's affection away from Fern and Iris. So I'm the one who has been moving the orchid photographs. I pasted the black tape over the eyes, and I destroyed the one you brought me. I always hated that orchid mask.
>
> However, you don't frighten as easily as I hoped, and you don't give up. As I must give up now. I can't do any more, and I can't carry the burden that's been placed on me. All I want is to go to sleep and have everything stop hurting.
>
> So now you are the one who must take this over and save them all. If you can. Be careful when you go to Derek's party.
>
> Alida

I read the words through twice in bewilderment. It was a relief to have an answer when it came to the photographs. There had been malice and an intention to upset me enough to make me leave. Perhaps because of my father's plan for changing his will. But I still understood nothing of what had driven Alida to this point of desperation.

"She doesn't really tell us anything," I said.

Fern shook her head forlornly. "I don't understand why she wrote to you. There was no letter for me, and no letter for my father. I looked in his room, and on his desk upstairs. Why did she write to you?"

"I wish I knew. Have you any idea what she's talking about? What's this burden she refers to?"

Fern went on shaking her head. "What will you do with the letter?"

"I'll give it to Cliff when he comes home. Perhaps he can figure it out. Shall we call the hospital now and see if he's there and if there's any word about Alida?"

"Yes—let's." She rolled herself off the bed and tripped over the long gown. Poppy must have been considerably taller. Hiking the skirt up from her ankles, she led the way to the telephone in her own room. I sat down in the chair she indicated, feeling that I no longer liked reproductions of flowers. They were so all-pervasive around Fern, as they must have been about her mother. And for me they had begun to seem eerie. I especially disliked a pair of elfin eyes that peered at me from the heart of a monster daisy painted in acrylic on the wall near my chair.

When Fern had dialed the hospital and asked for Alida's room, she handed me the phone. "I don't want to talk to anyone. I'm too scared."

It was Cliff who answered. He told me that Alida seemed to be coming along as well as could be expected, and they weren't keeping her in intensive care. She was asleep now. "How is everything at the house?" he finished.

"I'm with Fern. She's terribly concerned about Alida." I

offered Fern the telephone, but she shook her head. "She doesn't want to talk right now," I told him. "I'll stay with her until you and Iris come home."

When I'd hung up, Fern burst into words. "You don't have to stay with me! I'm going to work in the orchid house. Poppy always contributed an orchid display once a year to the Garden Club. It's time for that soon, and I want to think about it and get ready. Besides, if I'm there, maybe Poppy will tell me what to do."

Fern's preoccupation with Poppy and her supposed presence disturbed me, but there was nothing I could say. At least working with orchids might help to calm her.

I went downstairs and sat rocking on the dark porch, too tense to stay in my room waiting anxiously—though I wasn't sure for what. If Alida had, as she thought, left me her "burden," someone would surely make clear to me what it was. Whatever it might be would concern Cliff and his family—even concern me, who had come to this house so recently. Whatever she intended, I hated Alida's legacy.

I rocked for a while, finding the movement quieting, even though the night with its scents and whisperings from the garden was too heavily sweet—oppressive. At least the garden around me was not a thinking world. Only human minds were filled with unrest and plans for evil. Nevertheless, all the outdoors seemed to rustle with secrets.

When Marcus came through the gate and up the steps, I was enormously pleased to see him.

"Your father phoned and asked me to come over," he said. "He told me about Alida. Where is Fern?"

"She's working with her orchids and wants to be by herself. All this has her terribly worried and keyed up."

Marcus pulled over a chair, and I remembered the time back

home in my bookshop—another lifetime away—when I'd rocked in a more familiar chair, and he had stilled the movement. This time I stopped it myself. I had Alida's letter with me to show Cliff the moment he came home, and I handed it to Marcus.

"She left this for me. I don't know why, or what it means."

He took the sheet of paper to a patch of light that fell through the front door from the hall and read it through. Then he came to sit beside me again.

"I wouldn't worry about her meaning—if there really is one. Sometimes I think Poppy's death affected her more than anyone else. She built it out of all proportion in her mind."

"You think Alida tried to kill herself for nothing?"

"I think her own imaginings got the better of her. When she's well again, Cliff will talk to her. Until then, this burden, as she calls it, isn't yours to carry. You can't pick up anything so vague, even if you wanted to."

He was making me feel a little better, and it was good to have him here in the darkness near me. I remembered what Cliff had said at dinner—about that summing up of endearing and sometimes maddening details. I had a feeling that I might be adding them up about Marcus for a long time, whether this was wise or not.

"Haven't you any idea what she might be hinting at?" I asked after an interval of silence.

He waited just a moment too long before he agreed that he didn't know. The pause alerted me.

"You do know something?"

"Nothing that would make Alida want to take her own life. And nothing you need worry about."

I got up and walked to the far end of the porch, away from the tower that held my father's room. Bushes grew close to the corner post, and I pulled scented white jasmine toward me and breathed its cloying sweetness before I pushed it away.

"I wish somebody would trust me," I said, without turning.

He didn't answer, and that meant he wasn't able to trust me yet.

"How can I behave sensibly when I don't know what's going on?" I cried.

The gate creaked open as someone came up the walk. I hated the interruption, even though I already knew that Marcus wouldn't answer me. Keeping his own counsel was his most maddening trait—and not endearing.

He got up to turn on the porch light, and I saw that the intruder was Eddie Burch. For once he wore no cherubic smile of innocence, his expression blank and his eyes wary as he stared at Marcus. He didn't look at me at all.

"Hello, Eddie," Marcus said.

He didn't bother to return the greeting. "I just heard about Alida. How is she?"

"Doing as well as can be expected," Marcus told him. "Have you any idea why she did this?"

Eddie sat down on the steps, a picture of gloom. "She was a good lady," he muttered. "She was okay. A whole lot better than me."

This seemed a surprising admission, considering that the last time I'd seen him he'd denounced her thoroughly.

"You didn't answer my question," Marcus said.

"How should I know? She wasn't exactly chummy with me."

"Yet you did come to see her that day I caught you in the garden," I said.

He looked at me for the first time, his eyes malevolent under sandy brows. "I let you catch me. And what Alida wanted is none of your business."

"That's enough, Eddie." Marcus pulled him to his feet. "Let's go over to Derek's Place and have a drink. We both need it. Okay?"

Eddie nodded, still lost in gloom as he walked toward the gate.

Marcus turned back to me. "I'm sorry, Laurel. This needs to be taken care of. See if you can get some rest, and I'll call you tomorrow."

I'd chosen my road and was too far along to retreat gracefully. "I can't wait any longer! I need to know now."

Marcus was already propelling Eddie toward the gate. "I'm afraid you'll have to wait."

"Then let me come with you."

His look didn't find me endearing, and he simply pushed Eddie through the gate and followed him along the sidewalk. Marcus's car waited at the curb, and he put Eddie into the front seat, then went around to get behind the wheel. They drove off without a backward look for me.

For a moment I stood staring after the car, as frightened as I was angry. Whatever Marcus was involved in had its dark side. Key West had its dark side, like any seaport town. From the beginning, there had been murderers here, thieves, adventurers of all kinds, and of course drunks. It had been cleaned up a lot since the bad old days, though drugs still came in over the keys. Eddie Burch belonged to that seamier side, and perhaps because of this very darkness Alida had tried to kill herself. What Marcus's connection was I couldn't begin to guess, and that made me even more afraid.

I went slowly into the house, still carrying Alida's letter. Just before I went upstairs, I slipped it under the door of my father's room. I no longer felt like waiting up for him.

Upstairs, I left the light off in my room and stepped out on the porch overlooking the garden. I listened to palmettos rustling their everlasting clatter in the wind, and the heavy sweetness made me long for a breath of clean, bracing pine. Down in the orchid house, lights burned, and I knew Fern was still there. The soft night did nothing to calm my spirit.

If Alida died with all her secrets still untold, what then . . . ?

Only one thing I knew for sure—whatever was happening had begun long ago. But now the pace was quickening as events moved toward some climax that made me afraid.

The first thing I must do tomorrow was to see Marcus alone and convince him that I must no longer be shut out of whatever was happening. I was involved—committed—and he had to let me in.

9

I wasn't to see Marcus for three days. I tried to call his apartment early, but he didn't answer.

When I went downstairs for breakfast I found my father outside drinking coffee at one of the small tables. His "good morning" was grave as I sat down with him.

"How is Alida?" I asked.

He'd already been in touch with the hospital. "They think there's no immediate danger, but she's not recovering as quickly as she should. Maybe because she didn't succeed in what she attempted, and because of whatever drove her to try. Iris stayed with her last night and just came home a little while ago. She says Alida's in a state of not caring about anything—not wanting to live."

"Did you find the letter she left for me?"

"Yes, but I don't understand it. What did she mean about the orchid photos?"

I explained and he listened without much interest. "She can be a foolish woman. I'm sorry if she upset you."

The photos were no longer important. "Have you seen Fern this morning?"

"Not yet. I suppose she's asleep."

He ate dry toast and stirred his coffee absently.

"Have you any idea why Alida did this?" I persisted.

"She's been brooding ever since Poppy died. I've always felt she knew something she hadn't told me. Whatever it is, maybe I'd better not know." He looked dispirited himself.

I told him about Eddie Burch coming to the house last night and that Marcus had gone off with him to the Banyan.

"Eddie can be a nuisance, but I wouldn't worry about him," Cliff said. "In his own way, I think he still cares about Alida."

"I've been trying to call Marcus," I said, "but he doesn't answer."

"He's gone to the Bahamas. I sent him off to do a spot of research for me. He should be back in a couple of days."

With that I had to be content. The moment Marcus returned, I would try to see him and have everything out.

While there was no way in which I could fully recapture the feeling of that warm interlude with my father last night, and while this morning was different and filled with concerns that we weren't able to talk about, we had moved subtly into a closer relationship. Now I could bring up the subject of Derek's boat party and question whether it was a good idea.

"What does it matter?" Cliff said. "Derek wants to do it, so I'll go along. I don't feel up to opposing Derek these days, and it matters to Iris."

I put a hand on his arm. It was a hesitant gesture, but it seemed to bring him back from some distant place to which he'd retreated. He covered my hand for a moment with his own, and the gentle pressure of his fingers was something I would always remember.

Cliff finished his coffee, and I watched with a sense of sadness as he went off to work on a book he had lost interest in. I had come a long way from those years of resentment I'd grown up with.

For three days more I drifted aimlessly, frustrated by the lack of anything useful I could do. I phoned Stan in Bellport and learned that the bookshop was going on nicely without me. Though Stan demanded crossly that I come to my senses and return home at once. He wasn't interested in any developing relationship I might find with my father or in any new understanding of myself that I might reach. I ended the conversation as quickly as I could. Bellport seemed very far away —not only geographically, but as my life's center. The days I'd spent in Key West had changed my outlook on so many things that my old existence seemed strangely distant and no longer appealing.

When Marcus came home and called me up cheerfully on the phone, it was as though there'd been no disagreement the last time we'd met.

"Fern and I are taking you to Sunset this evening, Laurel. I've just talked to her, and it's all arranged. I'll pick you both up in half an hour. Okay?"

This wasn't what I wanted, but he said, "See you," and rang off.

I set the phone down on the hall table with a thump. He was behaving in his usual way—racing ahead with decisions, not waiting to hear what I wanted. He was putting obstacles in my path that I would have to find a way around.

In a little while Fern came to my room with word that we were to wait on the porch downstairs.

Since she'd been moping around for days, I was glad to see her looking more cheerful. From the first, she had refused to visit Alida in the hospital—for a strange reason.

"If I'm there and Alida dies," she'd told me, "I couldn't bear it. I want to see her, but it must be safe for her first." Apparently Fern had become even more superstitious about death and her own nearness to it.

At least attending the "happening" called Sunset was something reasonably peaceful for us to do. Or that was what I expected. It didn't turn out that way.

Sunset, of course, took place every night, by arrangement with nature, and the skies were usually clear. Even some residents, as well as tourists, turned out for the event.

Marcus, still cheerful and friendly in an impersonal way, took us to the pier an hour ahead of time. A crowd had already gathered, packing the space from water's edge to water's edge. Every possible manner of dress was evident, from gaudy visitors, to Key West's informality, to sailors on shore leave, and to a few hippie types that drifted in and out of Key West, long of hair and beard, and gentle in manner. Marcus said that residents often gathered more privately at another pier to watch the sunset.

In one corner a banjo player held court, collecting any coins the good-natured crowd chose to offer, and he was fine at fast renditions of old-time tunes—"Turkey in the Straw," "Oh, Susannah!" and something toe-tapping that he informed everyone he had written himself: "Mallory Square Blues." Two magicians worked together with their sleight of hand and somehow found elbow room. Even more remarkable, a juggler tossed balls in the air with never a slip. Most popular of all was the banana bread man, doing a good business with his wares.

There seemed to be a feeling of carnival excitement, and now and then someone even glanced at the sun, keeping track of its progress toward the Gulf of Mexico as it left a trail of gold and flame in the sky.

We must have been there for half an hour or more, packed in

by the press of the crowd, when I began to sense that someone was watching us. Once or twice I looked around quickly, but was never in time to catch anyone staring at us.

Perhaps Fern, always sensitive, felt it too. "Let's get out of this," she said. "Let's go over to the next pier, where there's more breathing space."

She did look a little green, I thought, and Marcus promptly pushed his way toward the back, pulling us after him. That was when someone gripped my arm. I jumped and looked around at Eddie Burch. He was plainly frightened, and he sounded breathless when he spoke.

"Let me come with you. Somebody's after me. Look—over there!"

This time I was quick enough to glimpse the tall, burly man whose head rose above the crowd not far away. He looked like the same man I'd seen breakfasting on Mallory Square with Derek, and I felt all the more uneasy.

"Hang on," I told Eddie, and we pushed our way after Marcus and Fern. When I glanced around again, I saw that we hadn't shaken the other man. There was something threatening, even brutal, about the way he moved through the crowd.

Eddie shoved past me to reach Marcus. "Get me out of this!"

Marcus recognized Eddie's fear, and he didn't hesitate. "Laurel, take Fern over to the next pier. I'll join you in a minute."

He moved fast, jerking Eddie out of sight around a building. The burly man had been blocked by a juggler, who didn't like his angry plunge through the crowd. It looked as though there might be a fight, and I hurried Fern away from the pier.

A strip of water divided the two piers, and we found our way to the street and went around to the other pier on a higher level. Here only a few people stood watching the sky, or looking down at the jammed spectacle we'd just left. From this new vantage point, I tried to locate the man who'd followed Eddie, but he'd apparently made his own escape from the crowd.

Fern had revived and seemed to have noticed nothing. Her attention was caught by a young woman flying a huge kite, making it dip and soar and dance. I watched too, but my thoughts were still on Eddie and Marcus. The tall man had looked liked serious trouble.

In a few moments Marcus reappeared and found us watching the woman with the kite. "Would you like to try that, Laurel?" he asked.

Fern was immediately eager. "Let's both try!"

For once, she had put on shorts and a shirt and looked less like a moth or an orchid. Her spirits still seemed to dip and soar like the kite, but she'd stopped looking green.

"What happened?" I asked Marcus.

He shook his head. "Not now, Laurel." He drew us toward the kite flyer, where several bystanders stood watching her, as well as the sunset.

"She's advertising a store that sells those kites," Marcus told us. "I know her, and she'll be glad to let you try if you want to."

I wasn't interested in kites, and I once more had the feeling of pressure rising toward some alarming event still to come. But there was nothing else to do but mark time for now.

The woman with the kite was tall and rather lanky, with brown hair she wore down her back in a thick braid.

"Hello, Connie," Marcus greeted her when we came near.

She smiled and nodded as Marcus introduced me, keeping her control of the diving kite. It was black and red, with a great spread of wings, like an exaggerated bat. At Marcus's suggestion, Connie transferred the cords to my uncertain hands and showed me how to make the kite perform. I hung on, pulling against its rebellious tug, and began to feel my control gaining. I could make this beautiful live thing do as I wished.

Fern knew Connie too and had flown such kites before, and when it was her turn she ran along the pier in the direction of the naval station, the kite following in the sky like some great darting predator.

"I'm glad we met," Connie said to Marcus. "There's scuttlebutt."

"There always is. Want to tell me?"

She glanced at me uncertainly, and he said, "Laurel's Cliff York's daughter from his first marriage. She's okay."

Connie nodded and went on. "There's talk about Derek Phillips finding a lot more treasure around that wreck than he's letting anybody know. Of course rumors always fly—like kites. But maybe he's asking for trouble."

"You mean with the government?"

"That's not the problem. There are always those around who watch for easy prey. Somebody ought to talk to Derek—maybe warn him."

"I imagine he knows whatever's going on," Marcus said. "But I'll tell him, if I get a chance." He glanced at me. "Don't say anything to Fern, will you, Laurel? But you might tell Iris, if you can."

Connie retrieved her kite from Fern, and when she'd reeled it in like a fish on a line, she wandered off.

"Connie Corson's a Conch from way back," Marcus said. "She's juggling two or three jobs around town right now."

Fern's eyes were still shining with excitement. "That was wonderful! I felt as though I were flying too!" As always, she was mercurial, ready to soar herself.

The sun had dropped low by now, and we found a spot

where we could look down on the heads of the crowd we'd mingled with across the strip of water. Everyone was quiet now, staring at the horizon. The sun dipped behind the black dot of an island, and the sky burned with a deepening fire. When the last sliver had disappeared, a burst of applause sounded from the crowd below, and from the few people on our side as well. I joined in the clapping, along with Marcus and Fern.

As we walked back toward Mallory Square, Fern came to a decision. "Tomorrow I'll go to see Alida," she announced. "Tomorrow I'll be brave enough. Will you come with me, Laurel?"

I told her I'd be glad to, and she went on, musing aloud. "The day after tomorrow is Derek's party. I'm looking forward to that."

"It's also a year from the day Poppy died," Marcus said.

"You don't think I've forgotten that?" Fern cried. "I'm glad Derek's doing this. It's good for Cliff, especially. And maybe for the rest of us too. Anyway, I'm going home now, and you needn't come with me—either of you. I'm still trying to select the right orchids to pick for the display at West Martello. Iris is no help at all right now. I'm doing this for Poppy. It's what she'd have wanted, and I'll give her orchids a beautiful showing. Have you told Laurel about the Martello towers, Marcus? When the time comes, Laurel, you must come with me and help with the orchids. West Martello is the spookiest place I know, and you'll love it!"

"I'll tell her about the towers," Marcus said, "but first we'll see you home."

She shook her head and hurried off alone. In spite of her troubling vulnerability, Fern could sometimes display an independence that no one could shake.

Now I would have my chance to talk to Marcus, and I was not going to be put off again.

He surprised me by pulling my hand companionably through the crook of his arm. "I'm glad to have you to myself for a while, Laurel. We need to talk about a lot of things. Will you have dinner with me now?"

Again the wind went out of my sails, and I wished he wouldn't be so disarming. "All right—I'll go to dinner with you. But only because we do need to talk."

The restaurant was called Lazy Afternoon, and it was tucked away in a garden on Simonton Street, adjacent to one of the old houses. Trees and a white picket fence shielded diners from the street. There were only ten tables in the garden, and since we were early, we had the place almost to ourselves.

Our small table was set near a grove of Norfolk Island pines, and other big trees surrounded the cleared space. Paper lanterns hung from branches overhead, shedding a gentle, romantic light, while the trees sheltered us from the wind, with only its whispering in branches far above.

Unfortunately, I didn't feel romantic.

"I must tell you about the East and West Martello towers," Marcus began.

I cut him off. "First, tell me about Eddie Burch!"

"I plan to," he said mildly. "I don't blame you for being upset about the other night, or about what happened on the pier just now. I'd rather not go into any of this, but since you've got yourself into a state of worrying I suppose you'd better know. First, let's order our meal."

My "state" subsided enough so I could study the menu, and when we'd ordered, Marcus began to talk.

"As you know, Poppy didn't want Derek to marry Iris. A few days before she died she must have confided some of her fears about him to Alida. Though Alida won't discuss this, she did try to pick up the fight against Derek, and she had some notions of her own. There've always been questions about where his money came from, though he has plausible enough answers. Alida got hold of Eddie and began to pump him about Derek to see what might surface. Eddie still has a weakness for Alida—though he can pretend he hasn't. He always felt a little in awe of her, so I guess he wanted to please her. He didn't have any proof of anything against Derek, but he has his suspicions."

"Who was that man who was after Eddie on the pier?"

"I didn't have time to see him, and Eddie didn't explain. He just wanted to get away."

"I think I saw the same man having breakfast with Derek the first time I went to Mallory Square. They seemed to be fighting about something."

"I'll sound Eddie out the next time I see him. You know, he's worked for Derek on and off over the years, and sometimes he's followed him from one place to another. Alida thinks that deep down he's never forgiven him for the vicious wound that caused his stiff shoulder. Anyway, he started to keep his eyes open, and recently he's come across bits of evidence that seem to connect Derek with possible drug running. Alida's eager to collect all the information about this that she can, and a few things are adding up. If Derek can be exposed before he marries Iris, Alida feels she can stop the marriage—which is what Poppy wanted. But now something seems to have happened that's made Alida give up. So I had to see Eddie the other night and learn whatever I could. Which wasn't much. He was already half drunk when he came to the house, and instead of loosening his tongue, the liquor made him maudlin. All he did was bemoan Alida's possible death. So I got nowhere."

"And my father doesn't know any of this?"

"He likes Derek and trusts him. Cliff has a gift for seeing only what he wants to see in his friends. So there's no point in bringing him into this until we have some real proof. I just hope it won't come too late for Iris."

Always there was a gentleness in his voice when he spoke of Iris—a gentleness that he never showed toward me. I stiffened my protective armor.

"You could have told me sooner what was happening," I said.

"I'd rather not have told you at all. This is dangerous ground, Laurel, and you'd better not get mixed up in it."

When I said nothing, he reached across the table to touch my hand lightly. "Let's forget Derek and Eddie Burch and that whole mess. Maybe you'd be willing now to hear about the Martello towers?"

I hadn't much interest in Fern's orchid display, but I did want to keep him talking, so I nodded and managed a smile.

As we ate our meal, Marcus told me about the two old forts. One—East Martello—was a museum now and was used for art shows. The other was occupied by the Garden Club. Over the years tropical plants and trees had been planted in the fort enclosure, and inside there were displays of flowers and smaller plants.

"It's a fascinating place with its old walls and underground rooms," he said. "Fern can tell you more about its history when she takes you there. And if Fern goes to the hospital to visit Alida tomorrow, I hope you'll go with her. I'm still worried about Fern. She's too tense and high-strung these days. Now too much seems to be pushing her toward—I don't know what. Especially with this crush she has on Derek."

"I feel that too," I said. "Do you have any ideas about the

rumors your friend Connie mentioned? If he's stashing treasure away, is he doing something illegal?"

"I'm not sure. We don't know enough."

I sighed. "I'll be glad when his boat party is over."

"So will I. I only wish there was some way to back out. Especially for Cliff. He's still set on going. I think he doesn't want to stay home that day, and he'd rather make it festive than gloomy. Laurel, how do you feel about him now—as a father?"

"Tentative, I suppose. Though I do think we're coming closer together."

"I hope so. It takes time. But I'm glad you're here, Laurel. I really am."

I shied away from the personal, not daring to trust myself. "Tell me what brought you to Key West in the first place. What were your parents like?"

He talked about them readily. His father had been a brilliant, much-respected man, mostly absorbed in his mathematical world. He'd been a professor in a Midwestern university.

"I don't think he was an especially good teacher, or that he even liked teaching. It was the way he earned a living, but he was more interested in his mathematical concepts than in his young students. He wrote three distinguished books that were published by a university press—and went mostly unread, except by experts. I admired him a lot, and was a little scared of him."

"And your mother?"

Marcus's expression softened. "She was a wonder. She could be excited about anything and everything. I suppose she wasn't really a pretty woman, but she seemed beautiful because she was so alive. Yet she knew how to keep a protective space around my father, so he could do his work. Maybe she'd be judged old-fashioned these days, but she loved her role as my father's supporter. They needed each other."

"She died first?"

"Yes—much too young—of some infection they'd know how to treat these days. Her death about finished him. He didn't want to go on without her. I don't mean that he killed himself deliberately—but I believe that he willed himself to die. He developed a tumor that couldn't be operated on. When he was gone too, I didn't have anything to hold me out there. I came to Key West mostly by chance. I suppose I was running away from everything that reminded me of happier times. Then I met Cliff and his family, and I began to make new connections."

I could ache a little for Marcus's loss. I knew what it was like.

"Poppy accepted me as a friend, just as Cliff did," he went on. "So I had something to hold me here. Of course I fell in love with Iris early on—while she was still in her late teens. That's over now. I wish she hadn't settled for Derek, but that's the way it is. I only hope it can be stopped in time."

He sounded melancholy and a little grim. We ate in silence for a while, until I became aware that he was studying me thoughtfully, and I raised a questioning eyebrow.

"A few weeks ago," he mused, "I'd never have talked to you like this. I wonder if you know how much you've changed, Laurel, since the time when I walked into your bookshop and first saw you?"

That startled me. "What do you mean?"

"You seemed awfully defensive. I suspected that a lot was going on in your head—but you were afraid to test yourself."

For an instant I bristled in the old way. "But I did test myself!"

"Right. And something's growing out of that testing, isn't it?

Nothing stands still. We go ahead, or we go back. You're reaching out more—toward your sisters. Or at least toward Fern. And toward your father."

Even toward you, I thought, feeling a bit grim myself.

"I do have more to care about," I admitted. "But it's scary too, because it makes me more open to—to damage."

"Isn't that a lot better than staying numb and playing it safe?"

I wondered if he was thinking of Iris and his own hurt.

The moon had risen over black treetops, adding its glow to the sentimental light of paper lanterns. By this time more diners had come in, but none of the clatter was evident that arose in a more enclosed space, and voices were soft at other tables.

"Stay open to hurt, Laurel," Marcus said gently. "It becomes you. Excitement becomes you too, and I've seen you light up a few times lately—where all your emotions except anger seemed battened down in your setting back home."

"It's such an accident that I'm here at all," I said, thinking again of the chance meeting of my mother and father. "Unless there are no accidents, no coincidences? Sometimes I wonder if things have to happen."

"I suppose we run into accidents and coincidences every day. What matters are the choices we make. If we let an important chance slip by without even trying, then what do we have?"

"What do we have if the chance is the wrong one?"

His sudden smile banished melancholy. "Right now, what it comes down to at this moment is two people having dinner together in a Key West garden. Shall we enjoy it?"

I returned his smile warmly, making my own choice in spite of myself. "I am enjoying it."

The dinner was perfection, and we finished with Key lime pie that was nothing like the imitations I'd had up North. Real Key limes were the secret, Marcus said, and this had the right Key West touch—tangy and sweet at the same time, so that each melting mouthful was a delight. The garden with its glowing lanterns was a delight too, and so was Marcus's presence across the table. There seemed a growing sense of wonder in me. I felt like one of those night flowers with petals unfolding visibly toward the moon. I wanted the moment to go on and on and never end—because this was the moment when I knew I was in love. This was what everyone had been talking about!

We walked back along Old Town streets toward my father's house, and the moon sailed with us, nearly full. My hand was in the crook of his arm and there was for me a new closeness I'd never felt to a man before. Marcus needed only to make a move—a gesture—and I would turn to him unhesitatingly.

He made no such gesture, except in a light, affectionate way. If I had put down my guard, he had not. At the gate he kissed me lightly and said he would see me soon. I watched him walk away, wanting so much more, and still not sure that he felt as I did. Though there had been times tonight when Iris no longer seemed to cast her shadow between us. As I came dreamily up the steps, I found my father sitting in darkness near the rail.

"A pleasant evening, Laurel?" he asked.

"A beautiful evening. Is there any news of Alida?"

"She's not doing well. I saw her this afternoon, and I think she doesn't want to live. Though she won't talk to Iris or me, or tell us why. She seems to have given up completely. In a way, I can understand that. Sometimes I feel like giving up myself."

"No!" I sat down beside him in a wicker chair. "You aren't the giving up kind. You have too much to live for."

"I'm not sure I care any more."

I hated that, but I didn't know how to change anything or anyone—least of all myself. For a time we watched the shifting patterns of light and shadow as wind stirred branches and ruffled shrubbery.

After a while I asked the hopeless question that so troubled me. "Why should Alida stop caring, and why should you?"

He didn't answer, and I knew he was thinking of Poppy and nearly a year ago. Only the lessening of pain would help him, but in the meantime he had to fight—for something.

"You have three daughters who need you," I said, "and you have a book to finish."

He said nothing, and there seemed no way past the barrier he'd built around himself.

Alida's despair was something else, and the things Marcus had told me didn't explain it. Her plotting against Derek through her ex-husband could have nothing to do with the "burden" she'd thrust upon me.

Out of my confusion I heard Cliff's sudden question. "Laurel, can you type?"

Had I reached him, after all? "I took a course once. And I've always typed my letters for the bookshop."

"You're right that my book should be finished. Would you be willing to help me out while Alida's away?"

"I'd like that," I said quickly. "If I can."

"It won't be easy. I write directly on the machine, and my typing is terrible. Then I revise constantly in pencil, so every page is interlined and scrawled on. I need new smooth copy that I can read over every day, so I can tell what I've written."

"I'll do my best," I promised.

"You're not being hired permanently." He smiled. "You

weren't cut out to be some aging writer's secretary. What about your painting?"

"I've done a little sketching since I've been here. Nothing much. Everywhere I look there's a picture that wants to be painted. But it's just for my own satisfaction—I'm not professional."

"Well, you'll have time for painting, once I'm caught up. My daily output isn't all that high these days."

His mood had changed completely, and even though I wanted to help, I felt a mild resentment. Mention of his daughters had done nothing for him. A reminder about his book had brought him to life. Yet in a way I could understand. He probably felt he could do nothing at all about his daughters, but he could finish his book, and writing was a way of life for him.

"I'll enjoy this," I told him. "Remember—I love your books. I have ever since I began to read them."

He seemed pleased. "You do? You never told me that."

It was a surprise to realize that I hadn't. So I told him then. About my favorite titles, about characters I remembered and plots I'd enjoyed. It seemed strange in so successful a writer, but I could sense the way he was soaking up my words, relishing them. The bridge was so easy, once I'd found it. Irrelevantly, I wondered what bridge led to Marcus O'Neill—an idea that made me jerk my thoughts back impatiently. Tonight, for a little while, I'd been lost in the spell cast by lanterns in a garden. Reality was a lot more grim. Reality right now was Cliff and his deep despair. If I could manage to lift that just a little . . .

He leaned over to put his arm about me and held me for a moment. "Thank you for coming, Laurel. I hope you'll never be sorry."

"No matter what, I won't be sorry," I promised, and wondered how reckless such a promise might be.

Upstairs in my room, I kept on thinking about the two men in my life. A good relationship with my father might be more possible than I'd expected. Marcus was something else, and I didn't know whether I would ever understand what he was like and how he felt.

That night I went to sleep remembering our dinner together at Lazy Afternoon. There had been no orchids in the garden where we'd dined, and I was glad of that.

In the morning, after an early breakfast, I presented myself upstairs in my father's study and found him at his typewriter. He was already involved with his characters and the scene he was writing, the closeness of last night put aside. Yet not entirely forgotten, for he smiled as he handed me a stack of papers.

"See what you can do in copying this stuff," he said. "You'll find everything you need in Alida's desk."

As he'd warned, it wasn't easy. Fortunately, Alida had a standard electric typewriter, as well as her word processor. I ran paper into the machine and began to decipher my father's writing. Some words almost defeated me, but I managed to get several pages done, however slowly.

Jumping into work in the middle of his narrative, I didn't know either the characters or the plot line, but the background of modern Caribbean piracy came through disturbingly. What he had written was obviously based on fact. When I had a chance, I must tell Cliff about what Connie Corson had said yesterday concerning Derek and his sunken treasure.

My typing speed picked up as I became more accustomed to Cliff's interlinings, and I moved along well, with my stack of pages growing. I was hardly aware of passing time when Iris came up the stairs carrying a tray.

She looked surprised to find me working in Alida's place, and she hardly greeted me as she went past. She wore white shorts again, and a red bandana halter that showed off her creamy tan and contrasted with her smooth black hair.

"I've brought lunch for two," she told Cliff. "I meant to join you. I didn't know you had a new secretary."

"I'm not hungry," he said. "I can't stop right now. You two have lunch together. Bring me something later, Iris."

She placed the tray on a small table that pulled out from the wall. "We might as well eat, Laurel. The muse can't be interrupted."

I'd had little occasion to see Iris alone, so I sat down to the meal intended for Cliff, even though her invitation was anything but cordial.

The muse, however, had already been interrupted, for Cliff left his desk and went to the piano. As his fingers roamed the keys, he picked out various tunes he knew by ear—bits of Cole Porter, Gershwin, Berlin, and again Scott Joplin. Idle snatches that made a disjointed musical accompaniment as Iris and I started eating Angela's shrimp gumbo and avocado salad.

"He does that to get his thoughts going again," Iris said under cover of the nostalgic music. "He can dream up whole scenes in his head while he's playing and then set them down on his typewriter. It's all right to talk now. When he stops, we'll have to be quiet. I've wanted a chance to speak to you, Laurel."

She looked beautiful and calm, but her hand shook as she buttered a corn muffin. Iris ran a lot deeper than Fern, and I couldn't help wondering how she would react if she knew that Derek might be involved in drug smuggling.

"I need your help," she added, sounding as though she dared me to refuse.

"I'll help if I can," I told her quietly.

"Fern seems to like you." She spoke as though this was hard to understand. "Perhaps she'll listen to you, when she won't to me. She's cooking up a plan that must be stopped. Derek and I hope you can discourage her."

"You'd better tell me the plan."

Iris glanced across the room to where Cliff continued to roam through snatches of familiar tunes. He looked rapt and far away, unaware of us, the music covering our words.

"Fern wants to bring Alida home from the hospital to this house. She's already had a room prepared for her near her own."

"So?" I said. "Why should you object to that?"

"You don't know Alida!" Iris's dark eyes flashed. "I'm fond of her, but I don't want her here. Not now."

"What does Cliff say?"

"He doesn't know yet. And when Fern tells him, he'll go along with what she wants. He always does. Anything for peace."

"Why don't you want this?" I asked directly.

The look she gave me seethed with impatience. "How can you come in here and take sides, when you know nothing? Nothing at all!"

"I don't think I've taken anyone's side. But it might help if you'd explain why you don't want Fern to bring Alida here."

"Because Alida can be dangerous. Fern's an innocent in some ways."

"Wasn't Alida your mother's good friend?"

Iris dipped her soup spoon so abruptly that liquid spattered to the rim of the bowl. "Alida hated Poppy. She hated her because Poppy had everything Alida wanted and would never have—including my father. She's made him depend on her, need her. And I don't for one minute believe that she meant to kill herself with those pills. That was just another means of worming her way into Cliff's sympathy—and Fern's. Fern's too trusting! Derek and I both think that the worst thing that can happen now is to see Alida brought into this house."

There was also a point that hadn't been mentioned—the fact that Alida was working against Derek, who might very well be aware of her plotting. Yet when I thought of Alida's action in tormenting me with Poppy's orchid photographs, I could see the pattern of an unbalanced, possibly vindictive woman. And there was still the matter of Derek's possible criminal activities that Iris might know nothing about.

"I don't know enough to make judgments," I said. "What do you want me to do?"

"Convince Fern that it isn't a good idea."

"Perhaps Derek could do that—she listens to him."

Iris flashed me an angry look. "I don't want Derek anywhere near Fern! My little sister has enough of an infatuation, as it is. She's constantly embarrassing poor Derek. And Cliff is helpless to do anything about it, even though he sees perfectly well how she's behaving."

I couldn't imagine a side of Derek Phillips that might be called "poor."

There was a pause in the music, and we both kept still, eating our lunch. Cliff had apparently caught none of our words, and after a moment his fingers wandered absently into an adaptation by ear of some old Jolson songs. I wondered aloud what on earth "Swanee" could do for his imagination, and Iris almost smiled.

"I don't think his mind is really on what he's playing," she said. "He's off somewhere else. If you're through, I'll take the tray downstairs."

"Have you heard the rumors that are going around about Derek's finds?" I asked. That, at least, was safe to mention.

She'd started to rise, but then sat down again. "What do you mean?"

I told her about our visit to the pier and of Connie Corson's "scuttlebutt."

"That's just Key West gossip," Iris said. "It's true that Derek's made a bigger find than he wants advertised yet. I went out there the other day to keep an eye on things because he asked me to. This is a tricky time for Derek, but it will be over as soon as he can get everything into a safe place. That will be right after the boat party tomorrow. I'm just glad Alida won't be able to attend that. You're going to the hospital with Fern this afternoon, aren't you? Please do as I ask, Laurel, and tell Fern it won't do to bring Alida here."

"How can I possibly tell her anything? I'll have to wait and see what happens. Fern seems to be busy right now with the orchids she's choosing for a display."

"Yes, I wish she weren't. I'd be glad to skip that this year. Fern thinks she's doing this for Poppy—as though it would somehow bring her back. I enjoy working with orchids, but they're not an obsession with me, as they are with Fern."

I rose as Iris picked up the tray, but before I could return to the typewriter Fern came running up the stairs. She'd put on a yellow sundress that left her arms and back bare, with red thong sandals on her feet and a straw hat on her head.

"Are you ready, Laurel?" she asked, ignoring Iris.

Cliff crashed his fingers on the keys and swung his stool around. "What is this—Grand Central Station?"

Fern ran over and kissed his cheek. "I'm sorry, darling.

Laurel promised that she'd go with me to the hospital to see
Alida this afternoon, and we'd better leave now, since Marcus
can drive us if we hurry. I've talked to Alida's doctor, and we're
going to bring her home as soon as possible. I've got a room
ready for her downstairs. She really shouldn't stay where she
is. She's not sick, and it's too depressing. But she mustn't be
alone. So it's all right, isn't it, darling? She'll be happier here."

"I suppose so." Cliff didn't look entirely pleased about the
plan. "What do you think, Iris?"

Fern broke in quickly. "It doesn't matter what she thinks!
She's always against anything I want. Poppy loved Alida, and
so do I."

"Well—all right," Cliff said.

Iris's outer calm no longer fooled me. She was angry beneath the ice, and I suspected that she hadn't given up her
opposition to having Alida move in.

When she'd gone, I picked up the stack of copy I'd typed and
took it to Cliff, who was at his desk again, rolling a fresh sheet
into the machine.

"I'll be back as soon as we return from the hospital," I
promised.

He waved me off, already lost in his imaginary world. "Fine
—fine. Run along."

As I went off with Fern, I had no idea of the surprise that
waited for us at the hospital.

10

When we reached the hospital, Marcus waited for us outside. He said too many visitors wouldn't be welcome, but I had a feeling that he didn't want to see Alida just then anyhow.

As we followed a long corridor, I could sense Fern's pleasure over the small triumph she'd won over her sister, and I wondered how much Alida might be used as a pawn between them.

"If it's possible, we'll bring her home right now," Fern said over her shoulder as I hurried after her.

"Are you certain this is a good idea?" I asked, catching up. "Maybe Alida needs more time to be away from everyone. Have you talked with her? Does she want to do this?"

"Of course she does! She knows she needs people around her now."

Fern burst eagerly through the open door of Alida's room. A stranger lay sleeping in her bed. When Fern would have rushed in to wake the woman, I stopped her.

"Wait! Let's go to the nurses' station first and find out what's happened. They may have changed Alida's room."

What had happened was quickly explained. Mrs. Burch had

been checked out of the hospital by her ex-husband, who had come to fetch her this morning. Miss Iris York had given the order on the telephone to release her.

Fern looked horrified. "Did Eddie Burch say where he was taking her?" she demanded.

The nurse had no idea, and we moved away from her desk.

"You see what my sister is like?" Fern said. "She's done it again! She tries to manage everything."

She headed for the nearest phone booth and left the door open. I waited while she rang the house and got Iris on the phone. I could hear her clipped tones, but not her words. When Fern hung up, she caught my arm and pulled me along toward the door.

"Marcus has to help us right away. So come along!"

She was too excited to make much sense, and when we reached Marcus in his parked car, I was the one who tried to explain.

Fern broke in on me. "We're going after them!" she cried, getting into the front seat beside Marcus, while I got into the back. Only a little while ago Iris had asked me to intervene so Alida wouldn't move into Cliff's house. Yet she must have already put this scheme, whatever it was, into effect.

Marcus made no move to start the car. "Slow down, Fern. Take a deep breath. Then tell me where we're supposed to be going, and what you want to accomplish."

Fern made an effort to recover herself and spoke more quietly. "Eddie has taken Alida out to Doubloon Key—Derek's island, Laurel. Iris says she's to stay there until she's fully recovered. Derek's housekeeper is supposed to look after her. That's what Iris *says*. Only it won't be like that! Alida's always hated Derek, and she'll hate being there. I don't know how

Eddie got her to go, but of course he'll do anything Derek orders. Iris is just doing this to keep her away from me."

"I doubt that," Marcus said mildly. "This could be a good solution."

"Then you don't know anything! It isn't good for Alida at all. So let's get your boat, and you can run us over to the island right away."

Marcus turned to look back at me. "What do you think about this, Laurel?"

He was great at asking my opinion when it didn't matter. I'd begun to wonder if Iris might be less ignorant of Derek's side interests than Marcus supposed and was deliberately spiriting Alida away, so she could take no action against Derek.

"I haven't any idea what's best for Alida," I said. "But I suppose we could go to the island and find out what she wants."

Fern was still excited. "She's been kidnapped! This isn't Derek's fault—it's Iris's. So we have to rescue her, Marcus!"

Marcus switched on the engine. "All right—one rescue mission coming up."

We drove to the marina where Marcus's boat was moored, and when we were aboard the *Seabird,* Fern began to calm down. She even pointed out several pelicans perched on pilings out in the water as we went past. She helped with the sails as well, and we were on our way. If it hadn't been for the questions about what was happening to Alida, it would have been a pleasant run.

The trip to Doubloon Key took more than an hour, and we knew that our approach had been sighted because one of Derek's Cuban helpers was waiting to assist when we docked. The island was low, except for a rise in the center, and it was covered with palmetto and a tangle of sea grape. Rising from the highest point was a compact stone house built of white coral rock. The roof was sharply peaked to allow for a runoff of water into underground cisterns, and the rooms beneath seemed to stand open to sea and sky.

We followed a shell path to wide steps that led directly into a living room stretching the width of the house. Great conch shells that melted from speckled brown to salmon pink at the heart made stops for each side of the screened double doors.

The room beyond was stunning—beautiful in its simplicity —and I could almost forget why we were here, lost in its effect upon me. Three sides were indeed open to sea and sky, with folding doors that made a wall to shut out storms when needed. The colors were shell white and the green of gulf waters that could be seen through open walls. Only the blue cushioned sofa was not bound in bamboo. Varnished bamboo chairs and small occasional tables were woven and bent in intricate designs that added their own golden luster to the color scheme. A huge Chinese vase, nearly as tall as a man, stood in one corner, filled with red-leaved branches of sea grape. Under a glass dome on a table grew a lovely little tree of white jade. There were no draperies or curtains, but only the shuttered doors, folded open now, so that water reflections rippled the white ceiling and mingled with patches of sunlight on pale azure walls. On the floor were the woven grass rugs called *pago pago*.

A steady breeze blew through, carrying the pungent scent of the sea. Sky and water seemed part of the room—its real decoration—a room that swam in light but remained cool and serene.

The contrast between Derek and his house seemed hard to reconcile. I'd have thought his rugged personality more at home in a bar, or on the deck of a ship, than in so harmonious and civilized a setting.

Fern spoke at my elbow. "It's a beautiful room, isn't it? Poppy designed it for Derek and picked out the furniture. That's one reason I love this house so much. But I'll never come here again if Iris marries him. Maybe that's why Poppy died."

"What do you mean?" I demanded.

Fern turned away at once, as though she'd said too much. From the rear of the house a Cuban woman whom Fern called Elena came to greet her in Spanish. Her English was halting, but Fern could chatter to her in her own language. The woman smiled at her, her black hair shining like satin in the sea light.

We followed her to an open, red-tiled area outside a rear door of the big room. A swimming pool shimmered blue under the sun, and on either side stretched two bedroom wings. As the woman started around the pool to the left, Marcus said, "I'll wait on the terrace," and again I felt his reluctance to see Alida. Fern and I followed our guide up shallow steps to a passageway that ran like a deck above the pool.

A door stood open on a small, charming bedroom, with wide windows that looked out over gulf waters. Here there were draperies with a tiny blue floral print, and again a grass rug from Haiti. The same blue print was repeated on the bedspread. A cane rocker and a bowl filled with colored yarns and white knitting needles invited a woman to comfortable leisure.

Alida lay stretched upon a flowered chaise longue, wrapped in a long blue cotton gown. Cushions had been piled at her back, and a book lay open across her knees, though she didn't seem to be reading. Somehow, she looked younger—and quite peaceful and sleepy. I supposed she'd been given sedatives at the hospital. Perhaps that was how they'd managed to bring her here.

Fern rushed to her chair and knelt beside it. "You shouldn't have come here, Alida! Why did you let Eddie take you away from the hospital without calling me? When we found you were gone, Marcus brought us over in the *Seabird*. We've come to take you home right away."

Alida glanced at her briefly and closed her eyes again. "Iris phoned the hospital and said Eddie was coming to pick me up. Iris didn't want me to stay at the hospital, and Derek offered his island."

This was still very strange. By the time Iris had come upstairs with her tray for Cliff, she had already made these arrangements. Yet she'd asked me to dissuade Fern from her plan. She knew we were going to the hospital, and she had said nothing. And where did my father stand in all this? Did he have any idea of what was going on, or was he content to let Iris take everything into her own hands so he could return to his work? Perhaps that was what writers did in the face of a crisis. Perhaps it was what he'd always done.

Fern paid no attention to Alida's words. "How could you possibly go anywhere with Eddie, when you can't stand him?"

Alida's tone grew dreamy, absent. Her defenses were down, and she mused aloud to herself. "Once, a long time ago, I could stand him. Though of course I always knew how different we were. Eddie was exciting in those days."

Fern's indignation increased. "Eddie's a drifter and a bum!"

"I suppose he is—now. The funny thing is that sometimes I think he still cares what happens to me."

"That's ridiculous—*him!*" Fern cried. She pulled a chair close to Alida's. "You don't belong here. I've fixed a room for you at home, and that's where we're going to take you. Right now."

For the first time, Alida showed some spark. "I don't want to stay in your father's house. I'm not a package for you to move around. I like it much better here. It's quiet and calm, and nothing will be asked of me. Your sister has promised me that."

"Why can't you find it peaceful at our house?"

"Because there are too many—currents. Here there are none. I can drift along and pretend I've never had any other life."

"But you do have another life! We need you. What about Cliff? How can you drop his work right in the middle like that?"

This time she answered more sadly. "I'm sorry. But Cliff will find someone else."

"He already has," Fern pointed out. "Laurel's taken over your desk and your work."

Alida glanced at me, undisturbed. "I hope you'll please him."

Something in her had given up to the point where even Cliff's work no longer mattered.

"I know why you won't come home," Fern wailed. "You've seen Poppy too, haven't you? Just as I have! Only you're afraid, while I want to see her. I want it with every bit of me. If only she'd just come close enough to talk to me—to us. Then she could forgive us all for not saving her."

If Alida had given up with Cliff, she hadn't quite abandoned Fern. She sat up and reached for her hand. "Stop that! You haven't seen anything, and neither have I. But she's haunting our lives just the same. She's haunting you and me and Cliff. Perhaps even Iris. Somehow we've got to let Poppy go. That's why I've come here. To see if I can—just let go. We need to talk about this, Fern. Really talk. I think I'm strong enough now. So let Marcus take Laurel back to Key West. Then Derek can send you home later. Or you can even stay here with me for a few days, if you like."

This new suggestion seemed to quiet Fern. "Maybe I will. You go back with Marcus, Laurel. And tell Cliff we're here. If Iris comes over later, she can bring me a bag."

There seemed nothing more for me to do, but as I started to leave, Alida spoke again softly, half to herself. "I don't know what I ought to do. I wish I really could be born fresh without anything having happened before. But it isn't going to be like that."

"No, it isn't," I said. I wanted to ask her about the "burden" she'd mentioned in the note she'd left for me, but this was something I couldn't speak about when others were around.

She nodded wisely, as though there had been some significant exchange between us, though I had no idea what she meant.

"If I don't see Cliff again," she added, "just tell him—oh, never mind. There really isn't anything I can say to him. Or anything I can do."

Fern bent over her. "Don't talk like that! Of course you'll see him again. You aren't even sick any more."

Alida lay with her eyes closed, scarcely breathing. The usual touch of rose on her cheekbones was absent, and her pallor seemed ominous. Alida had wanted to stop breathing—had tried to stop—and the way she looked now was all the more disturbing.

"Come outside for a minute, Fern," I said.

Below us on the terrace Eddie Burch was talking to Marcus,

and I put a hand on Fern's arm to keep her from running down to speak with them.

"You'll need to watch Alida now," I said. "The sea is all around, waiting for her. Be careful."

"I know," Fern said. "That's one reason why I'm staying. Besides, Derek will be coming over soon . . ." Her eyes sparkled, and I turned away from her open, defenseless yearning. How foolishly we all bound ourselves into the very chains that could destroy us.

I walked toward Marcus, knowing very well that I was bound, and that perhaps he was too, when it came to Iris.

Eddie looked solemn, conspiratorial, and he glanced at me impatiently, not welcoming my approach.

"I'll do what I can," he said. "But no promises. I got a stake in this too, don't forget."

He walked off, and Marcus waited for me. I told him that Fern had decided to stay on Doubloon Key.

"Then we'd better get back," he said. "It's clouding up, and weather reports promise a blow coming out of the gulf. This isn't the season for a real window rattler, but even in Key West it can rain."

When we'd cast off from the dock, I helped with the sails, and when we were on our way, Marcus talked impersonally about hurricanes. I watched him sail the boat skillfully across a new choppiness in the water, taking advantage of the wind, and I knew that he talked to keep me from asking more questions than he cared to answer. The air never did seem to stay cleared between us.

"*Huracan,*" he said, "—that was the name the Arawak Indians gave what's called a typhoon across the Pacific. And that Far East word came from *tai-fung,* Chinese for a great wind.

Down here we have waterspouts too—nasty for boats, if one comes along."

"All very informative," I said, "but not what I really want to know. Why didn't you want to see Alida?"

"I'd just upset her more, because of what Eddie's getting into with Derek. She's begun to get scared."

I had to be satisfied with that.

I watched the gray, lace-trimmed waves and the whipping palm branches as we neared land. The pelicans, for once, had gone elsewhere.

By the time we reached the car it had begun to rain. Big drops at first, and then the downpour of a tropical shower. At Cliff's house, we stayed in the car for a few moments, hoping for a break.

"You'll keep an eye on your father now, won't you, Laurel?" Marcus said. "Tomorrow will be the worst day for him to get through. I wish you could get him away for a few days until he's beyond this bad stretch of time. He might listen to you. Perhaps a quick run to the Virgin Islands would do it. Though you'd need to hurry."

"I don't think he'd go. Derek's party's tomorrow, and he's counting on that as a distraction."

"It's the wrong kind of distraction."

"I think so too." I sprang my question while Marcus was off guard. "Has Eddie found out anything useful?"

His eyes could remind me more of winter sometimes than of warm gulf waters. I'd never known a man who could freeze up so quickly. I should have been warned earlier—I should have kept still. But when did I ever?

It was hopeless to stay out here in the car, so I said good-bye and dashed through the rain. When I reached the porch I didn't look back, and after a moment I heard his car drive away.

Someone had been busy shuttering the house, but storm sounds came through from everywhere. Tree branches thrashed in the garden, and rain clattered at every window. Behind the rain sounds the wind whooped, and the house shuddered under its impact. Nevertheless, when I reached the hall, brushing wetness from my shoulders and hair, the inner vacuum of the house held me for a moment in its unnatural stillness. It was like the instant before a storm breaks—this time a human storm.

Into the stillness that was only the holding of a breath came the sound of voices from the living room, strained and off-pitch. Iris sounded angry, and Cliff's voice was sharper than I'd ever heard.

I stepped to the doorway to look in.

"The same thing's happening that happened before!" Cliff cried. "It's the same struggle. I can feel it boiling up all around me, just as it did before Poppy died. She was afraid of something. If you know what it was, tell me!"

"What you're doing is foolish," Iris said. "I hate to listen to it. There wasn't any struggle. Poppy made that all up because she didn't want me to marry Derek. She wanted him for herself! That's what you've never been willing to face. She wanted to punish him because he wouldn't look at her. She even threatened to have him sent to prison. As if that would have stopped me! The last time I saw her I told her that if he went to jail I'd marry him anyway. No matter what he's done, I'll marry him. You know what a fight Poppy and I had that last morning. It's time for you to face what really happened!"

Neither of them had looked at me, and I listened, fearful of the effect of Iris's words on Cliff. Yet at the same instant I had a strong sense that she was holding something back. In this pouring out of the "truth," there was still more that she concealed—perhaps even lied about.

But I couldn't bother with Iris now. Cliff had reached for a chair and lowered himself into it as though his bones had turned fragile, and I ran to his side.

Iris's rage dissolved as quickly as it had risen. "Cliff, I didn't mean that! I'm worse than Fern when I get angry. I just pop off with words."

She *was* worse than her sister, I thought, and her words were far more damaging.

Cliff didn't answer, and Iris looked at me, beseeching and guilty. "Stay with him, Laurel. See what you can do."

I spoke to her as she passed me. "Marcus and I have been out to Doubloon Key with Fern. Why didn't you tell me you'd persuaded Eddie Burch to take Alida to Derek's island?"

She paused long enough to answer. "I wasn't sure she'd go. And if she wouldn't, I still thought you might persuade her not to come back here with Fern."

There was nothing to say to that. She went toward the door, and I turned to Cliff again. The moment I saw him, everything else ceased to matter.

"You'd better call a doctor," I shouted to Iris, and she ran back into the room.

Cliff's head was bent into his hands, but he'd heard me. "No doctor. I'll be all right." He looked up at Iris. "I've forgiven a lot, but not lies like this. You were always jealous of your mother because you could never be half the woman she was."

"In your eyes no one ever could," Iris said, and this time she went out of the room and up the stairs.

"If I'd ever believed that Derek would make a move in Poppy's direction, I'd have killed him," Cliff said, not really speaking to me. "And I never had any doubts about Poppy. She belonged to me."

Iris was still on the stairs, and she had heard. Her words drifted back to us. "You needn't worry. Nobody needs to look very far to see that Derek is mine, and has been for a long time."

I heard her climbing the stairs, and the moment she'd gone, Cliff pulled himself together and sat up. Was he a play actor in real life, as well as a manipulator of characters in a story? I knew him so little. In fact I didn't know him or any of his family well enough to read behind their emotional words and actions. Sometimes I seemed to be caught up in the pattern myself— the make-believe, if that's what it was.

"How is Alida?" Cliff asked. "Is she willing to stay on the island?"

He seemed to have a faculty for shutting out what he didn't want to hear, and after his first outburst he had done it again.

I tried to follow his abrupt transition. "Alida needs to be by herself in quiet surroundings for a while. Derek's house is very beautiful." I remembered that it was a house Poppy had helped to design, and stepped away from dangerous ground. "I wish I knew what's really troubling Alida."

"Probably nothing more than usual," Cliff said. "It doesn't take much to worry her." He made a helpless gesture and dropped his hands limply, his brief show of assurance gone. "I'd better get back to work." That, as always, was the thing that would save him.

I followed him into the hall and saw Iris still at the top of the stairs. She must have stayed there to listen, and I wondered what we'd said that might interest her. Only then did I remember that I had a message for her.

"Fern is staying on the island with Alida," I told her. "Alida asked her to stay, and Fern said you could bring her a bag the next time you go out.''

Iris looked down at me grimly for a moment and then went off toward her room. Cliff and I climbed the top flight to his study together, and I saw that he leaned heavily on the banister.

Once more at his desk, he sat down and began to reread the last pages he had written. I marveled at his ability to immerse himself so quickly in a world that existed only in his imagination. There would be no point at all in suggesting a trip to St. Thomas now.

I returned to Alida's desk to go on with my transcribing. It was difficult to concentrate because my thoughts floundered helplessly. Even the rain blowing in gusts across the roof was a distraction, and so was the wind that hurled itself at shuttered windows. Yet when the storm sounds ceased abruptly, the sudden quiet seemed disturbing—breathless and stifling.

With my fingers still on the keys, I thought about what Marcus had said—that accidents and coincidences were always happening, that the important thing was how we dealt with whatever might occur. But this left an awesome choice in human hands. Every pebble dropped in a pond caused widening ripples that could intercept other ripples and reach distant shores that were never dreamed of or intended by the hand that dropped the pebble. Perhaps wisdom was always hindsight. What was I doing right now that might affect the future? I wanted to help my father and to help Fern—but what could I do when others were making ripples bigger than mine, widening arcs that I could neither avoid nor stop?

Cliff spoke to me down the room, and I looked around the screen. He hadn't lost himself in his writing, after all. "It's no use, Laurel. I can't work today. The storm's blown over, so I'm going for a walk."

"I'd like to come with you," I said quickly.

He made no objection, and I followed him downstairs to the front door.

All the green world outdoors dripped and pattered. The wind had carried itself away, and a patch of blue sky was visible. In a little while all the wetness would begin to steam away.

There was purpose behind Cliff's movements, and I didn't ask where he was going but kept up with him as he turned down the sidewalk with long strides. It was time, however, to make a few ripples of my own.

"Do you know a woman named Connie Corson?" I asked.

"Sure—what about her?"

"When Marcus took Fern and me to watch Sunset yesterday, she was on the next pier flying one of those kites she advertises. When we went over to join her and Fern took a turn with the kite, Connie told Marcus there was scuttlebutt going around about Derek and what he's bringing up from the wreck."

"So?" Cliff didn't slow his steps.

"Connie told Marcus that there are rumors about Derek's find being a lot bigger and more important than he's telling anyone. She seemed to feel there might even be some danger threatening him."

We were about to cross the street, but Cliff stared at me for a moment and then changed his direction without warning.

"I was going to see Derek," he said. "But maybe we'd better make another stop first. There's a place you ought to see anyway—the house Ernest Hemingway owned down here for some thirty years."

I didn't know why we were suddenly going sight-seeing. I'd read about Hemingway's productive years in Key West, but what did that matter now?

The house on Whitehead Street was Spanish colonial in style, and it occupied a large spread of tropical garden filled with varieties of palms. The original owner had built of local coral rock, instead of the usual wood, and the house was a big square of beige stone amidst all the green. Wide verandas—I liked the word "veranda" much better than "porch"—surrounded the levels above and below, and arched wooden doors and windows opened all around. The public was invited, and tours were going through. Cliff was waved in and I found myself walking slowly down a central hall, looking into the rooms we passed and out across a rear garden.

In spite of my concern for what Cliff might intend if he looked for Derek now, I was caught by the spell of this house. It was here that Hemingway had lived with Pauline, here that he'd written *A Farewell to Arms, For Whom the Bell Tolls, The Snows of Kilimanjaro,* and so many other books. Every room was filled with furnishings, rugs, tiles that he must have brought from Spain and Africa and Cuba.

Cliff, however, had seen all this, and he had some other purpose in mind. He made a quick circuit of the lower floor, and as he started toward the stairs, a young woman came down, winding up the tour she was leading. It was the woman we'd met on the pier—Connie Corson.

When the group had thanked her and the last visitor was gone, she came over to us.

"Hi, Cliff, Miss York. Anything I can do for you?"

"Any place we can talk for a minute?" Cliff asked.

"Meet me out in front. I'll be with you right away."

We waited for her on the veranda, and I noticed a slab of

coral rock that was part of the house, with tiny sea growth embedded in the stone. Cliff went down the steps into the garden, and when I went with him I began to notice the cats.

Everywhere there were cats—dozens of cats! Some moved lazily out of our way, while others examined us haughtily without stirring. One great tawny creature lolled in a decorative wrought-iron chair and dared us to usurp his place.

Cliff smiled at my surprise. "The cats are supposed to be descended from those the Hemingways owned. That's probably apocryphal, but they make a nice, legendary touch. They're fed and pampered, and I'm afraid the tribe increases, in spite of giving kittens away."

We followed a pink concrete walk, and I paused to look down, entranced. Tiny paw prints could be seen, daintily embedded in pink cement, and I could imagine ancestors of the present cats treading this walk when it was newly laid and leaving their paw signatures behind.

Connie came running out a side door, her long brown braid over one shoulder. Today she wore a printed Mother Hubbard that enveloped her lean body.

"Shoo!" she said to several cats, and we sat down on a bench.

"I've just learned what you told Marcus about rumors concerning Derek," Cliff said. "Since we're closely involved because of Iris, perhaps you can tell me what you've heard?"

Connie seemed hesitant. "You know how things get embroidered around here. There's talk about gold chains and gold bars. Pretty remarkable stuff. Derek says none of this is true—but of course he'd have to say that until he gets it all safely into a vault somewhere. Otherwise, almost anything could happen."

"Any other details?"

"No details at all, really. But it's a bit scary if all this is getting around."

"Thanks," Cliff said. "We'll see if we can catch Derek now."

We left Connie to her next tour and headed toward Mallory Square and the Banyan bar. Cliff was looking grim again, and I didn't think it was Derek's possible treasure that interested him most right now, though he might use what he'd learned from Connie.

"Are you really going to help matters?" I asked when the Banyan sign came into view just before the square.

He spoke gently. "Laurel, I need to know. After what Iris said a little while ago, I know I have to find out the truth. It's not knowing that's the torment."

I put my hand on his arm as we stopped near the entrance. "Will it be enough to know—if the knowing is bad? I hope you didn't mean what you said to Iris back at the house—about what you'd do to Derek."

He looked tired, yet implacably driven, and he didn't answer me. He shook off my hand and went inside. Why this should surface now, when he'd chosen to be blind in the past, I didn't know. Perhaps this was one of the "dangers" Marcus had meant about the anniversary of Poppy's death. I followed Cliff inside, feeling both alarmed and helpless.

The bar was downstairs—a long, bare room, high-ceilinged and hung with whirring fans. There were a few tables and a great length of counter, where a number of Key Westers were having convivial drinks. Behind the bar a somewhat lurid mermaid swam across a mirror, her green hair streaming and one eye slyly closed in a wink. On the walls around the room—walls interrupted by several full-length doors—hung old posters of Key West, celebrations long in the past; even one that showed the day the Overseas Railroad had come to the island.

"Derek's Place" suited him a lot better than his splendid house on Doubloon Key. Everything seemed in character here, while on the island one had the feeling of a beautiful, rather grand pretense. I wondered if that was the great attraction Poppy's family held for Derek. They didn't need to pretend because they could be anything they pleased and had been over the generations.

Cliff waved me toward the stairs at the rear. "Go on up, Laurel. Find a table and wait for me."

I hated to leave him, but there was nothing more I could say, and I climbed the flight of wide pine stairs that curved upward to the room above. The restaurant was cooled with a breeze from a dozen or more ceiling fans, and windows stood open on all sides. Pine beams pitched the roof, and bare wooden tables were set with place mats that were also maps of Key West.

As a waitress led me toward a center aisle, I saw Iris sitting at a table near a window. She beckoned me over.

"I'm waiting for Derek," she said. "Though he's probably too busy to join me for a while. What are you doing here, Laurel—come and sit down."

Once more, she made me uneasy, but I slid into the chair opposite and could hardly keep from staring. She looked far less elegant than usual, her pongee silk wilting and her lipstick smudged.

"Cliff's downstairs looking for Derek," I said. "I came with him because I'm afraid there may be trouble."

Iris grinned. "I'm not surprised. Now I suppose they'll have a bang-up fight. It's been coming under the surface for a long time, though Cliff keeps his feelings battened down. A fight is supposed to settle everything—men!"

I sat down a bit anxiously, glanced at the menu the waitress set before me, and ordered conch chowder to send her away.

"Is there anything we can do?" I asked.

"We can bake cakes, or knit socks. Or load the muskets when the Indians come."

Iris was neither a cake baker nor a sock knitter, but if there were muskets, I suspected she would be quite willing to fire them herself.

"We can't just sit here waiting!" I said.

"There's nothing else to do. Cliff's a haunted man, and until he lays his ghosts, he won't really come back to life. Now he thinks Derek is one of them."

"What you said to him didn't help."

She went right on. "When I saw Cliff this morning the first thing he said was, 'This is the last time I can ever say that Poppy was alive a year ago.' He's been brooding all day, and he's ready to stir up trouble. I gave Angela and Pedro the day off and told them to stay home tomorrow too—since we'll all be out on Derek's boat."

"You didn't help much in calming him down," I repeated. Perhaps "haunted" was the word for Iris too.

"He knows I fly off when I'm pushed." She sounded defensive. "He makes allowances."

"I don't think so. He came here to confront Derek. He told me he had to know."

Apparently Iris couldn't face her own actions, and she changed the subject abruptly. "Everything will be better when tomorrow is over. For more than one reason. I'm going out to the island tonight with Derek to help get things ready. Though of course he's bringing in caterers to set up the food. I'll come over on the *Aurora* in the morning and pick you up. The caterers will come out by boat later. Have you been aboard the *Aurora* yet?"

I shook my head. At the moment I wasn't much interested, and I kept listening for sounds from the stairs.

"The *Aurora*'s a dream—a power yacht, and very fast. Starting at dawn tomorrow, Derek will be over on the *Dolphin* getting everything up from the bottom. He already knows what's down there and has the places marked. Though the storm this afternoon could have shifted sand, so the job may be harder than he expected and take longer. He'll use his divers as long as he can. There's a limit to how many times a diver can go down in one day."

Iris sounded as though she might be bolstering her own courage, reassuring herself.

"Once it's over," she went on, "once everything is safe in vaults on the island, then Derek and I can be married. I don't want to wait for a big wedding and all that nonsense. I just want Derek for my husband as soon as possible."

She closed her eyes, and her hands were clenched on the table. What Iris wanted she would have, no matter what.

"Who's coming to this treasure party?" I asked.

"Only us. Cliff's family. We're the ones Derek wants to impress, I think. And for Cliff that will be party enough. Though of course Marcus will be there—he's one of us."

"Then the rumors we've been hearing about treasure really are true? I mean, there's talk about gold bars and chains and all sorts of fabulous items."

Iris glanced around quickly, but the nearest occupied tables were some distance off and the room hadn't filled up.

"It's true enough."

"Why hasn't be brought these things up as he found them? Isn't he taking a chance to wait?"

"This way he'll make one trip. And it's all safer on the bottom of the ocean, with a ship to guard the area on top. The

Dolphin's an old scow, but she's fully armed, and Derek can trust the men he keeps on board.''

"Men like Eddie Burch?" I asked.

She gave me a quick look. "What do you mean?"

"I don't know. It's just that Eddie keeps turning up, and I don't like him."

"He's okay. Despite their old trouble, he's been devoted to Derek for years, and if he really got out of line, Alida could handle him." Iris broke off. "Look who's coming, Laurel."

I looked around and saw Derek and Cliff approaching down the room. Derek's arm was around Cliff's shoulders, and Cliff was laughing.

"So much for mayhem," I murmured. "Maybe they have better sense than we thought."

"It's a bit early," Iris said, as they reached our table, "but sit down and join us for dinner. There's no cooking going on at home."

Everything wasn't quite as congenial as it seemed, however. Derek gave Iris a cool look, and he didn't sit down when Cliff did. "I'm busy downstairs right now. I'll grab a bite at the bar and see you later."

I caught the hint of alarm in Iris's eyes. "We're still going over to the island tonight?"

"That's the plan," Derek said and walked away.

Iris turned her quick anger on our father. "You told him what I said! When I was only making things up!"

"Of course I told him. I had to know what you were so mad about." Cliff looked at her thoughtfully. "Derek thinks you may be the one who's developing envy and jealousy. Perhaps you always were jealous of Poppy. And maybe of your sister Fern."

Iris looked so shocked that I felt sorry for her. Perhaps the one thing she'd always counted on, been sure of, was Derek's almost fatuous affection.

She rose from the table abruptly. "I'm not hungry. I'll come back later and meet Derek. Right now I want to telephone Alida."

Cliff let her go, but she looked so upset that for an instant I wanted to run after her to make sure she was all right. I hadn't expected to feel any sympathy for Iris. But even as I thought of following her, I denied my own intuition. There was nothing I could do or say that would help her now, and she would certainly repulse any such effort from me. So I stayed with my father, where I wanted to be.

It wasn't until much later that I wondered if events were as much affected by what one didn't do as what one did. If I had followed Iris, might I have prevented her call to Alida—or at least delayed it until she felt better? If she hadn't made the call, perhaps Alida wouldn't have taken the desperate step she did, and then some of the awful things that followed might never have happened. Or would they have happened anyway, in some other pattern?

All this was hindsight. We are seldom warned at the time when we most need it. I sat at the table with my father, glad to see him more cheerful and glad enough to be with him, never dreaming of the storm Iris was about to stir up.

11

The *Aurora* was magnificent—not a large yacht, but nevertheless a white sea queen whose prow raked the water dramatically. The deckhouses were in two layers, the top one offering good visibility for the helmsman. An oddly shaped funnel served in place of a sail, and above the waterline a row of white circles indicated portholes. Aft, a sun deck overlooked the stern, and its teak boards already burned hot in the sun.

We had left Key West around nine in the morning, and we were all on board except for Derek, who had gone directly from the island to the *Dolphin*. Iris, Fern, and even Alida had come from Doubloon Key to meet Cliff, Marcus, and me in Key West.

The moment I'd come aboard, I'd sensed an odd disquiet—as though those on the boat were apprehensive about something. Iris looked enticing and cool in white piqué shorts and a lemon shirt, her hair bound back with a white band. Her perfection was marred, however, by her restless, nervous air—so unlike the calm I'd first thought typical of Iris. I wondered if she might have learned more about Derek's activities than she could accept.

Fern had wrapped herself inappropriately in a filmy creation that blew about her in the wind and was the color of those woodsy ferns for which she was named. There seemed an unearthly quality about her today, as though she had little connection with gravity, never losing her balance when the yacht rolled in the swells and floating along without clinging to handrails or lifelines like the rest of us, who were mortal. She stayed near Cliff when she could, showing a yearning and anxiety that was obvious and which probably embarrassed him, since he was hardly a demonstrative man.

I felt that Alida shouldn't have come. She looked pale and ill and spent her time stretched out in a deck chair topside, with her eyes closed much of the time. Iris had brought her along reluctantly, and only because Alida had insisted on being part of the day. Whenever Cliff was in sight, she opened her eyes and watched him anxiously, her apprehension contagious, so that uneasiness lay heavily on all three women and began to affect me as well. Though I had no certain idea of what there was to fear. As I realized later, all their fears were different.

Chairs had been set out for us on the sun deck, where we could look down and watch as treasure was brought up from the bottom of the sea. Divers from the *Dolphin* had been working since dawn, and when we anchored near the wreck site a power launch came over to put aboard all that had been collected earlier.

The stern of the *Aurora* was quickly puddled with sea water and strewn with chunks of coral. Now when divers went down, they came up directly to the *Aurora*, climbing an improvised platform and depositing additional treasure on each trip. There was no longer any question that this wreck was the Spanish galleon, the *Santa Beatriz*. Much of her cargo had been registered in Spain, and what had not been marked for the King's taxes was probably contraband.

I stood at an upper rail with Marcus beside me, more conscious of him than ever on this beautiful day I wanted to share with him, yet feeling that we had moved away from each other. The preoccupation of all the men was entirely on the main event—the treasure—while the women focused mainly on the men. Perhaps because they worried us more than all that gold.

Derek had come over with the first load and was supervising the astonishing trove as it was brought up and dumped casually into the stern of the *Aurora*. Heavier pieces were either left on the *Dolphin* or remained on the bottom for later retrieval.

For a time we were all struck into awed wonder at the sight of so much ancient gold. Only Alida didn't seem to care. She watched Cliff, and when he wasn't nearby she lay back in her chair, shaded by an awning, indifferent to all else. She really looked like death, and though Iris and I took turns keeping her company, she didn't respond. Sooner or later, I must find out what had happened on the island after I'd left. Fern would know. But right now Fern too was hypnotized by the gold.

The sun struck a yellow dazzle from the piles of treasure. There were a great number of gold bars, and probably two or three dozen long chains with carved and twisted links, all ringing as only gold can as each chain was dropped on the heap. Large gold plates stamped with elaborate designs had been recovered, and there were more gleaming piles of golden doubloons. Gold, as Marcus had told me, never tarnished like lesser metals and always looked like gold, even after all these hundreds of years.

Derek brought a few special items up for us to look at and handle. He was bursting with energy today and flashing even more confidence than usual, so that he seemed overpowering and a little frightening. None of the women's uneasiness had touched or dampened his enthusiasm as the collection grew.

Marcus watched, always the observer today, and not entirely happy about Derek's triumph.

I could understand now why Iris had looked displeased about the gold medal I had found. That was a fluke, since nothing was supposed to be brought up until this staged celebration today.

"Why are there so many gold chains?" I asked Derek, weighing the heaviness of a chain in my hand.

"They could be used like money," he said. "Every link had a value and could be spent separately. Chains were supposed to be ornaments worn by Spanish noblemen, so this was a good way to smuggle in gold without being taxed for it. I expect there was a lot of greasing of palms, since there's plenty here that was never stamped for the King's taxes."

He put a doubloon in my hand, and I saw the Spanish shield on one side and the cross on the other. For me, the *Aurora* seemed peopled with ghosts that drifted out of the gentle swells and clung to the rails, peering at us with hollow, accusing eyes.

I tried to shake off the macabre fancy. There was enough else to concern me now. I gave back the doubloon, remarking on how heavy the gold was.

"Sure," Derek said. "Gold's two and a half times as heavy as iron, and eight times the weight of sand."

As time passed, the scene grew monotonous as far as I was concerned. One couldn't keep exclaiming over each new item the divers brought up. Especially since Derek already knew what was down there, and it was no surprise to any of his crew. Where the original finds must have been greeted with tremendous excitement, this was, to some extent, an anticlimax.

I wandered about the decks and in and out of cabins, exploring the *Aurora*'s luxury. Marcus and my father were talking together on the leeward side. Iris stood where she could continue to watch Derek giving directions as divers came aboard. Eddie Burch, out of his diving gear now, darted about on idle chores, as tense and nervous as though our uneasiness had infected him too. At least he kept carefully away from Alida, though once I saw him standing where he could look up at her deck chair, his face expressionless.

Fern stood at a rail, where she watched the endless movement of the water, looking a bit like a figurehead, with her filmy dress blowing back from her body. When I approached her, she turned away almost sadly, as though there was nothing she could possibly say to me.

Hampers had been brought aboard filled with food for lunch, and we ate on deck, or wherever we were. Derek didn't stop to eat at all, still alert to every detail of the continuing parade of treasures from the past.

It was late afternoon when the caterers arrived in their own boat, and the diving ceased. Derek's divers went back to the *Dolphin,* except for Eddie Burch, who stayed with us. The caterers set our dinner out in covered dishes, kept hot in the dining area of the big saloon, and then went back to shore. We helped ourselves from the buffet and sat down at a long table. This was a family party, and the crew didn't join us. Of our own group, only Alida remained on deck because the idea of food nauseated her.

Iris had brought sprays of orchids aboard, and their splendid colors glowed down the length of the table like waxy jewels.

At my place, a single blossom recalled the photograph that had been destroyed in Poppy's bedroom—a reminder I could do without. Whenever possible, I averted my eyes from the flowers, though I knew this was a weird fancy I'd developed— that an orchid could watch me.

The swift darkness of the tropics was all around us. The engines were running now as the *Aurora* moved away from the wreck site, though Derek said there was still more to be brought up at a later time, and the *Dolphin* would remain on guard. In my last moments on deck I'd noticed that the *Dolphin*'s lights were growing distant astern, and I knew we were running for Derek's island. There would still be an unloading tonight by his crew, since Derek was anxious to get his treasure into waiting vaults on Doubloon Key.

Derek poured champagne and toasted the success of his long venture. He was affable and hearty now, and if the strain that had touched the rest of us had reached him, it wasn't visible. As I watched him, I could more and more imagine his being engaged in something as horrific as the drug trade, and I wondered if some knowledge of this lay beneath the uneasiness I felt aboard the *Aurora*.

I began to listen again as Derek spoke.

"I haven't been given enough credit for respecting an historic site," he said. "The old controversy goes right on between the treasure hunter, who puts up the cash and makes retrieval possible, and the historian, who's always afraid something valuable will be damaged or sold before records are complete. I have put up the money, as you all know, but nothing will leave Doubloon Key until the archeologists are satisfied."

Though we joined in Derek's toast to the *Santa Beatriz*, I was still aware of the underlying disquiet, and it seemed to be growing. By this time it had reached Cliff and Marcus too, and when Derek sat down, my father spoke to him across the table.

"It's possible that no historic wreck should be salvaged by anyone but the archeologists. Then what's found would furnish scientific information and not be damaged as it is brought up. And it would be kept in museums for everyone to enjoy. I remember a phrase used for the marauders who strip sunken wrecks and sell what they find for profit: 'Piranhas on a carcass.'"

There was a stunned silence around the table, and everyone except Fern stared at Cliff. She had picked up an orchid and was turning it about in her fingers. My father had finally taken a stand and was flinging down a challenge to Derek. But what he was talking about wasn't any rape of the *Santa Beatriz*.

Derek took no outward offense, his smile affable enough, but I didn't like the cold light in his eyes.

"I'm sorry, my friend," he said quietly, "but I can't agree. Your archeologist can take forever sifting teaspoons of sand. He'd be at this for years after the wreck was found. And while he was being so careful, storms would scatter whatever was left, and most of the wreck could be lost. My way is better—and cheaper. The historians will get their turn, now that the job's accomplished."

Cliff said nothing more, but I could sense the satisfaction he'd felt in opposing Derek, and I didn't think he was through yet. More was surfacing than gold from the bottom of the sea.

Fern was the one who sprang to her feet now and held up her glass. The *Aurora* rolled slightly, and she steadied herself with one hand on a chair. She loved moments of drama, and when she spoke I knew that she too was challenging Derek.

"Here's to beating the curse!" she cried. "You all know what I mean—the curse of death and bad luck that follows anyone who disturbs ancient bones, whether they're in a wreck or a tomb. But you'll overcome that, won't you, Derek?"

She sat down abruptly without sipping her wine, spilling a little on the tablecloth. No one else drank to her toast, but Derek smiled at her across the table.

"Of course we'll prove the old stories wrong. And now let's start before our food is cold."

Fern didn't look at him. She picked up the white orchid again and fastened it in her hair. "The curse is already working. I can feel it, even if none of you can. Last night I dreamed about Poppy."

I glanced at Cliff and saw his closed look. All day he must have been dealing with memories that wouldn't leave him alone, and perhaps all his long-buried resentment against Derek had begun to come out.

In spite of our discomfort, we did our best to enjoy the meal. But though the food prepared for us was delicious, no one seemed hungry. I think all we wanted was to reach the island where we could get safely ashore. Just being in close proximity to such piles of gold was unsettling. Of course I'd seen the arms on board earlier, the crew keeping watch, and even Derek wore a pistol strapped to a belt around his shorts.

We'd eaten only a little when the first jarring warning came with a bump against the *Aurora*'s side. We started and looked at one another as something struck again and scraped along near the waterline. Shouting broke out on deck, and a woman screamed. Alida! Derek jumped to his feet, but before he could reach the companionway, Eddie Burch appeared, wild-eyed, his fringe of hair standing up above his ears.

"Pirates!" he screeched. "We've been boarded!"

"Get the lights off!" Derek shouted to him, and ran for the stairs with his gun in hand. Cliff and Marcus went after him.

After a moment of stunned silence while we stared at each other, Fern ran up the companionway, and Iris and I followed.

We all huddled together in the door for a moment, and I had a glimpse of the nearest deck before the lights went out.

A man stood alone a few feet away—a big, rough-looking fellow. The bandana he'd worn over his face had slipped, and I saw him for just a second. I knew I'd seen him before. Then darkness came down, blinding me. All around there was shouting and confusion, and several shots were fired.

"I've got to find Alida," Iris cried, and slipped away before I could stop her. Fern went after her. My eyes were becoming accustomed to moonlight that washed the decks, and I glimpsed my father in his white suit running toward the bow. Without thought, I started after him. Someone I never saw put out a foot and tripped me. I sprawled full length and lay stunned on the wet, slanting deck. I felt spray on my face as the yacht dipped in a swell. The engines had stopped, and the uproar all around seemed to be receding.

I pushed myself shakily up from the planking and found no one nearby. The man I'd seen had disappeared. I was near the foredeck, and as I clung to the wet handrail, I could just make out my father's white suit ahead of me in the bow. A shadowy figure stood beside him, but I couldn't see who it was. Then Marcus found me and pulled me back when I would have gone to Cliff.

"It's already over, Laurel. They had the advantage of surprise. Now we'll have to do what we're told." He raised his voice to call to my father. "Come with us, Cliff."

Now I could see some of the men who had come aboard—all in seamen's caps, with handkerchiefs tied across their faces, guns in their hands. Derek's crew had been outnumbered, and he had been quickly disarmed. All of his treasure from the sea was about to change hands.

We were pushed roughly toward a rope ladder that dropped

to the water, where a dinghy waited for us, bobbing on the waves. Spray soaked me as I clung to rope rungs and lowered myself into the little boat. Iris and Fern were already there, and for once Fern was clinging to her sister.

Derek himself brought Alida down, and in the light of stars and moon I saw his glazed look and the glitter of his eyes. I think he hardly knew what he was doing. Iris took over with Alida while Marcus and Derek picked up the oars.

"Wait!" I cried. "Cliff isn't here. Someone has to find Cliff!"

It was already too late. Our small boat had been pushed away and the *Aurora*, her decks and portholes as dark as any ghost ship, was picking up speed as we watched her move away.

Fern came frantically to life. "We can't leave Cliff!"

I tried to put an arm around her, though I felt frantic too. She pushed me away angrily. "You don't care! You never knew him for most of your life—he's *my* father!"

But there was nothing to do, and no one spoke after that. Derek and Marcus put their backs into rowing. The *Aurora* had vanished in the darkness, but her fluorescent wake remained, ghostly in itself, marking the path she'd taken away from us toward the Caribbean. The lights of Key West glowed distantly against the sky. Doubloon Key was nearer, and its own lights beckoned us.

As we crossed the swirling waters of the wake, something on my side of the boat bobbed into view, and I shouted to Marcus, "There's a man in the water!"

Marcus rested the oar on his side, and I peered into the black water where something white floated just beneath the surface. Without any doubt, I *knew*, and my heart seemed to stop beating.

"It's Cliff!" Fern screamed, trying to lean over the side of the boat.

Marcus pulled her back and reached to grasp the collar of Cliff's white jacket, hauling him toward the boat. Derek helped to pull him in, while our little boat tilted and dipped. They laid him across a wooden seat, and water streamed from him. But there was no possible room for lifesaving techniques. Fern, her dress already soaked, knelt where she could hold his head and shoulders in her arms, the white orchid shining in her hair in the moonlight.

Marcus and Derek began to row toward the island with renewed effort. Iris sat huddled over, hugging her knees with both arms. I felt too stunned to believe in what was happening. It was all too awful and unreal—like a terrible dream.

Someone in the boat began to moan—a high-pitched keening sound, like a mourning for the dead. Iris sat up and shook Alida. "Stop that! You're not helping. Stop it, Alida!"

The woman froze, clinging to the side of the boat, and her dreadful moaning stopped.

I spoke to Marcus and Derek. "When you need a break, I can row for a while."

After that, Iris and I spelled the men when they rested, and the lights of the island dock came closer. We could see the house now on its rise of ground, with all the lights ablaze, as though whoever was there expected us.

When we neared the dock, however, no one came to help with the boat.

"There's no one here," Derek said bleakly. "I had my men on board the *Aurora.* God knows what's happening to them now."

Marcus sprang out and tied up the dinghy at the dock. Then

he and Derek lifted Cliff onto the boards and began to work over him.

The moment I climbed out of the boat, I ran for the house with one idea in mind—a telephone. But that had been taken care of too. I found Derek's housekeeper wringing her hands and weeping helplessly. The telephone connections had been cut. Whoever had been here had also turned on all the lights. In her fright, Elena's English had vanished.

While I was trying to make sense of what she said, Iris came up to the house and stood staring at me blankly.

"Cliff?" I asked.

"I think he's dead. They're still trying."

Iris could understand her, so Elena gave her a garbled account of men in masks. She was still wide-eyed and terrified, but at Iris's urging, she went off to make coffee for us all.

There was still a two-way radio kept for emergencies, Iris said. She knew where it was and how to use it. When she finally raised the Coast Guard, Derek had come up to the house, and he explained to them what had happened, asking for help for Cliff.

It was already too late. He could have been dead when they pulled him from the water. We were all in a state of shock, and worst of all, helpless. Strangely enough, Alida seemed to rally first. She asked Marcus to carry Cliff into one of the bedrooms. Then she found some dry clothes for Fern and sent her off to change.

I wished I could cry, but there seemed only a blank emptiness inside me. I was too stunned for tears. After a time, I went outside to look for Derek. He had gone to wait at the dock, where lights still burned, and was watching for the first sign of a Coast Guard boat. I noticed the swelling bruise, crusted with dried blood on his forehead.

"You're hurt," I said.

"It's nothing. Somebody hit me."

I didn't know whether he was the right person to talk to now, because of his own loss of a fortune. Nevertheless, I had to put into words something that was troubling me—a question that had to be asked.

"How could Cliff have fallen overboard?"

"Who knows?" Just then, I didn't think Derek even cared. "I suppose if he tried to tackle one of those ruffians, he could have been thrown over the rail."

"The last time I saw him there was someone with him," I said. "All I could see was his white suit and a figure beside him at the rope handrail. But I don't think they were fighting."

"Look, Laurel, I'm sorry about Cliff. And I know I'll be sorrier as time goes on—we were friends for a long while. But right now I can't feel much of anything. I'd better look for Iris. What's happened has changed everything."

I didn't know what he meant, but I understood that he couldn't focus on Cliff in his dazed state. I followed him up to the house, aware of a pleasantly balmy evening and the rustling of palm fronds in the wind. A familiar, peaceful scene— where there was no peace.

Marcus stood out on the front terrace, staring across the water as Derek had done. He started to speak when Derek reached him, but Derek went past without a word.

I dropped wearily down on a step and asked the same question I'd asked Derek. At least, Marcus listened.

"I've been wondering too," he said. "The police will want to know who might have been with Cliff. Though we may never find the answer."

That sounded ominous. "Whoever was with him seemed to be talking to him quietly. All the fighting was going on somewhere else. Do you know if anyone was wounded? What do you suppose will happen to the crew?"

"If these pirates get away with the *Aurora*, it may be a long time before anyone knows. There were only a few men in Derek's crew."

For a little while we were silent. Then I said miserably, "Too late can come so suddenly."

Marcus nodded, and I knew he was grieving too. Perhaps Cliff had been more like a father to him than he had to me.

I tried to rouse myself. "What will happen to Derek now?"

"I expect he's broke. He must have put everything he had into bringing up the *Santa Beatriz* gold. And he'd borrowed heavily besides. Cliff put a lot into the venture."

I hadn't known that. This would be a loss to Iris and Fern as well.

"Isn't there anything left down there in the sea?"

"Mostly the big pieces that haven't much except historic value. Cannons, musket balls, and any parts of the ship that didn't rot away. Probably silver coins buried in clumps of coral. Some things were left on board the *Dolphin* too, but all the gold was brought over to the *Aurora*. I wondered about this scheme of Derek's from the first, but he had to do it his own way. He's always gone for big, dramatic gestures, but he'll pay for this one."

I wanted to touch Marcus, to have his arm around me—I wanted someone to comfort me, but he seemed too far away to reach.

"What if this was the way Cliff wanted it?" he said at last.

"No! I don't believe that! I think he was even beginning to look ahead a little. What he wanted most was to get past the date of Poppy's death."

Marcus sighed. "He didn't make it, and there's no use speculating. Let's wait for the autopsy—it may tell us something."

Alida came out the door, and for the first time I thought of Eddie Burch. Was he still aboard the *Aurora?*

"Come inside," Alida said. "There's coffee, and Elena has fixed some sandwiches. Even if we aren't hungry, we'd better try to eat. We had very little dinner, remember. Derek thinks the Coast Guard will be here soon." I had the feeling that Alida was holding herself calm and capable by sheer effort.

We followed her into the big kitchen, with windows all around that looked out upon dark water. Reed blinds could be pulled against the sun in daytime but were rolled up above black openings now.

Iris sat at the kitchen table talking earnestly with Derek, whose attention seemed to be elsewhere. Fern huddled on a stool near a counter, the bruised orchid still clinging to her hair. Alida spoke to her, and when Fern looked up I saw with dismay the wild light in her eyes. Fern needed a doctor and something quieting as soon as possible. When she looked around at us, I had the feeling that she was blaming us all for what had happened.

She burst into words suddenly. "How can you think about eating, when Cliff is dead? None of you cared about him the way I did! I loved him more than any of you did!"

Alida put a hand on Fern's arm, but when she spoke her words were sharp. "We all cared about him. So don't take the grief all to yourself."

Fern slapped her hand away angrily, masking her pain. But before she could answer, Derek leaned toward her and spoke sternly.

"Stop that, Fern. No more!"

She drew back from him. "Don't you touch me! You killed him! You all killed him!"

Derek looked at Iris. "You'd better take care of your sister before she loses the rest of her marbles."

Iris didn't move. "Fern won't listen to me."

There was no one else to try, and Fern's hysteria was getting out of hand. "We really are all hurting, Fern," I said. "Maybe we need to help each other now."

She stared at me for a moment, and I saw her terrible need. Fern was the little girl whom everyone had loved—Poppy, Cliff, and even Iris. And now she needed help, desperately. Not sure of her reaction, half expecting to have my arms struck away, I put them around her and held her gently. For a moment she resisted, and then her body went limp. Her head with its tangle of tawny hair came down on my shoulder, and her tears were a release. I wanted to cry with her—and couldn't.

In a little while she stopped, reached for a box of tissues Alida had placed on the counter, and began to mop up her tears. I looked around the room at all of them—all strangers to me, really. Alida had retreated behind her stoical expression. Iris observed me with clear suspicion, not trusting me at all. Derek had already forgotten everyone in the room. He picked up a sandwich and walked outside to where he could watch again for the Coast Guard boat. Only Marcus tried to smile at me—but he was a stranger too right now. I had lost all sense of reality.

We drank too much coffee and waited for what seemed an endless length of time. Once Alida tried to get Fern to lie down, but any effort to push her brought on signs of hysteria. She sat near me and seemed to take some comfort in my presence.

When we heard the sound of the boat approaching, Derek

and Marcus hurried down to the dock. The rest of us waited at the house.

There was a doctor aboard, and of course the police. Word of what had happened to the *Aurora* had been on the air, but no sign of her had been reported. When last seen she'd been heading full speed toward South America, and there were thousands of places scattered across the Caribbean where she could put in and hide. Of course there'd been no word of Derek's men either, and now there were families ashore who must be notified of what had happened.

Since Fern's need was greatest, the doctor took care of her first and then examined Cliff's body.

We were asked to give what details we could of the piracy. Derek did most of the talking, with the rest of us corroborating what he said. We had no answers concerning Cliff's death. I mentioned seeing someone with him on the *Aurora,* but everything was confused at that time, and no one knew who it might have been. Or at least no one was ready to admit to being with him. After a couple of hours the boat left with Cliff's body on board. At the last minute Derek decided to go back to Key West with them, assuring us that he'd send for us the first thing in the morning.

Fern and I took the guest room with twin beds. The doctor had given Fern an injection and left medication with Alida for use in the morning. I helped Alida get her to bed and removed the wilted white orchid from her hair. Iris brought us extra pajamas that she kept on the island, but she offered no help with her sister. When Fern was settled, Alida went off to the room she'd been occupying, and we saw no more of her till morning.

Iris fixed nightcaps for herself, Marcus, and me, and we sat outside on the cool terrace until the mosquitoes moved in. We talked very little, and I think we were all considering what it would be like and how different our lives would be when we returned to Key West. For the first time I found myself thinking seriously of escape—of going North. But there was still Marcus to hold me here—whatever that was worth.

When I was tired enough physically, even though my mind was wide awake, I went into the room where Fern lay sleeping, her hair a bright tangle on the pillow. Strain and tension had faded from her face, and she looked young and vulnerable.

I undressed, turned out the lamp, and fell into bed. For a few moments I lay staring into the dark, hearing the sound of waves on the shore of the island, hearing the now familiar rattle of palm fronds. I didn't want to relive the terrible experiences of that evening. I didn't want to think about my father. Luckily, my weary body lulled my mind, and I fell asleep quickly.

I must have slept for two or three hours before the dream that I'd dreaded began—that dream of orchids Fern had warned me about. It was unbearably vivid and real. The time was night, and the only lights that burned were in the orchid house. I stood with all those flowers crowding around me, watching. Now I knew they had eyes and could whisper among themselves. There were so many of them in bloom—hundreds, it seemed. And among them one great empress orchid was larger and more powerful than all the rest. Her color was as golden-tawny as Fern's hair, and there were red streaks along her petals—as though some animal had clawed them and left lines of blood in every mark.

In the dream the empress orchid spoke to me with a voice I recognized, even though I'd never heard it before. Poppy's voice.

"There's no way for you to get out. You can try the door—

pound against it until your knuckles bleed. No one will come. Your father is upstairs playing the piano, and he won't hear. The others don't want to hear—they want you to die. I want you to die."

I knew I was dreaming, yet I couldn't escape, couldn't wake up. The only way out lay through a door that would never open.

"Look!" The word was suddenly there, put into my mind, and the tawny flower seemed to have swelled in size—a bloated parody of an orchid. I saw the glass flask on the shelf before me, with a growth of seedlings crowding it, and I knew what I was supposed to do. I must free the plants, so they could be repotted and continue to grow.

I must pick up the flask and break it. And I knew what would happen when I did. But someone was at the door of the orchid house calling to me, warning me. The voice was Cliff's, and a feeling of gladness surged up in me. My father would get me out of this terrible place—he had come to save me. A warmth of love flooded through me.

Yet somehow the flask was already in my hands and had shattered into daggerlike shards.

I cried out and threw myself across the bed, wakening to reality. There was no orchid house, no jammed door or broken flask. But neither was Cliff alive, and there was no gladness left in me. In that waking moment I knew how much I had lost.

12

Days had passed since Derek's fatal "celebration," and nothing would ever be the same again.

In the first shock of what had happened, numbness had kept me from feeling anything but bewilderment and disbelief. It wasn't real—it couldn't have happened. Now pain was like a throbbing nerve that would not let me be, that met me at every turn.

I had just begun to find my father, just begun to love him. Perhaps he had begun to love me too, and if only there had been time . . . Always after death, "if only" becomes the most haunting and futile phrase, yet, for me, its torment never stopped. I went on with everyday life, but there was always the aching underneath.

In the days that followed no trace had been found of the *Aurora*, or of Derek's crew who had stayed aboard—Eddie Burch among them. Fear for the men was increasing as the news media played up this drama of modern piracy with an avidity that was all the more distressing because we were involved.

Of course we'd been questioned and interviewed, but now

there was no "head of the house" to take charge of all this. Neither Iris nor Fern wanted to deal with what faced us, and Alida drifted in and out, as lost as anyone else. Derek was busy with his own disaster and saw little of Iris at first. I was sure he didn't really care about Cliff's death, and I disliked him all the more for his callous indifference.

While Marcus kept watch over Iris, he was in no position of authority, and I was an outsider whose presence was barely tolerated. I knew very well that both my sisters were merely waiting for me to go home. But I didn't know where "home" was any more.

We learned quickly enough about the cause of Cliff's death. He hadn't drowned but had suffered a massive heart attack before he went into the water. This could have been caused by shock when the *Aurora* was boarded. Or it could have been brought on by anything at all. No one came forward to admit to being with him at the rail that evening, so we couldn't be sure of what had brought on his fatal seizure. The doctor said his heart had been weakening for some time, and the moment had simply come for it to stop.

These were the bare facts concerning what had happened. They were brutally simple and revealed nothing of what we were experiencing.

Perhaps the prosaic matters of each day were what kept us all from exploding into an anguish that I knew my sisters were feeling too. Marcus's very grimness told me what he was suffering, and Alida looked like death itself—despairing and without hope. How much Eddie's disappearance had affected her, there was no telling. None of us could open up and talk to one another. For me, this was the most difficult part of all—that I was walled in by myself. I'd never known before what loneliness really was. Not even when my mother had died.

Another devastating piece of news was the revelation that Cliff had gone ahead with his changed will and done the very things I'd begged him not to do. The orchid house was to be mine. Even Clifton York's books, with their continuing royalties, were left to me, because, as the will stated, I was the one who "cared most about them." The house was to be my home and Iris's for as long as we wished to stay. Eventually it would belong to Fern. There was still probate ahead, but the legacy had been made, and nothing could stop the legal wheels from turning.

I tried to reason with Fern and Iris, to make them understand that I wanted none of this. However, refusing a legacy wasn't as easy as all that. Especially since Iris told me flatly that neither she nor Fern would touch what had been left to me.

My immediate impulse was to run away—to throw up my hands and go home. No one needed or wanted me here, and all I longed for was to get back to that time before Marcus O'Neill had walked into my bookshop. Only my father had really held me here, and now that tenuous bond was gone. I'd been fooling myself about Marcus, and it was time for a clean break and a new beginning. My life back home hadn't been all I'd wanted, but it hadn't been filled with the turmoil and pain that had engulfed me here. With this sort of reasoning, I tried to fool myself.

If there had been a time when Marcus and I had moved tentatively toward each other, that was changed now. His main concern was clearly for Iris, and I could see how gentle and tender he was with her, how understanding of her new uncertainty toward Derek—just being there for her to lean on. He talked to me often enough, but casually, and he seemed to take it for granted that I would be all right.

Cliff had left instructions for cremation, and this was done quickly. When his memorial service was held, much of Key West came, and I realized for the first time how many friends he'd had, even though he had withdrawn since Poppy's death.

For a while our emotions continued to seethe below the surface—all the pent-up anger and resentment that we'd held back until now. Then the whole stir boiled over, and the lid shot sky-high.

The first real explosion came one night at dinner about ten days after Cliff's death. Iris had invited Marcus to join us that evening, and even Fern, who often ate in her room or at a counter in the kitchen, joined us. From the start it was hardly a friendly meal. My sisters barely spoke to me, now that they knew about the will, and Marcus's concern seemed to be wholly for Iris.

I have no idea what we ate at that meal—food had ceased to matter. But as we were finishing our coffee, Fern suddenly let her fury spill out in an attack on me.

"How could he give you my orchids!" she cried. "How could he do anything so cruel? Why did he hate us that much? I always loved him, and I thought he loved me."

"He didn't hate you, Fern," Marcus said gently.

"Of course he hated me, or he wouldn't have done this." She turned on me again. "You poisoned him! You never cared about him for all these years, the way we did. We were his real daughters, and look how he's repaid us!"

Her words cut through whatever defenses I'd tried to raise around myself. Cliff had been cruel to me, as well as to my sisters, in what he'd done, though Fern wouldn't see that.

"Why don't you go home?" she ran on. "Go up to your icy North, where you belong! Why don't you leave us alone? We never wanted you here in the first place."

Perhaps her rage was justified, and it left me helpless. I

couldn't remind her of that orchid she had sent to me by Marcus at a time that seemed so long ago.

"You haven't any answer, have you?" she demanded, when I was silent. "There's guilt all over you—I can see it. Because you've got what you came here for—you've taken Cliff away from us!"

She was weeping wildly now, and she jumped up from the table and ran out of the room. Iris laid her napkin aside, and I felt her suppressed fury when she spoke to me.

"Fern is right. Everything she's said is true. I cared about Cliff's books. I cared about him." She stood up and followed Fern out of the room.

Marcus had watched as if he were a bystander, and suddenly I was more angry with him than with either of my sisters.

"I've had enough!" I said. "They're both right, and Cliff should never have done this. There's nothing to hold me here, and I'm going home as soon as I can."

"Your father wanted you to stay." Again Marcus spoke quietly, and I felt that I'd have liked him better if he too had raged.

"Then he was a foolish, misguided man," I said. "I don't know and I really don't care what his purpose was. I just want to get away."

"Your sisters need you. Even though they don't realize it now, they need you."

"That's ridiculous! I know them better than that."

"I'm not usually so wrong about people," Marcus went on gravely. "But apparently I was wrong about you from the first. Though I still remember what you said to me at the airport in Miami when you flew in from New York. You said you didn't back out of things."

I stared at him furiously. My mind was made up. I would

board a plane to Miami and then catch the first flight I could for New York.

"I am backing out," I said. "That was a foolish boast. I'll go home tomorrow. I have a bookstore to look after and a life that's important to me. I don't need what's happened here."

"What about Fern?"

"What can I do? Cliff finished everything for me with my sisters when he left me the greenhouse."

"Don't you see how deeply Fern is suffering, first over her father's death, and then because of what she feels is a slight? If you stay, you'll find a way to reach her. That's what Cliff was counting on."

"He had no right to count on that!"

"All right," Marcus said. "Have it your way. I'll be going along now. There's nothing I can do for you here."

I realized suddenly that I might never see him again, and I went with him to the door. He held out his hand, and I gave him mine, wishing vainly that I could make him understand.

"The trouble is, you've imagined me as someone who doesn't really exist," I said.

He let my hand go. "You're probably right, Laurel. I hope you find the answer to your fantasies."

That could never happen now. Not with Cliff gone, my sisters detesting me, and Marcus lost forever.

I watched him walk away and get into his car. When he'd gone, I went inside to my father's room and sat down in Poppy's great fan-backed chair. It was as though I wanted to defy her in some way that I didn't understand. But I couldn't sit there for long, and I moved instead to Cliff's leather armchair and curled up in it. Now, at last, I could cry. I let all my grieving pour out in sobs that shook me. For a long time I cried there in the darkness of his room. Then I went upstairs and packed my suitcases.

In the morning, when I was ready to leave, I knew there was one more thing I had to do. One thing I must take away with me, no matter how I felt about my father's actions.

I hadn't been up to his study since he'd died, and I went to the foot of the stairs, hesitating because I wasn't entirely sure why I was going there now. Did I really want more pain? Yet this was something I must do.

I'd just started up when I heard the music. I froze, listening. Someone was playing Scott Joplin on my father's piano. Shock held me for only a moment, and then I ran up the stairs.

Alida sat at the piano. I hadn't known she could play, but now she was picking out the music lightly, perhaps by ear. She lacked my father's touch, but something of her own pain came through in what should have been lively music. As I went quietly down the long room toward her, Alida heard a board creak and stopped playing to look around.

At once she stood up to face me. "What are you doing here? You have no right to come into this room—not any more!"

"Of course I have a right," I told her. "Perhaps more right than you have. There's something I want from my father's desk."

"Aren't you keeping enough as it is?"

"I'm not keeping anything—I'm leaving. My father wrote me some letters years ago when I was a little girl. Letters that my mother returned to him. He kept a few of them, and I've never read them. I'd like to have them now."

She sat down at the piano, still watching me suspiciously.

I pulled open a bottom drawer and began to look through it. Underneath a blue notebook lay the packet of letters, and I took it out. Before I put the notebook back, I opened its pages idly, to find that it was a journal in which Cliff had kept a partial record of his current work. Dated notes indicated his progress and listed scenes still to be written in a particular chapter.

"You're not to read that!" Alida left the piano and came toward me indignantly. "That's his private journal. He never wanted even me to look at those notes."

Now my interest was caught, and I turned more pages until the dates ran back to the time of my coming to Key West.

"Give me that book!" Alida commanded.

I shook my head. "Perhaps my father would want me to read this. Haven't you felt him here in this room, Alida? Can't you sense that something of him is here right now?"

She stopped with her hand outstretched, staring at me. I turned the pages and began to read.

> My eldest daughter has come to this house. She is all I could hope she would become, and I have a feeling that she is strong. Stronger than Iris or Fern. I believe she can save this house and help her sisters if she finds herself. Though she's not ready yet.
>
> Someone must take hold. I no longer care enough. Perhaps Laurel can bring me to life, since she's bursting with life herself. She doesn't fully realize this yet, and she's still suppressing her own feelings, holding back too much. This is because of her mother, who was a narrow, oppressive woman.

For an instant, the old, defensive anger rose in me. I had never allowed anyone to criticize my mother. Not even me. But perhaps it was time. I had to face the fact that there was truth in his words. I read on.

Janet was a destructive woman who tried to bend everyone to fit into her own limits. I hope Laurel can be freed eventually from her influence.

Both her sisters need her, though neither they nor Laurel understand this. I have changed my will—for which no one will thank me—because it is the only chance of helping my two younger daughters. Without Laurel, they will tear each other apart—both loving the same man, and both loving Poppy's orchids as well.

His pen had hesitated at this point, leaving a mark on the paper. Then he finished with a single sentence:

Those beastly, murderous orchids!

After that the journal returned to a casual work record, and I found only one more personal note: "Our mistakes are always paid for."

For a little while longer I sat with the book in my hands, and my father seemed very close. What if I carried out his wishes— or tried to—instead of fighting them?

I held out the book to Alida. "Sit down over here, please, and read this."

She took the journal from me reluctantly and sat in the red morocco chair. I watched her read what he'd written about me and saw the trembling of her lips.

"Help me, Alida," I said. "Tell me what I must do."

"How should I know? With Cliff gone . . ." Her voice broke.

"There must be something," I said.

"You're going away—so why don't you just go?"

Strangely, some of the turmoil in me seemed to be quieting

—as though part of it had been caused by my own decision to leave.

"Maybe I'll stay," I told her. "I think I must do what my father wanted—or at least try. It won't be easy. But I don't know where to start. Tell me a first step I can take, Alida."

As she watched me, some of her antagonism seemed to fade. Perhaps Cliff's words had reached her too.

"You could begin with Fern, I suppose," she said.

"How? She's furious with me."

"You could reach her through the orchids. Neither she nor Iris have been near the orchid house since they found out about Cliff's will. If you could coax her back . . . Before—everything happened, she was planning a special orchid display at West Martello. Get her to go on with it."

Remembering Fern's anger, I didn't know how I could persuade her to do anything. Yet some unexpected determination was rising in me. I had never really wanted to leave—I'd just been running away, if I was honest with myself. And I didn't like running scared, giving up.

"All right," I said. "I'll try. I'll see if I can get Fern to listen."

Alida still looked suspicious, and I studied her. Perhaps this was the moment when she might be surprised into answering some questions she had sidestepped until now.

"Once you asked for my help," I reminded her. "You left a note for me that said I was to take over a burden you couldn't carry any more. I've never understood what that burden was. Can you tell me now?"

She was still on guard. "It doesn't matter. We've gone way past that point. There's no more need for you to do anything."

"What happened on Derek's island after Marcus and I left that day? Derek and Iris came over, didn't they? Did Derek do something to upset Fern?"

She looked pale and stricken, almost about to give in, so I asked another question quickly.

"Iris went to make a telephone call while she was with me at Derek's place. Did she call the island? Did she talk to you?"

"I don't know anything about it. I was resting."

I would get nothing more out of her now, and I switched to something else—something I'd wanted to ask ever since that night on the *Aurora*.

"When we were on Derek's yacht, you were up near the top deckhouse, so you must have had an overall view. What did you see? I mean, is there anything you haven't told the police?"

She seemed relieved at my change of course. "Nothing that matters, really. There was so much confusion, and those men had their faces covered. There was only one I caught a glimpse of, and I'm not sure about him."

"Tell me," I said.

"You remember that day we met in Mallory Square? When we left, Derek was having breakfast across the street. A big, rough-looking man was with him, and they seemed to be quarreling."

"I remember," I said. "I saw the same man again when Marcus took Fern and me to the pier for Sunset. Eddie came running to Marcus, terrified because this fellow was chasing him. And I think I saw him on the boat too. I haven't told anyone, because all I got was a quick impression, and I couldn't be entirely sure."

"He's the same one," Alida said.

"Have you mentioned this to Derek?"

"I don't speak to Derek at all, if I can avoid it."

She'd never liked Derek, but this seemed extreme. Something had happened on the island to bring her dislike of him into the open. However, she was willing to tell me nothing more right now.

"I'll see if I can find Fern," I said, and left her sitting forlornly in the red chair. As I started down the room I turned back as something else occurred to me.

"What about my father's last manuscript, Alida? How far along did he get with it?"

"It was nearly finished."

"Do you know how he meant to end it?"

"He made some special notes about that, and I have them in my desk."

"Then perhaps you should finish typing the manuscript, so you can send it to his publisher. If you include his notes about the last chapters, maybe they can find someone to finish it."

She seemed to think about this, and her expression lightened. "His work shouldn't be wasted. But with Fern not caring, and Iris concerned with—other matters, I felt I had no authority."

"Please work on it," I said. "You're the only one who can. And, after all, Cliff left his books to me, so I have the right to ask you to do this."

"All right—I'll do it. This is the one thing left that I can do for him."

For years back, the guiding light in Alida's life had been Cliff. It might not be wise to trust her on anything else, but on this one thing she would be dependable.

"Thank you," I said. "We'll talk again."

"Then you're really not leaving?"

"At least not right away."

As I went downstairs with Cliff's letters in my hand, a new vigor seemed to flow through me, recharging and energizing me. I wouldn't let Cliff down, and I wouldn't let myself down.

Now I could move with purpose and a new determination. As soon as I'd unpacked, I'd look for Fern and see what I might accomplish.

I didn't need to look far, for the door of my room stood open, and Fern was once more sitting on my bed. She had rehung the two remaining orchid photographs, so there was no space between them, and was regarding them with satisfaction. When she heard me at the door, she turned with a faltering smile.

"I'm sorry, Laurel. I shouldn't have snapped at you the way I did."

I felt a little wary over her about-face. She could change too quickly to be trusted. "It's all right," I said, and put Cliff's letters away in a drawer.

I couldn't look at the orchid photos without remembering the dream I'd had on the island. Fern, however, didn't seem to notice my avoidance of them.

"They belong there, don't they, Laurel?" she said. "So I put them back, since this was Poppy's room and you'll be gone soon. You won't care." She nodded toward the open suitcases on my bed.

So this was why she'd relented toward me.

"I've changed my mind," I said. "I'm going to stay for a while, at least. Because Cliff wants me to stay."

She stared at me, wide-eyed, and I explained matter-of-factly about the journal I'd found in Cliff's desk. She heard me out, accepting what I told her more easily than Alida had.

"That's wonderful! I wish he would speak to me in some way."

"Perhaps he's speaking through me. I think he'd really like you to go ahead with the orchid display you were planning for the Garden Club. It's something only you can do properly."

"Do you think I could? I've missed my orchids, but Iris said I had no right to them any more."

"That's foolish. You're the one who has the most right, and if you don't do something they'll all die. When is this display supposed to be ready?"

"A lot too soon. Day after tomorrow. But I can never be ready in time, and Iris won't help. All she worries about right now is Derek. She's so foolish to trust him."

I asked my question quickly. "Why have you changed your feelings about Derek?"

"He's a dreadful person! I know that now." She huddled on the bed, pulling up her knees and drawing the woodsy green of her dress around her.

"I thought you were fond of him?"

Her look of anguish was so acute that I couldn't press her any further. Something had disillusioned her about Derek, and I could only be thankful.

"Perhaps I could help you get the orchids ready, if you'll show me what to do."

She came out of her huddle and got off the bed. "All right! If you'll help, then let's go!"

I wished I could put aside my own feelings as quickly as Fern seemed able to do. At least the new surge of energy that I'd felt continued high. There was some purpose to my life now and immediate tasks to accomplish, even though the eventual goal still wasn't clear. If I tried to help Fern, then somewhere in the fog ahead might lie the answer to my father's death. It wasn't possible for me to leave Key West until I knew why it had happened, and if I kept moving, perhaps the mists would clear. Whatever it was that still lay hidden, I had to know. I owed him that.

I followed Fern down the back stairs. I mustn't think of the word my father had used for the orchids—*murderous*. That was his illusion. The flowers themselves were beautiful and innocent, and they'd had nothing to do with Poppy's death.

13

When we reached the back garden we heard sounds from inside the orchid house, and Fern ran to the door and pulled it open. I was close behind her.

Iris and Derek stood at the far end of the central aisle, and I saw in dismay that Iris was deliberately uprooting orchid plants and dumping one after another into a large trash container. Derek appeared to be watching with open satisfaction.

Fern flew down the aisle and hurled herself upon her sister. "Iris! What are you doing? Those are our best vandas you're destroying!"

Iris shook her off and picked up another plant. Derek, clearly enjoying himself, reached for Fern and held her, imprisoning her arms. Though she squirmed and struggled, he held her in his grip until she went suddenly limp and began to weep bitterly.

No one noticed me near the door until I walked toward them. "Let her alone!" I told Derek.

He glanced at me in surprise, and Fern wriggled free, to dart off a little way to safety.

"Why are you doing this?" I asked Iris.

She picked up another plant as though she hadn't heard me, pulled it raggedly from its pot, and threw the bright bloom into the trash with the others. Fern cried out as though she felt the outrage along her own nerves.

Showing no emotion, her expression blank, Iris picked up the next pot. I took it out of her hands and replaced it on the shelf.

"I don't know what you're doing," I said, "but it's got to stop. Maybe we can go somewhere else and talk, and you can tell me what this is all about."

Iris looked at me directly for the first time, and I saw the bleakness in her eyes as she tried to pull herself together and answer me.

"You can't come into this house and take over what belongs to Fern and me!" she cried. "You've no right, no matter what Cliff's will says. You probably wangled that yourself. Derek is with me on this, and I mean to see that there won't be an orchid left by the time you get your—legacy."

Somehow I managed to speak quietly. "There are laws against destroying property that belongs to other people. This orchid house isn't yours any more."

Derek laughed. "You're going to turn your sister in—have her arrested?"

"Not if she stops what she's doing. Fern, can these orchids be saved?"

Fern came closer, keeping a wary eye on Derek, and leaned over the edge of the trash container. One by one, she began fishing out orchids, to examine them. Some of the petals were bruised, but the roots seemed intact, and she went to work repotting them, her movements feverish, as though she raced against time to save their lives.

"You could help her," I said to Iris. "Fern says the orchid

display at the Garden Club is coming up soon, and she wants to put on an exhibit in Cliff's name and Poppy's honor."

Iris threw an agonized look at Derek, who had stopped looking idly amused. He spoke to me directly.

"Iris is right. I've told her she should do this. There's no sense in leaving these plants for you to take over. Cliff must have been losing his marbles to change his will the way he did. If you think you're going to stay on, you'll have a fight on your hands, and I don't think you've got the stomach for it."

I wouldn't let him blow me down. "I don't think destroying everything Iris and Fern have created is going to help anything."

"Tell her, Iris," Derek said.

Iris had paused with an orchid pot in her hands, looking at me strangely.

"Go ahead, Iris. Tell her," Derek repeated.

Her hands were shaking, and Fern reached to take the pot from her.

"I've invited Derek to move into the house," Iris said. "There's been no one to take charge since Cliff died, and he will know how to manage everything."

Fern looked her outrage. "You can't do that! It's my house, and I don't want him here. Laurel, tell him he can't stay!"

There was nothing I could say. In one stroke Iris had handed over the reins. She would marry Derek, and he would have every right to stay in the house if he liked. Fern's futile objections would never stop him, no matter who owned the house.

"What I'd like to know," Derek said, "is what you've got against me, Fern. We used to get along fine."

Fern wiped grimy hands across her cheeks, leaving smears of earth, and her eyes snapped into angry life as she stared at him. "I think you probably caused my father's death! I think maybe you planned it all along. You wanted to hurt him!"

"Fern!" Iris protested. "You know how Cliff died. He could have had a heart attack any time. What happened on the *Aurora* brought it on. You can't blame Derek."

"I do blame him—for everything!" Her voice was rising in near hysteria. "I'll always blame him. What has happened to those men on the ship? They're probably dead by now. What's happened to the *Aurora*?"

Derek's grin had a steely edge. "As a matter of fact, the *Aurora* returned to port late last night. I was aboard her until a little while ago."

We all stared at him.

"You didn't tell me." Iris seemed to come out of her daze.

"Why should I trouble you about all that unpleasantness? You've got enough on your hands here. Only three of the men came back with her."

"Was Eddie Burch with them?" Iris asked.

"No. Some of the men were dumped off on various islands. It may be a while before they can even get in touch. The pirates left in another boat that was waiting for them, and they took all the gold with them. That's all I know right now."

Fern turned her back, as though nothing he was saying mattered. "Iris, I want to do this orchid display, and I can't do it alone. This is for Poppy. You know it's for Poppy."

Derek had clearly lost interest in what must have seemed a minor skirmish. "Do as you please, Iris. I've got a lot to attend to now. Tonight I'll bring my things over from the island, if you'll get a room ready." He kissed her lightly and went off.

For a moment Iris looked after him with something less than affection, and I wondered if Derek would manage in his insensitive way to set Iris free of him, as he'd done Fern.

"I'm sorry," she said to Fern. "I'll help with the display."

They went to work together. Perhaps they'd move in some positive direction and stop fighting each other now. This was what Cliff had wanted.

Angela came to the door just then. "Miss Laurel? There's a phone call for you."

When I went into the hallway and picked up the phone, I heard Marcus's voice. "Laurel? Can you find Alida and come over to my place right away?"

I stared at the phone. He hadn't mentioned my plans or the plane I'd meant to take today.

"Laurel? Are you there? Get hold of Alida right now and bring her over here. Don't waste any time. I'll see you."

As usual he was gone before I could argue or ask questions. He was simply taking it for granted that in spite of what I'd told him, I wasn't going to leave. He'd been as sure of me as that! However, there'd been an urgency in his voice that I couldn't ignore. I went upstairs and found Alida working on Cliff's manuscript.

"Something's happened," I told her. "Marcus wants us to come over to his place right away. He didn't say why."

Alida turned off her word processor, took her handbag from a drawer, and stood up. She was ready to come without question, confident of Marcus.

As we walked the few blocks, I told her what had happened in the orchid house and that Fern would now go ahead with her plans for the display—with Iris's help. I also told her that Derek was moving into the house.

She missed a step, almost tripped, and took hold of my arm. "That's dreadful! That means he's really going to marry Iris. He'll expect her money to rescue him, and somehow he's got to be stopped."

We'd reached the big white house with its fantasy of turrets and towers, and we went up the steps together. There was no one about as we climbed the inside stairs. When I knocked on Marcus's door, he opened it, looking relieved when he saw Alida.

"I'd meant to leave for New York this morning," I reminded him.

"Of course you wouldn't leave while everything was up in the air," he said curtly. "Come in, both of you."

His calm assumption left me wondering about *me*, as I followed Alida into the room. When Marcus had closed the door behind us, I heard a sound from the kitchen area, and Eddie Burch came out looking shaky and uncertain—much the worse for wear.

Marcus eased him into a chair and put a cup of coffee in his hands. If Eddie had been thin before, now he looked scrawny in his khaki shorts and torn shirt, with stubble growing across his chin and his eyes watery with fear.

Alida pulled over a chair and sat down beside him. "Tell me what happened," she said.

After a gulp of coffee, Eddie began to talk. "They threw me overboard after they got rid of the rest of you in the dinghy. They meant me to drown, but one of Derek's crew managed to drop a life preserver into the water. I guess it was dark enough so nobody saw when I swam to it and hung on." He took another swallow of coffee while we waited.

I glanced at Marcus, whose bright hair seemed more on end than ever. Perhaps I should have gone North while I had the chance, but somehow Marcus had known that I wouldn't leave.

He was watching me, his mouth pinched into a half smile. Already, he knew me too well.

Having finished the coffee, Eddie went on. "There isn't

much more to tell. I don't know how long I was in the water when a boat came by and picked me up. She was bound for Dominica, and they put me ashore in the Marquesas. I let everybody think I was still out of my head, and I didn't tell them anything. I was too scared. When I could, I hopped a boat for Key West and came straight here."

Marcus spoke to me. "As I've mentioned, we're pretty sure Derek has a drug smuggling operation going on up the keys. Eddie's been picking up information that may help to blow the whole thing."

"You'll need to act quickly," Alida said. "Derek's moving into Cliff's house. That means he'll marry Iris as soon as he can, and she will do whatever he wishes."

Marcus looked grimmer than ever. "We haven't got enough to act on yet. I don't know how speedy we can be."

"If Derek catches on to what you're doing, your life won't be worth much," Eddie said. "Any more than mine is." He put his empty cup aside and stared at me. "Somebody pushed your father into the water. I saw it happen."

Alida moaned softly, but I didn't look at her. This was what I'd feared. I took a deep, steadying breath. "Tell me who it was."

He hesitated, staring at the floor. "I saw it happen, but I couldn't see who pushed him. When those fellows started to board, I rushed down to the cabin to tell Derek. Then everybody came out on deck, and there was a lot of confusion and noise. By that time I didn't know where anybody else was. All I wanted was to ease out of sight. I saw Cliff's white suit plain enough at the rail, and somebody else was with him. I saw him go over. But that's when somebody grabbed me, and I went into the water on the other side."

"Cliff died of a heart attack," Marcus told Eddie. "He didn't drown. So no matter whether he was pushed or not, he was dead before he hit the water."

"Just the same, I think somebody tried to kill him," Eddie said.

Alida had listened in silence. She looked so stricken that my attention was caught.

"Do you know who was with Cliff?" I asked her urgently.

She shook her head. "It was never meant to happen! It was all a mistake—a terrible mistake!"

"What haven't you told us?" I demanded. "Where were you when this happened?"

She made an effort. "You know where I was. I was on the top deck, and I could only see down into the stern. I couldn't possibly see what happened up forward. I'm only guessing."

As usual, Eddie Burch seemed to have an ambivalence toward Alida—perhaps drawn to her, yet resenting her at the same time. A touch of malice came through when he spoke again.

"You weren't up there, Alida—not when everything started to happen. I saw you heading forward right after we were boarded."

Alida looked as though she might go to pieces all over again, and that wouldn't help us now.

"What matters right this minute," I reminded her, "is what to do about Eddie. Do you have any ideas?"

With immediate pressure removed, Alida relaxed a little, though she threw a nervous glance at Eddie. "I don't know what to do about anything. I shouldn't even be here now, wasting my time. I ought to get on with typing Cliff's manuscript."

"Eddie wanted you to know," Marcus told her quietly. "He has a lot of confidence in your good sense, Alida. Anyway,

Laurel's right. We need to figure out where Eddie can hide safely for a while. If you want me to, I can keep him here for a few days. We need you to stay around, Eddie. You're a big part of the case against Derek."

Eddie squirmed uneasily, and I suspected that he was a weak link in whatever chain Marcus might be welding. Eddie Burch had reason to hate Derek, but he was mainly interested in saving his own neck. Now, however, he seemed to make up his mind about something.

"Okay, I'll lie low for a few days and keep out of Derek's sight. But not permanently. I got a score to settle with him myself. Anyway, I need to get something right away, Marcus. In the yard at Cliff's house—something I hid there that time I came to see Alida. I need to dig it out to show you. Maybe we could get over there before Derek moves in?"

"Evidence?" Marcus asked.

"Maybe. I swiped it from Derek's cabin on the *Dolphin*—a lot of dates and navigational directions."

Marcus spoke sharply. "Why didn't you bring it right to me?"

At times Eddie had a way of looking brightly innocent. "No chance to get it till now—that's all."

Or perhaps he'd been playing both sides and waiting to see where his advantage lay?

"Well, let's get it now, and I'll see what you've found," Marcus said, and I knew that the same thought had occurred to him.

Before we could leave, someone knocked at the door, and Marcus went to open it a crack. I heard Iris's voice from the hall, and Eddie ducked into the bathroom out of sight.

"I need to talk to you, Marcus," Iris said.

He opened the door. "Sure. Come on in and join the party."

If she felt dismayed at the sight of Alida and me, she hid it as she sauntered into the room, looking beautifully cool and contained. Again I noticed the flash of the large sapphire on her right hand—the ring that had belonged to Poppy.

"What's up?" Marcus asked, bringing another chair for her.

"I hadn't planned on making a public statement," she said. "It can wait till you're not busy."

Before Marcus could answer, Eddie came out of the bathroom, looking disreputable and much too cocky. Perhaps, like Derek, he liked the edge of danger.

Iris gasped at the sight of him, and he grinned. "Right—it's me. They fished me out of the ocean, and I came back to Key West by the first boat I could catch."

"Does Derek know you're here?"

"Not yet, he doesn't."

"Then I'd better phone him right away. He'll want any information you can give him."

"I don't want to talk to him. I don't know who threw me overboard."

"Let me use your phone, Marcus," Iris said.

Marcus put his hand over hers as she started to pick up the phone. "Just wait a minute. It's possible it was Derek who had Eddie thrown into the water from the *Aurora*, so don't be in a hurry to call him."

"I don't believe that. I must call him."

Her affection for Derek, if it had faltered briefly, had clearly returned, and she was again on his side.

"Let's talk a bit first," Marcus said, and she turned reluctantly from the phone and listened while he explained the plan to keep Eddie with him for a few days, and asked her to wait about telling Derek. He didn't mention any possible drug-running information.

She heard him through, frowning, undoubtedly torn between what she felt was loyalty to Derek and what Marcus wanted of her.

"I don't know," she said when he finished. "You're suspicious of Derek—and that's wrong. He's lost everything, and he needs my help and support right now."

Eddie had begun to squirm again. He was suspicious of us all, except perhaps for Marcus. Alida watched Iris as though she was intent on reading something that wasn't evident to me.

"Iris, will you at least go along with this for a day or so?" Marcus asked.

She gave him a lost look from great dark eyes, and I could see him melting. "All right. I'll trust you, Marcus. I have to."

"Then it's settled," he said. "Eddie wants to pick up something over at the house, so I'll drive you all home, if you like. Then I'll bring him back here."

Iris didn't move as the rest of us rose to leave. "I haven't told you what I came to say, Marcus. I'm going to marry Derek at the end of this week. We have the license, and it's all set. I—I wanted to tell you myself."

Alida ran to put her arms around Iris. "No—you can't do this! You mustn't. Poppy had every reason to know that Derek can't be trusted. You know what her reasons were."

Coolly, Iris withdrew herself from Alida's arms. "I only know what you've told me. Derek needs me more than ever now."

"I can stop you," Alida said.

Iris shook her head. "I don't think so. No one can."

I watched Marcus's concern for her with a growing sense of loss. There had been times when he and I had enjoyed being together. He'd even looked at me as though something real was coming to life between us. But now, more than ever, I knew how little it had meant. Rebounds were dangerous. Trying to heal one's wounds with a new, lesser love never worked for either one.

In the car, Alida and I sat in back, with Eddie between us, and Marcus put Iris in the front seat. There was no comfort for me in knowing that she would soon be lost to Marcus. He was still in love with her, and I didn't want to witness his pain or admit my own. We might easily be drawn into comforting each other, and that wasn't what I wanted.

At the house we left the car in a hurry, in order to get Eddie out of sight. Marcus came with us, still helping Iris. Since I was ahead, I was the first one to step through the front door. As I did so, Derek Phillips came out of the living room. He gave me an appraising look and stared past me at the others. There was no way now to hide Eddie Burch.

Derek pounced on him at once. "When did you get back? Why didn't you get in touch with me?"

Iris drooped on Marcus's arm, and Alida closed her eyes, rejecting what was happening. Eddie looked as though he might have bolted if Derek hadn't taken hold of his collar.

That was too much. "Leave Eddie alone!" I cried. "He's half starved, and he's sick. He doesn't remember anything clearly right now, and he needs to rest before you ask him questions. He's going to stay with Marcus for a few days."

"I'll decide what to do about Eddie," Derek said.

"It's already been decided," I told him.

Marcus spoke quietly. "You'd better listen to Laurel, Derek."

Derek seemed to enjoy being angry. Once he might have frightened me, but now I had to stand my ground.

"You have to accept the way it is," I told him.

"You haven't any authority in this house," Derek snapped.

"Oh, yes she has!" Fern had come running down the hall from the back garden. "Laurel's our older sister, and she's got better sense than Iris or me. She's in charge here, and what she says goes. Isn't that right, Alida? Isn't that right, Iris?"

I wasn't sure how lasting any support from Fern would be, but it was welcome right now.

Alida opened her eyes and stared at Derek. "You really must let Eddie get some rest—Laurel's right. And he's not going anywhere."

Iris had said nothing, and Eddie solved the impasse neatly by going limp in Derek's hands and slumping to the floor. Marcus picked him up and carried him over to the couch.

For the first time Iris stirred herself. "It will be all right, Derek. He'll be there when you want him." She threw me a quick look that carried an unexpected appeal for help.

"That's the way it has to be for now, Derek," I said.

He wasn't the accepting sort, and he stalked out of the house without a word for any of us. I suspected that he would never take defeat—he'd simply attack from a different direction. It was easy to believe that he'd had Eddie thrown overboard, for his own reasons.

Iris dropped into a chair, clearly shaken by the fact that she too had stood up against Derek. But I could imagine what might lie ahead, with Derek moving in, marrying Iris, carrying out successfully whatever illegal affairs he was mixed up in—and turning Iris into a helpless victim. Unless he could be exposed very soon and his plans thwarted, we'd all be under his tyranny, and there could be much worse to come. In the meantime, I meant to ally myself with Iris and try to strengthen her beginning rebellion.

Marcus had bent over her, but now he looked at me, and I

saw approval in his eyes. "You're doing what Cliff wanted, I knew you had it in you."

I hadn't known myself, so why should he? Anyway, whether I liked it or not, I'd been put in very shaky charge, so that others were looking to me for help and support. All I could do was try.

Alida and Marcus took Eddie outside, since he'd recovered as soon as Derek was gone, and I supposed he would retrieve whatever he'd hidden there. Iris, still looking stricken and bewildered, went off to her room. Fern stayed behind, her eyes shining.

"You didn't let him bully us, Laurel! I wanted to applaud."

"Save that for later," I said. "We haven't done anything yet."

How did one ever know what was the wise thing to do at any crucial moment? If cruel actions could destroy, so could foolish ones.

I remembered Cliff's words in his journal: *Our mistakes are always paid for.* The cost of mistakes could be high, and that was frightening.

Fern slipped a hand through my arm. "Come help me with my orchids, Laurel."

All I could do was try, I thought again, as I went with her to the orchid house.

14

This was the night when we were to work on the display of orchids at West Martello. Derek was with us at dinner, having moved into the house the previous evening, to the distress of everyone except Iris. Her brief rebellion seemed to be over, and she was acquiescent with Derek, yet strangely indifferent. Except for Marcus, who hadn't been invited, everyone was at the table. Even Alida had come down to join us for the meal.

I still felt doggedly determined, in spite of Derek's open opposition, and once more I began to push for answers.

"That night on the *Aurora*"—I spoke to him directly—"I'm sure I saw someone standing with my father before he went into the water. Apparently others saw this person too, though nobody wants to talk about it. Did you see anything, Derek? Anything that would give us an answer?" All I wanted was to prod him and watch his reaction.

He rejected my question without much interest. "I had my hands full with all that was happening. Anyway, what does it matter now?"

I persisted. "I suppose any of us on board that evening could have been with him. So why doesn't anyone want to admit it? Until we know who it was, and what happened, we won't know what caused Cliff's heart attack."

My own words brought the scene back to me sharply—that sense of darkness and confusion, the shouting and shots, and the movement of the slanting deck. I remembered the way I'd been tripped and had fallen. I remembered the last glimpse I'd had of my father, never dreaming that I'd never see him alive again. Pain could strike so swiftly, and I was never on guard.

"It could have been one of the crew, I suppose," Alida said.

I doubted that, since Derek's men were all occupied at the time with the boarding. In any case, it was no use. Whoever held the secret wasn't vulnerable to my prodding.

Right after dinner, Derek left for his bar, and the rest of us went to work helping Fern load her selection of orchids into Iris's station wagon. With Derek gone, Eddie had come over to help us, summoned by Alida.

A tension seemed to have grown between him and Iris. By this time, I was well aware that her cool, subdued manner, even her indifference, could hide a passion of emotions, and I caught a glimpse of her anger as we carried orchids out to the car. She avoided being near Eddie, but once when he nearly dropped a pot, she spoke to him sharply, and I saw him scowl.

At least I found that tonight I could treat the orchids merely as beautiful plants. Once we were away from the orchid house and its uneasy atmosphere, the flowers seemed innocuous, and my imagination was quiet for a time.

I knew a good deal of fascinating history about the East and West Martello towers by now. They were copies of invincible Corsican fortresses built in Europe's Middle Ages. East Martello had survived best and was now a museum and home of the Art and Historical Society. West Martello had supposedly been used for target practice by the U.S. Army before World

War I, and much of it lay in ruin when restoration began. The very ruins had been plundered over the years for their bricks.

The site where the West Martello had been built was itself historical in a terrible way. This was where yellow fever victims had been buried as well as slaves who had died in ships coming over from Africa. Some four hundred bodies had been uncovered by construction workers, who couldn't take it and walked off the job. Nevertheless, the fort was built.

Originally, Congress had authorized the building of four forts—Fort Jefferson at Dry Tortugas, Fort Taylor at Key West, and the two Martellos. The Union officer in charge of the construction program (and the Army forces in Key West) took control of the city by taking over Fort Taylor. This in spite of the island's pro-Confederate sentiments. It remained the only Southern city that never left the Union, and its strategic position as the Gibraltar of the West caused some to believe that if the Confederates had taken Key West, the outcome of the war might have been a stalemate.

By 1955 both forts were long obsolete. Key West's Garden Club, looking for a more suitable home, arranged to use West Martello. Members went to work clearing out trash, rubble, and vermin and got rid of a forest of high weeds. New plants and trees had turned the enclosure of the fort into a tropical garden, with paths winding through. Now the place was an attraction for visitors and enjoyed by Key Westers.

The flower show had come to be held in March every other year, but special displays were put on the year round. Poppy York had of course been a member of the Garden Club, as were her daughters, and she'd loved to provide orchids once or twice a year. This was the project that Fern and Iris intended to carry out in their mother's honor. The display would be set up this evening, after West Martello closed for the day.

I found the old fortress a gloomy, unnerving place in my present mood. Lights had been left burning for us inside, and a big wooden door with great locks and hinges was opened for us by the woman curator, who was just leaving.

Because a hill of earth covered one side of the fort, I had the feeling of going underground when I went through the door. A row of vaulted rooms—casemates—reached out from the entry room, connected by narrow brick archways that were windowless. This was a type of construction that went back to Roman days, hundreds of years before steel and concrete and much too vulnerable for today's weapons.

The floor under my feet was slate, and rosy bricks formed the walls. Overhead more bricks arched the low ceilings, and the air seemed cool and still—oppressive. Our voices reverberated in an unsettling way, as though the farther reaches of the fort held a chattering but invisible throng. Plants and flowers softened the harsh quality of the rooms, but for me it seemed a haunted place, burdened with tragic memories.

Excited about what she was doing, Fern had led the way in eagerly, carrying pots of orchids. The rest of us followed, bringing in more boxes of plants. The place assigned for the Poppy York display was one of the old fireplaces built deep into the walls—fireplaces intended not for warmth, but for the heating of cannon balls.

"I wish I could have been at the first Garden Club show," Fern said. "Though of course it wasn't held here in those days. The judges were Ernest Hemingway, Elmer Davis, and John Dos Passos. With the help of what they called Southernmost Swill Punch, I guess they got carried away and pinned a ribbon on every exhibit in the show. There were write-ups in papers all around the country. Famous people are always getting Key West into the spotlight. Like my father."

Though Iris made some attempt to help and would have been as expert as Fern in doing the arrangement, she seemed at times like a somnambulist, drifting in some dream that held her in its spell. I suspected that her thoughts were mostly with Derek, but I'd begun to wonder what course they were taking, and if some of the bloom had worn off her infatuation.

Only when her eyes rested on Eddie was there a spark that seemed ready to burst into flame. Once when I caught her alone for a moment, I asked what was the matter—what had Eddie done to make her so angry?

For an instant she looked startled because I'd read her so well. Then she whispered, "Don't trust him. He'll make trouble if he can. Derek thinks he's up to something. And he's brought Alida nothing but unhappiness."

Her words shocked me—more for their intensity than for what she said. When she saw my reaction, she tried to laugh, as though she'd meant nothing serious. Yet I had the strong feeling that currents were moving in Iris that she still held dammed. I wondered if she even knew their true direction. Perhaps not Eddie, but something else was making her angry. The spark never seemed to last, though, for she dropped quickly into apathy again.

Once the car had been emptied, they didn't need me, and I found a door to the garden that now occupied the outdoor enclosure of the fort. I walked into the mild evening with its scents of tropical growth, laced by a tangy hint of the sea. The area had been thickly planted, with brick walks and sandy paths winding between trees and shrubbery. Here and there a light burned, but the garden was mainly a place of shadows, patched by radiance from the moon.

I wandered idly. In the center of the garden stood a brick ruin that had once been the watchtower of the fort. As I walked under a brick arch and followed another path, I found this mysterious, haunted place more and more disquieting. Too many dark memories had stained this earth.

Now I had time to feel alone—too far away from the others. A faint rustling reached me, as though someone might have followed me out here but was staying back in the shadows. Probably I'd just heard some small nocturnal animal, or it might even be palmetto bugs—that polite term for outdoor cockroaches—rustling among the shrubbery. Yet my feeling of being followed persisted.

"Who's there?" I called. There was no answer. I had reached the outer rim of a garden that had begun to seem wild and junglelike, and I turned back toward the lighted doorways of the fort.

At that moment a shadowy figure stepped from behind a tree, blocking my way. I gasped, and when he put a finger to his lips, I saw it was Eddie Burch.

"Ssh!" he said. "They watch me all the time. They don't want me to talk. It's not just Derek—it's the women. They're afraid of what I might know."

He sounded a little wild, so that I wondered if his recent experience had left him unbalanced.

I spoke as soothingly as I could. "You can talk to me, Eddie. You can tell me what you saw that night on the *Aurora*."

He stepped out of shadow into moonlight, his eyes shining in the white oval of his face.

"Not here," he said. "They're watching me."

"They? You mean they're all in this together?"

He shook his head. "I don't know. Sometimes it seems like they are—protecting each other. Other times I don't know. My head still feels sick a lot of the time."

"No one's watching us now, Eddie. They're all inside. So tell me what you saw."

He turned away, looking over his shoulder. "The trouble is I can't guess why it happened. That's what bothers me—it doesn't make any sense. So maybe I'm crazy—maybe I didn't see anything, after all."

He suddenly ran off into the nighttime wilderness of the garden. The place had set its spell on him too, and I could only wait and hope to catch him in some more familiar atmosphere.

I was eager now to get back inside, and I hurried toward the nearest door. When I stepped into the room with the fireplace, I saw that the display had been completed, and no one was there.

The bank of orchids looked beautiful in its arrangement of single blooms and lovely sprays, the colors blending, yet individual, and all framed by the old bricks of the fireplace.

Another wide brick archway framed a section that was open to the sky. This could have been where the brickwork had been damaged by guns. A dome of latticework had replaced the ruined roof and let in air and shadowy moonlight. Here plants and pots were placed against the brick walls and rose in tiers, offering a bower of greenery. Someone had called this the "bird cage" room because of that overhead latticework.

I stayed for a little while, waiting for someone to come for me. The echoing rooms were silent now, and I wondered where everyone had gone.

As my uneasiness grew, I retraced my way through brick arches, to find each casemate empty until I reached the reception room near the door. There Alida sat on a small chair, her hands folded and her eyes closed. She heard my steps and looked at me without speaking.

"Where is everyone?" I asked.

"Derek's searching for Eddie," Alida said. "He's afraid Eddie's trying to get away. Iris and Fern are out there looking too."

"Derek? He's here?"

"He came right after you went out. He wants to take Iris somewhere tonight, I guess. Eddie *would* have to disappear."

"I saw him a little while ago. He seemed upset—almost irrational."

Alida nodded. "He's frightened. Derek scares him."

"Maybe I can help find him," I offered. "He can't have gone far."

She gave me a sour look, discounting my usefulness, but I went outside anyway. In the garden Derek was shouting Eddie's name, but there was no answer. Out there in the dark, he could easily hide in a dozen places.

I followed a path, calling to him. "Eddie, we're ready to go now. Where are you, Eddie?"

A faint sound reached me, and I whirled to catch it. The others were moving about on the far side of the garden space, but this sound had seemed closer. Had it been a groan?

I walked quickly toward a part of the enclosure that I hadn't explored, and Alida came out to join me. There appeared to be a pavilion of some sort rising hugely against one wall, with massive concrete steps running up on either side.

"What's that?" I asked her. "Where do the steps go?"

"The old powder magazines are over there. The steps were built during World War I as emplacements for coast artillery."

I moved toward one concrete flight and heard the sound again. I ran toward it, but Alida was already ahead of me, dropping to her knees beside Eddie.

"He's hurt," she said. "Call the others!"

I shouted for Iris and Fern, and Derek heard me and came as

well—all apparently from different parts of the garden. The moaning had stopped. As Marcus had done earlier, Derek picked up Eddie's slight body and carried him into the fort. There was a terrible bleeding wound on one side of his head. Now it was Alida who moaned. When Derek went to telephone and had talked to the police, I called Marcus and was able to catch him. He promised to come at once.

Alida held Eddie in her arms, and he died quietly without regaining consciousness. I was near enough to watch her, and there seemed no pity, no grief, no shock of horror in her expression. She simply watched him sigh his last breath, then let him go and stood up. Fern was crying—probably with fright, since she'd never liked Eddie—and Iris stood apart. Apart from life, as well as death? When Derek touched her, she drew back a little.

Only a few minutes ago Eddie had been alive, and I felt stunned by the suddenness of what had happened. I even wondered if I might have pushed him to a farther point than he could endure. It seemed so unlikely that a man who was a diver, and presumably surefooted on a deck, should slip to his death off those wide concrete steps.

The police came quickly, and Marcus arrived a little after. He gave me a searching look, decided I was all right, and went directly to Iris, who still waited apart from the others while Derek talked to the police.

The questions in my mind wouldn't be quiet. What could have so frightened Eddie that he had run away from me in the garden?

Since no one appeared to have been near Eddie at the time of his fall, there was no particular suspicion of anyone present. Why Eddie had been on those steps that led to nowhere was still an unanswered question. I might have thought that someone was pursuing him, but if that had been true, surely he'd have called out for help.

When the police had finished with us and Eddie's body was taken away, Iris left with Derek, and Fern went home with Alida.

Marcus drove me, and when we were in the car, I poured out my doubts about what had happened. "Eddie was afraid," I said. "Someone could have pushed him off those steps, but that's only a hunch. I haven't anything to go on."

"I have the same feeling," Marcus agreed. "Be careful, Laurel. Maybe it wasn't right for you to stay in Key West, after all."

We'd reached the house and were sitting in the car outside the gate. "It's too late to have second thoughts," I said quietly. "You were the one who wanted me to stay."

"To help Iris and Fern recover and take up their lives. Not to get involved in what could be murder."

That was the word I feared. Poppy had not been murdered. My father hadn't been murdered. Now Eddie Burch, too, had suffered a fatal accident.

"If only he'd talked to me," I said to Marcus. "He almost did —when I was with him in the fort garden. But he was either too scared, or too crafty. I think he knew who was with Cliff on the *Aurora*. Marcus, what are we to do? Iris will marry Derek, Fern will bury herself in orchids, and Alida in my father's book. But what's the future for any of them? Ever since Poppy died, everyone connected with Cliff has pulled away from any sort of social life. They don't see the rest of Key West any more, though it's a small town, and there must be a lot of social mixing. But no one comes to Cliff's except you. What's wrong —what is really wrong?"

"It's like a blight they can't escape," Marcus said. "If Derek is pulled out of the center, where he's planted himself, the pieces may fly into a healthier pattern."

"How can that be managed?"

"I'm almost ready to go to the FBI. That paper Eddie lifted gives us something to go on. I wish we'd had it sooner. Maybe Eddie was holding out to sell what he knew to Derek."

"Does Alida know?"

"If she does, she's not talking."

"What about Iris?"

Marcus looked so depressed that I wished I hadn't spoken her name. I opened the car door, and at once he reached across to stop me. "Would it help if I stayed at the house tonight?"

"What point would there be in that?"

"Maybe *I* would feel easier if I stayed."

"We'll be all right. I don't think anyone is after us."

He let me go and drove away. Perhaps he was realizing at last that Iris had moved far beyond his reach or help.

Fern sat alone on the porch. The moment she saw me, she ran to the steps.

"I'm glad you've come, Laurel. I hate being alone tonight."

"Where's Alida?"

"She wanted to go home. I guess what happened to Eddie began to hit her, and she wanted to be by herself. Laurel, who do you think did it?"

So Fern, too, had her suspicions.

"Do you know why Iris was angry with Eddie?" I asked.

"Iris? Sure—Eddie had it in for Derek because of what happened a long time ago. That stiff shoulder he carries. But what difference does it make? We were all mad at Eddie some of the time. He was a creep. It's Derek we need to watch. He went out in the garden looking for Eddie—maybe he found him."

I had no answer for that. During the rest of the evening her restless movements took her from room to room. I stayed with her so she wouldn't be alone, and she seemed glad of my presence. At least she avoided the orchid house, and I was grateful for that.

Later in the evening, I followed her upstairs to Cliff's study, and there, sitting at his desk, she finally broke down and cried. She wanted no comforting from me, but only to have me there. I had cried like that too, and as I sat in the red leather chair watching her, I began to feel angry with my father. What had he really done for any of his daughters? His life had been his writing, the endless stories that stirred his imagination and poured out through his typewriter. But even as I thought these things, the feeling subsided. I couldn't judge him. Perhaps I was angry only because anger helped the hurt a little.

"Cliff loved us so much," Fern said. "He was a wonderful father."

So that was the fantasy with which she comforted herself, and perhaps now it was the only way for her to go.

"I know how fond of you he was," I agreed gently.

"You don't know anything!" she cried in sudden reversal, and jumped up to run the length of the study and clatter down the stairs.

Sitting alone in the big room, with only the desk lamp burning and one light at Alida's end, the piano silent, I felt forlorn and much too lonely myself. There seemed no protective fantasy that I could build. I'd found no way to approach either sister. Iris held herself away from any emotional contact, and Fern was never the same for two minutes. In a moment I'd be weeping with self-pity, and I didn't want that.

I got up resolutely and turned on more lights. Then I went up the narrow stairs that led to the roof and out through the trapdoor. When I'd climbed out onto the platform, I found the night quiet, the wind holding its breath for once, even in this high place. Trees that usually whispered in the garden below were hushed, their branches still. The roofs of Key West shone under the moon like pale silver, with lines of streetlights marking the crisscross of the ways below. The town was far from asleep, however, and sounds of partying came from the direction of Mallory Square and the tougher end of Caroline Street. So many of the streets, I'd noticed, were named for women.

As I stood looking down, a car stopped before the gate to the house, and Derek helped Iris out. He put an arm around her, and she clung to him for a moment. "I'll be back," he said. She ran out of sight beneath the pitch of the roof, while Derek got back in his car and drove away.

I went quickly down the stairs and reached the second floor as Iris came up. She stared at me for a moment, as though trying to make up her mind.

Then she said, "There's something I want to show you."

I followed her to the front of the house. This was the first time I'd been invited into her room, and I found it different from what I might have expected—the opposite of Fern's flowery retreat, and almost cell-like in its plain, unfussy state. It was a tailored room, neat and trim, but somehow impersonal, and with little of the clutter that grew around most humans. Perhaps the clutter was inside Iris, and this room was another effort to seem serene.

In spite of her father having been something of a collector on his travels, the only ornament in the room was a large black and white shell with spikes all over it. A few books stood between African bookends—perhaps a gift from Cliff who had traveled in Africa. Since I always read titles, I looked at these and found they were all by English writers of another day:

H. G. Wells, *The Forsyte Saga* in all its volumes; a novel by Arnold Bennett, who was mostly forgotten these days; Hugh Walpole's *Rogue Herries*, Priestley's *The Good Companions*, and even *The Scarlet Pimpernel*.

"Those were my grandfather's books," Iris said. "My mother's father. I still read them."

She sat on the edge of the bed with its unpatterned cream-colored spread and motioned me to a small wing chair.

"I never knew my grandparents. What was your grandfather like?" I asked.

"He was a sea captain, and he only came home now and then. The rest of the family never approved of him. It used to be a close family, but they're all gone now. He read a lot on the voyages he made in the twenties and thirties—novels like those. For some reason, he never liked Conrad. Perhaps the sea he knew was different. I used to sit on his lap and listen to his stories whenever he came home—such magic stories. He died before Fern was old enough to remember him."

"What about your grandmother?"

"She was supposed to be a great beauty in her day— magnolia skin and all that. I think she wanted to go on the stage, but of course this was frowned on. She was always busy with charities and social affairs, as I remember. Amateur theatricals. I don't think she liked children a lot. Everyone loved Poppy— except her mother. Cliff was the outsider who came in and turned into a magnet that attracted everyone. My grandmother didn't approve of him at first because he didn't have a regular job. She'd have liked Poppy to marry someone she thought important. It didn't matter that Poppy made the right choice for herself."

"Did she?" I asked softly.

"Of course!" There seemed an unexpectedly sharp note in

Iris's voice, and her manner became less dreamy, more focused. "Don't believe any stories you hear about Poppy—she was a happy wife."

The words were so emphatic that I wondered if Iris might be trying to convince herself first of all.

"What do you think about what happened to Eddie Burch tonight?" I asked.

Her beautiful eyes widened, and I could sense the tensing that gripped her. "What do you mean? What could I possibly think?"

"Do you believe it was an accident?"

"Of course it was an accident! What else? Maybe he'd been drinking." Her control had slipped for a moment, but she recovered quickly. "No one was near him. Derek was never far removed from me, and neither was Fern. So who else was there, except of course for Alida and you. Alida would be a tigress if someone she loved was threatened, but that wouldn't be by Eddie. So where were you?"

I answered her quietly. "I waited inside for a while, because I didn't know where you'd all gone. Then I found Alida in the room where we first came in."

"So don't go fantasizing like Fern!" she said sharply.

I let that go. "What do you want to show me?"

She seemed to remember why I was here and went to pull open the top drawer of a bureau. From it she took a steel tool about five inches long. It was of smooth, rounded metal, except for its wedge-shaped tip that made it a chisel. I took the piece from her and looked at it blankly.

"What is this supposed to be?"

"Yesterday Alida found it in her desk upstairs, and she brought it to me."

"I don't understand."

"No, I suppose you wouldn't. It was always kept in the toolbox in the orchid house. Alida says this is the metal wedge that was used to jam the door of the orchid house, so Poppy couldn't get out. That's what she says."

I turned the cold metal about in my fingers. "Alida told me that she found the door jammed and removed the wedge. Cliff wanted to avoid unnecessary questions by the police, so he warned her not to talk about it. Alida also told me that the wedge disappeared a few days later."

"So now it's come back? Why?"

"Do you think it's a threat? A warning to Alida?"

Iris dropped the chisel onto the desk. "That's all you can make of it?"

"Should I make something more?"

"Why not? Fern says you're in charge, doesn't she?" There was mockery now.

"I don't feel in charge. But I do think we need to get back to some sort of normal life. Perhaps it's different for you—since you'll be marrying Derek. You'll move away soon, won't you?"

Her eyes didn't meet mine. "Perhaps not. Derek has grown fond of this house. He may even want to live here permanently." She stood up to move restlessly about the room. "Of course we'll have to make changes. Derek likes Cliff's rooms best, though they'll have to be done over to suit us."

My surge of indignation surprised me. I had no right to feel so irritated. Iris could do as she pleased in this house, unless Fern opposed her.

"I suppose this is Derek's idea?" I asked.

"He usually gets what he wants. After all, Cliff's rooms are the largest, most comfortable rooms in the house."

I held back the sharp words on my tongue. "I've never

understood why your mother's room was so far away from Cliff's. Had they separated?"

"I don't want to talk about that. Poppy just liked a place where she could be alone when she wanted to be."

"I'm not sure what I'm supposed to do about anything," I said. "Especially about that chisel. Why did you show it to me?"

"Oh, go away!" Iris said impatiently. "You're no help at all."

She wanted something of me—perhaps only some reassurance that she couldn't ask for directly and that I had no idea how to give. How could I offer reassurance when I had so little myself?

I told her good night and went out of the room, feeling even more disturbed than before. Iris had meant to influence me in some way—but she hadn't been clear enough so that I could even guess what she wanted. Whether the reappearance of the metal wedge meant anything, I had no idea.

As I moved about the room that had been Poppy's, I felt as restless as Iris had seemed. A moment of that terrible night on the *Aurora* came back to me vividly—when I thought I'd recognized the man Alida and I had seen breakfasting with Derek that morning in Mallory Square.

I took out my sketch pad and turned to the quick drawing I'd made of Derek and the stranger. The man certainly looked like the one both Alida and I had seen on deck that night. The same man who'd been pursuing Eddie. Had Derek known that he was on board the *Aurora*?

But there was nothing I could do about any of this. Looking for something to occupy me, I remembered Cliff's letters that I'd brought from upstairs, and I took them out to read.

They were quite dear letters from a father who tried to write cheerfully to a lost daughter and conceal his own pain. I cried a little as I read, and now I could let the last of old resentments go.

When I'd put the letters away, I still felt restless and unable to settle down. I needed to walk—to do something active—so I went downstairs through the quiet house. A light shawl had been left on a chair near the door, and I threw it around my shoulders. The air was mild and still, the sky starry, and a stroll might help me to sleep. I needn't go far from the house.

I walked briskly, more comfortable than I'd felt outdoors in the garden at West Martello, yet with something at the back of my mind troubling me. Something far more trivial than what had happened to Eddie, yet in some way pertinent. It concerned the metal wedge. What was it Iris had said that bothered me?

I couldn't recall her exact words, and I walked along, trying not to think at all.

15

The hour was after midnight, but people were still about on Key West streets, and the bars were busy. Residences and restaurants and occasional dark shops were mixed together in this old island district. A few sailors had come ashore, and they greeted me cheerfully when they passed, but didn't bother me.

Then I saw a man coming toward me who seemed both drunk and angry. He was arguing to himself as he walked, and sometimes he waved his arms threateningly. I crossed the street to avoid passing close to him and kept a wary eye in his direction. Though he didn't notice me as he paused under a streetlight, I recognized him with a shock. This was the man whose face I'd sketched—and had only just looked at in my own drawing—the man I'd glimpsed among the pirates who'd boarded the *Aurora* that night. If this was the same man, he might be a key to what had happened, and I'd better not let him out of my sight. If I could find out where he was going, I could call Marcus.

I crossed the street again and was in time to see him turn up a narrow alleyway. The maps I'd seen of Key West had shown me the strips of short, blind alleys that opened off some of the main streets, cutting into the heart of a block. This one looked dark and unsavory. The houses appeared dilapidated, the tiny yards weed-grown. Reconstruction hadn't reached into all the byways yet.

The tall man weaved ahead of me until he came to a ramshackle, single-story house, its paint weathered and its shutter slats broken. The house stretched back almost flush with the alley, and as I hesitated, the man turned into a rear porch entrance. I didn't like the feeling of any of this, and my instinct was to turn and run. But there was too much at stake, and I walked cautiously past the end of the house before I looked back. The alley ended abruptly—blind and a trap, with no way out in that direction.

Streetlights hardly penetrated, but I could make out two dark figures against the blackness of the back porch. One must have been waiting for the other, and they were speaking softly, so I couldn't hear their words. I lost myself quickly in deep shadow near the house, poised to run at any moment.

One of the men raised his voice angrily—just loud enough for me to distinguish the words. "You'd better not try anything if you want your pay." The voice was Derek's, and I tensed in alarm.

"I've got my pay," the other said insolently.

Without warning, Derek hit him, and I saw flailing arms as the fellow went off the open porch and crashed to the ground. Moving like a shadow myself, I crept around the corner of the house and fled back to the street. I walked two blocks as fast as I could go, while my thoughts clamored. When I paused to see where I was, I recognized the street and knew I could find again the house where I'd just been. Right now, however, I must get to Marcus.

Most of the Old Town houses were dark and asleep, and

there was no place where I could phone. It was easier to walk a few more blocks to where Marcus lived.

The big house with its conspicuous towers and gables was easy to find, and most of it was dark too. I walked through the yard along one side and was relieved to see a light burning in Marcus's window. The front door would be locked at this hour, and I didn't want to rouse everyone in the house, so I searched the bushes for a small stick. Then I aimed high at the lighted window screen and threw it hard. The stick sailed toward the target and clattered on the screen. Nothing else happened, and I could hear Marcus's typewriter, shutting out other sounds.

I looked for a heavier bit of broken branch and waited for a pause in the typewriter rhythm. When I hurled my second stick into the air I heard it land with a satisfying thwack against the screen.

A chair was shoved back in the room above, and Marcus came to the window. He couldn't see me in the shadowy yard, but I called to him softly. He tapped the screen and disappeared. I went around to the front of the house, and a few moments later he came down to me. He'd brought a flashlight, and when he'd turned it on my face he took hold of my shoulder to steady me.

"You're shaking. What is it, Laurel? What happened?"

For just a second I hung on to him, wanting supportive arms around me. But there was no time for such weakness now, and I told him quickly what I'd seen and where I'd left the two men.

"I'll have a look right away," he said. "Go up on the porch and wait for me, Laurel."

"I will not," I said, and I saw his grin in the light from the street. He was getting used to me.

"Okay, come along. Maybe two of us will be safer than one, anyway."

We hurried up the street, and when we came to the slit of alley, we slowed and slipped into a patch of shadow that lay against the house. The rear porch was dark and empty. Marcus went ahead, and I reached out to touch his back as we followed through the weeds to rickety steps. No one lay on the ground below the porch, and the door stood open on darkness.

"I'll have a look inside," Marcus whispered. This time he didn't ask me to wait, and I climbed the steps right on his heels.

When we were inside, he closed the door behind us and turned on his light. The room had been a kitchen once, but it was empty now, the sink chipped and grimy. This was a shot-gun house, with room after room in a straight row from back to front. The next room had been used as a dining room, and the flashlight beam led us on.

"There's no one here now," Marcus said.

We went through to the front, our steps echoing on bare pine floors.

"I think this is a house Derek used to own," Marcus said. "It may still belong to him."

Though rooms were at a premium in Key West, no one seemed to be occupying the house now. There were no possessions, no traces of former residents. Marcus opened a closet door in the long hall that ran along the row of rooms and turned the light upon a cardboard carton. It seemed to be full of old newspapers. When Marcus would have closed the door, I stopped him, prompted by some curious intuition.

"Look under the papers," I said.

He lifted them out, a layer at a time, and from between the folds of the last paper something slipped out and clattered heavily to the floor. We stood staring at the puddle of golden links shining in the flashlight's beam. When Marcus picked up the chain and held it out, I knew it was one of those that had been retrieved from the *Santa Beatriz*.

"The man who was talking to Derek said he had his pay," I said. "Maybe this is what he meant. Maybe he has more where this came from. I know he was one of the pirates."

"I'll take this with me," Marcus said, and wrapped the links of chain into a crumpled newspaper.

"What are you going to do?"

"I'm not sure yet. The next step may be tricky because we still don't know quite enough to take action against Derek, but there are some people I can consult. Don't say anything about this, Laurel. We don't want to set him running."

"Of course not."

"And don't go sneaking around in places like this alone at night."

"I didn't do it for fun."

"I know." He put an arm around me as we walked back to my father's house, and at the gate he kissed me. While it wasn't a brotherly kiss, I didn't think it was the way he'd have kissed Iris.

"I'll be in touch," he said. "Do take care, Laurel."

He waited near the steps till I'd let myself in with my key, then went off, walking quickly. I hoped he would take care too. These were dangerous and probably desperate men.

I got ready for bed as quickly as I could, and this time I was tired enough to fall asleep. Not until nearly daylight did I come suddenly awake with something clear in my mind. It was the matter of the steel wedge that had been used to shut Poppy into the orchid house. I knew now what it was that had bothered me about the chisel when Iris had shown it to me. It was supposed to be kept in a toolbox in the orchid house, she'd said. So how did it come to be outside, where it could be forced into the doorjamb? Unless someone was in the orchid house with Poppy that day—someone who might have seen the accident with the glass flask and had deliberately picked up the chisel to carry it outside, where it was used to jam the door. If that was really the way it had happened, then Poppy had been allowed to bleed to death by someone who knew very well how badly she'd been cut.

The next morning I slept late and woke up sluggishly. Too many unpleasant memories were ready to rush through my mind to engulf me. It was better to get up and find out what was happening.

When I'd showered and dressed, I went out on the back porch and looked down into the garden. Two people were there, breakfasting together. Derek and Fern were talking as cheerfully as though there had been no recent antagonism between them. Yesterday Fern had been avoiding Derek, as she had done ever since that fatal trip on the *Aurora*. Now they seemed to be the best of friends.

I went in search of someone to consult—Alida, if she were here. However, it was Iris whom I met as she came out of her room. She looked distraught, even a little wild, and I wondered if Marcus had told her what had happened last night.

"What's wrong?" I asked.

She grasped my arm almost fiercely and propelled me toward my room. "We need to talk—where no one will hear us."

The pictures Fern had rehung on the wall caught Iris's eye as we walked in, and she shivered, turning her back on them, her words pouring out in a rush.

"Last night, after Derek came home late, I went to his room

because I had something to tell him. I'd decided that I couldn't marry him, and he had to know without waiting any longer. In the beginning, I thought that what Alida had told me about Derek and Poppy wouldn't make any difference. I thought I loved him enough to overcome anything. But I've been waking up to the way I really feel. Laurel, I think I was in love with what I thought was his love for me. He seemed so exciting and different from any men I knew."

She broke off and was silent for a moment. When she went on she sounded more resolute.

"After a while I began to see that I was more like a goal to him—something to win, to achieve. Not a real woman. And I didn't want that. So I told him last night in his room that I wouldn't marry him."

"How did he react?"

"He was furious. For a minute I was afraid of him. Then he seemed to pull himself together, and he said, 'I don't need you any more—so get out!' Do you know, I'd even told him that I knew about his affair with Poppy, but he didn't care. It was as if Poppy mattered to him only in a strange, perverse sort of way. After what happened between them, she must have hated herself. Alida says she would have nothing more to do with Derek. He went away, but from then on I think he wanted mainly to hurt her, to punish her. That's why he came back to Key West after all these years. Perhaps he thought he could pay her back by marrying me, by charming Fern. I'm afraid he nearly succeeded. But Fern has changed toward him too, and he knows now how I really feel. When I walked out of the room, he let me go, but I'm not sure what he may try now."

"Maybe you'd better see who's having breakfast together down in the garden." I motioned her toward the porch door.

She stepped outside, and I stood near her at the rail. Derek was holding Fern's hand, and she was crying softly, happily.

"Oh, God!" Iris pulled me back inside. "Come downstairs with me, Laurel. We have to put a stop to this."

We hurried down the back stairs together and burst out upon them. Derek looked up in surprise, and Fern stared through her tears.

"Let her alone!" Iris cried. "I know what you're up to. If you can't have me, you'll go after Fern. You'd like to get your hands on Cliff's wealth, wouldn't you? Well, it's not going to happen!"

After his first surprise, Derek seemed undisturbed. "Oh, I don't know. Fern understands now that I've always been more than fond of her."

Fern looked up, her eyes still brimming. "Isn't it wonderful, Iris? Wonderful that we can find each other—when I thought it would never happen."

"Don't be an idiot!" Iris snapped. "You know—but he doesn't. So stop pretending it's not true. Derek, Poppy told Alida the truth that she never told you. You can't make any move in Fern's direction—she's your daughter."

My knees turned suddenly weak, and I dropped into a chair abruptly.

Derek stared at Iris. "What are you talking about?"

"It's perfectly true. Alida has all the facts. They've been haunting her for a long time. I wanted her to tell you. I even phoned her that time when she was on the island and asked her to tell you everything. Only she didn't—she told Fern instead. So Fern knows, even if she pretends she doesn't."

"Don't believe it, Derek!" Fern cried. "Cliff was my father. I told Alida it couldn't be true. At first what she said put me off, and I couldn't talk to you. But now everything inside me tells me it's not true. The way I feel about you isn't the way I feel about Cliff. I can tell—"

Derek stopped her. "Wait a minute, Fern. We'd better not kid ourselves. I expect it probably is true. But that doesn't mean that you and I can't get to know each other in a new way. Maybe when I get used to the idea, I'll even like having a daughter."

Iris saw what he was doing, and so did I. If he couldn't reach Fern and use her in one way, he'd do it in another. Iris started to protest, but this wasn't the time, and I drew her into the house. There was a better way to fight Derek—Marcus's way.

"Did Cliff know about this?" I asked when we were in the hall.

"No, I'm sure he didn't. Alida has been carrying her secret around for a long time, and she would never have wounded Cliff by telling him. But she finally had to stop me from marrying him. Who knows what Fern will do now, if Derek turns on his charm and plays father?"

"I don't see how Poppy could have—"

"Alida said it was only a temporary fling. She was piqued by what she thought was Cliff's neglect, and she reached out to Derek. I think she never forgave herself, from what Alida says. Alida was her one confidante. Fern was conceived while Cliff was away on a trip, and she couldn't possibly tell him and wreck her marriage. She really loved Cliff. So she juggled dates, and of course she never told Derek either. But this was why she didn't want me to marry him, and why Fern's infatuation upset her so much. At first when Alida told me, all I wanted was to go on caring about Derek. But somehow I couldn't."

A temporary fling, I thought, with all these terrible consequences that would leave their stamp upon the future. Fern was still Poppy's daughter, but she hadn't yet been able to face the loss of Cliff as her father.

"What are we to do?" Iris sounded desperate.

"Give her time. We can both talk to her, try to help her. You're still her sister. Besides, there's going to be a way to trap Derek, if Marcus's plans work out."

We'd walked through the house to the front porch, and we stepped outside just as Marcus came up the steps. He saw Iris's face and looked at her questioningly.

"I'm not going to marry Derek," she said.

"I'm glad," he told her gently.

I could sense his compassion, his sadness for her, even though this break with Derek was what he wanted.

"We won't have to worry much longer about Derek," he went on. "Sit down a minute, and I'll tell you what's happened. Laurel, does Iris know about last night?"

I sat in a porch chair, but Iris stayed where she was, near the door. "You said not to tell anyone, and I haven't."

"It doesn't matter now." Marcus drew Iris gently to a chair and sat down beside her before he turned again to me. "The police have picked up Jim Simpson—the man you followed last night. In order to save his own skin, he's been talking as fast as he can. Derek staged the whole hijacking himself. A few of his own men were in on what happened, and they made off with the treasure. I gather they got rid of all those who weren't with them. How, we may not know until some of them turn up."

This was astonishing news, but good in a way, if it incriminated Derek.

"How did he dare to trust those men on board the *Aurora*?" I asked.

"They needed him and his contacts in order to sell the gold in South America. If he manages to skip the country, he'll be free of his debts, and of the complications and interference that might prevent his doing what he likes with the treasure here. Right now, of course, this house is only a screen for him to hide behind until he can get away. Simpson came back to Key West to let Derek know where the gold is hidden. He and Derek were going to join the others, and they meant to get out of the Caribbean as soon as they could. But Simpson and Derek never hit it off very well, and last night there was trouble. When the police took Simpson in and he saw the gold chain we'd retrieved, he knew the game was over, so he began to talk. There may be murder charges, and he wants to be in the clear."

"Derek's down there in the garden right now," I said.

"The police will move soon to arrest him. Even if he leaves the house, they'll pick him up. He can't get off the island. I've got to get back to the station now, but I wanted you to know—both of you." He took Iris's hand. "You'll be all right, honey—just give it time. Derek's mixed up in drug running too, and they'll get him on that. This hijacking crime will hold him here for what's coming next."

I went down the steps with Marcus. "There may be another murder charge," I pointed out. "Eddie could have seen Derek on deck that night with Cliff. He could have seen Derek push him into the water. If Cliff guessed what Derek was up to—" I paused because it was hard to go on. "I mean, if Cliff found out what Derek was up to, he could have had a heart attack before he went overboard. And if Derek guessed what Eddie had seen . . ."

"It's all possible. Derek would have had his chance at Eddie when they were in the fort together. We'll talk more later, Laurel. Just hang on." He kissed me on the cheek and dashed off.

I went thoughtfully back to where Iris sat stunned, not moving. Speculation was still running wild in my head. It was even possible that it had been Derek who had shut Poppy into the orchid house and had started the whole terrible chain of events. If Poppy had decided to tell Cliff the truth to save Iris, Derek wouldn't have stood still for that.

But right now I had to shake Iris out of the stupor she seemed to have dropped into. "Derek will be taken care of—but what about Fern? She's the one who needs our help now."

"There's nothing more I can do," Iris said limply.

That left only me.

I went to the porch and looked down into the garden. The table below, where Fern and Derek had breakfasted, was empty, their dishes and cups still uncleared. He was nowhere in sight, but as I stood there Fern came out from beneath the porch and walked to the door of the orchid house. The problem of Derek now belonged to the police, but Fern's safety and sanity had to be my concern.

I ran quickly down the back stairs.

16

Fern stood looking sadly around at her orchids. She tried to smile at me as I came in. "It's hard to tell them good-bye, Laurel. I don't think they want me to go."

Her words left me more fearful than ever, not knowing how to dissuade her. "Where are you going?"

"With Derek, of course. Wherever he means to take me. I guess he really is my father. I couldn't accept that at first, but he's been talking to me, and I think he wants to be my father. He's never had a child."

How was I to tell her that this happiness she reached for was only a mirage? Yet it must be done.

"There's something you have to know, Fern. The police are going to arrest Derek very soon. That hijacking of the *Aurora* was staged. Derek must have planned to have us all on board so we'd serve as witnesses later. But it's Derek who faked what happened, and he had all that gold from the *Santa Beatriz* taken to a Caribbean hiding place. And now—"

She broke in on me. "Yes, I know! Isn't it wonderful? Wasn't he clever to pull that off?" Her eyes glowed with admiration. "He's a real pirate, Laurel!"

"Listen to me," I said. "Please listen. We don't know how many men may have died—that's what's ugly and real. And we think Derek has been running drugs up the keys besides."

She didn't care in the least. Nothing I'd said had impressed her. She touched the petal of a vanda lightly, and I knew she was still telling the orchids good-bye. Yet when she turned back to me, her lips were trembling.

"Now I have to let her go too—and that's terribly hard. Laurel, look what I've found."

She gestured toward a work shelf, and I saw with a sense of horror the object she had placed there. It was a monster orchid made of papier-mâché, painted pale green with a crimson lip and speckles of the same color cast across the green of upper petals. This was the very mask of the picture that had hung in Poppy's room, and now I could see the entire head. All but the orchid face was an intricate mass of darker green leaves. It must have taken hours to create so beautifully, though now it was shabby and dusty, with tips broken from some of the leaves.

"I just wish she wouldn't watch me like that," Fern said. "I thought she'd be happier if I brought her here—but you can see the way her eyes follow everything I do. She's still angry with me."

Empty slits were visible just under the upper trio of curling petals—slits through which Poppy's eyes had once peered. I felt chilled in the sultry air, and I knew I had to stop this.

"Fern, listen to me! That's only a mask she made for a party a long time ago. It has nothing to do with your mother."

She seemed not to hear me. "I found it in an old trunk with some of Poppy's things. It's a wonder it wasn't completely crushed. I've been looking for it for a long time."

I had to bring her back to the present. "You must listen! It's what Derek has been doing that matters now."

"I expect she really did love him more than she did Cliff." Fern's tone was dreamy, lost.

I wanted to shake her into awareness, and I took her by the shoulders to make her face me. "Eddie Burch was helping Marcus to expose Derek. That's why Derek may have killed him at West Martello. Eddie could have seen Derek with Cliff that night on the *Aurora*, when he pushed Cliff into the water. So Derek had to be rid of Eddie. That's what's real, Fern. It's even possible that Derek had something to do with shutting Poppy in here on the day she died."

This time I'd caught her attention, and she was staring at me wide-eyed. Suddenly she began to laugh. "How silly you are, Laurel! Derek wouldn't do any of those things—it's ridiculous! I'm sure he's lived a violent life, but he'd use a gun—or maybe a sword. Laurel, you aren't even half a sister to me, so don't start making up stories and telling me what to do."

How could I reach her? A toolbox rested on a shelf, and I went to rummage through it. Someone had returned the steel chisel that Iris had shown me, and I took it out and held it up for Fern to see.

"Do you know how this was used?"

She shook her head, but her look was wary. She would be on guard against anything I might claim. Nevertheless, I went on.

"Derek could have been in here with Poppy the day she died. He turned up very quickly after they found her. Perhaps he saw her cut herself and took the chance to stop her from going to Cliff with the whole truth about him. He could have gone out, jammed this wedge into the door, and left her to bleed to death. That's the terrible truth that you may need to accept about Derek."

Fern snatched the chisel from my hand. "What a liar you are! None of that is true. Derek wasn't even here that day. But I was, Laurel. So what do you think of that?"

I stared at her blankly. "You were here when Poppy cut herself?"

"Of course! I saw it happen. I was terribly upset with her. She was going to talk to Cliff. She said she knew something about Derek that would make Cliff send him away. This meant I would never see him again, and I couldn't bear that. Poppy was transplanting seeds from a flask, but she was so upset that she didn't wrap newspaper around the glass when she broke it. So she cut her wrist badly by accident. Probably because she was so nervous. Blood spurted all over the orchids, and they all started to whisper. It was as though they told me what to do. So I got this chisel out of the toolbox and wedged the door shut. When I was sure she couldn't get out, I went back to the public library, where I was looking something up for Cliff."

"You meant her to die! You left her to bleed to death!" I felt sick with shock—not only for the deed, but because Fern was lost in a terrible fantasy that put her beyond the reach of reason and reality.

She nodded at me in sad agreement. "I really didn't think about it then. The orchids told me, and I—I just did what they said. I didn't know how awful I was going to feel after she really died, and I knew it was my fault. I nearly died of grief myself then. And I was afraid someone would find out. I knew Alida took the chisel out of the door, and later I found it when I looked in her desk upstairs. So yesterday I put it back so I could worry her and make her stop bothering me about Derek."

I had no words to deal with what Fern was telling me. There *were* no words to deal with madness.

"It was all sort of confused," she ran on. "You have to understand that, Laurel. It was like the time on the *Aurora* when I found Cliff alone on deck just as the boarding started. That was when I told him Derek was my father. Alida had explained everything to me out on the island, and I couldn't stand it. I was angry with Cliff for not taking better care of all of us. So when I told him, I just threw myself at him and pounded on his chest—and he went backwards overboard. There was only a flimsy handrail out where we were. I guess he was already dead from the shock of what I'd told him by the time he fell. I didn't mean to hurt him, Laurel—not any more than I meant to hurt Poppy."

I was convinced at last of this horror. Now I wanted only to get away—to find Marcus, who was sane and healthy and who would help me deal with something so horrible.

"I suppose you want to know about Eddie?" Fern sounded almost cheerful as she went on.

There was no help—I had to hear it all. "You'd better tell me," I said.

"But don't you see—that was different. I loved Poppy and I loved Cliff, but I hated Eddie. He was no good at all. He knew I was on deck with Cliff that night. He saw me. Alida did too, but she wouldn't have told. He was trying to get me to pay him to keep quiet. To get away from him, I climbed the steps to the gun emplacement at West Martello. But he followed me right up there. He was plenty scared of Derek that night, but not of me. So I just had to push him off when I got the chance. And you know something, Laurel—it gets a little easier all the time. It took so little effort afterwards to fool everyone. Of course Derek doesn't know any of this, and he mustn't ever know. He's my father, and he must love me the way I love him. Though maybe I always knew we were alike—deep down."

"He'll have been arrested by this time, Fern," I said quietly. "You can't go anywhere with him."

"Do you think I'd believe anything you tell me? Do you think I'll stand around and let you weave your lies about Derek—and about me?"

She could no longer tell the difference between what was real and what wasn't. Yet I knew with a terrible conviction that all the earlier things she'd told me were so, and I wondered if she would try to stop me if I walked out of the orchid house. But how could she? I was bigger and probably stronger than she was. There was no way she could stop me physically.

However, she still stood between me and the door, and there was an eerie quality about her now, as though she were one with her orchids, the evil orchids of my dream—my father's "murderous" orchids.

She put a finger to her lips and whispered. "Listen to them, Laurel. Hear them rustling? They're terribly excited, just the way they were the day Poppy died. They know. They know it's going to happen again—just the way it did before."

Suddenly she broke off and turned fiercely toward the orchid mask.

"Stop watching me!" she cried. "I can't stand it when you watch me like that!" She snatched up an empty brown pot and smashed it down on the fragile orchid head. It crushed with a brittle sound, and bits flew across the shelf and skittered on the floor.

I had to get away as quickly as I could. I tried to slip past her, but she flew into startling action. With a swift, graceful movement, she leaned toward a basket of trash under a shelf and brought out something that glittered in the sunlight pouring in from overhead. It was the neck of a broken glass flask, with naked, jagged edges. Almost in the same movement, before I realized what she intended, she snatched up my hand and brought the sharp daggers of glass strongly across my wrist.

I felt a tiny aching of pain and watched the pulsing of blood.

Fern rushed to the door and went through, slamming it shut behind her. I heard the sound as she jammed in the steel wedge that would hold me here in the orchid house.

There was an instant of déjà vu. This was my dream—shut in among the orchids, with my blood spattering the petals. I could almost hear them whispering among themselves—these descendants of the blossoms that had once tasted Poppy's blood. Now they were waiting for me to die.

I pushed the dream away. A box of paper towels stood on a shelf, and I caught up a wad and pressed it tightly over the artery. I held both arms above my head, still pressing as hard as I could with my uninjured hand. Poppy had panicked. She'd been too frightened to do anything but pound on the door and call for help. I wouldn't panic, and I knew I could stop the flow of blood, even though I'd begun to feel a little faint and dizzy.

Orchids that had been white and pale mauve were streaked with drops of scarlet, and blood was trickling down my arm. I pressed harder, fighting my own weakness. I hadn't lost much blood, so I was causing this reaction with my own mind—increasing the frightening weakness. Fear could destroy me, and I fought it back.

The orchids were harmless—only beautiful flowers. I mustn't let them build this terror in me. Perhaps they did tremble and whisper in the face of terrible deeds, but they meant me no injury. I told myself over and over that the wound was closing, that my own blood was clotting to save me.

After a time I took my numbing arms down and removed the wad of paper cautiously. The bleeding had stopped. I took no chances. I applied pressure again, found a stool to sit on, and waited for what seemed an endless length of time. Like Poppy, I was shut into the orchid house, and I knew there'd be no use in trying to open the door—no way to attack the enveloping wire shield. I kept my eyes away from the bits of colored papier-mâché on the floor. I didn't want to start imagining eyes watching me.

If I shouted, no one would hear, since they hadn't heard Poppy, but I tried shouting anyway. No one came, but I was no longer frightened. The orchids around me seemed to have quieted, as my own mind quieted. I tried to remember things that would help me—that theme my father had been writing about in his book, and that I'd thought of so often lately. The way a single act, large or small, could start ripples that went on and on until they touched distant shores. The course of future lives could be changed in one tiny instant. Cliff's neglect of Poppy, her brief infidelity to Cliff, had brought me here to be trapped by Fern—who was the result of that infidelity. Yet, as Marcus had said, this wasn't inescapable destiny. Human beings could make their own choices. Perhaps Poppy had even chosen to die—we would never know. I, at least, chose to live, and the things I did from now on would affect other lives—so I'd better not act blindly. Since I'd come here, I'd been cutting across ripples that others had started. But it was possible to change the future before it happened. Children of mine would be born, and they would affect others because of my choice. Awesome, but inspiring as well. I felt a new surge of hope and energy.

Suddenly someone was at the door, pulling out the wedge of steel. Marcus and Iris were running toward me, and Marcus looked more frightened than I'd ever seen him.

"I'm all right," I said. "My wrist was cut, but I've stopped the bleeding."

They both put their arms around me, and Iris was crying.

"I shouldn't have let you go and talk to her alone, Laurel. But I couldn't help the way I was—I was dead for a little while."

I could take no more right now, lest I go to pieces altogether, and I pulled away from them. "Where is Fern?"

Iris turned unhappily away, and Marcus answered me. "Alida's with her now. After Derek was arrested, I came straight back here and found Fern outside in the street babbling about all the people she'd killed. I took her upstairs to your father's study, and Alida's calming her down. When she said you were in the orchid house and dying, I dashed right down and met Iris on the way. Laurel, is anything of what Fern was saying true?"

"I'm afraid it is," I told him.

Iris said, "I'll go upstairs and see if I can help Alida. Now that you're all right, Laurel—" Unexpectedly, she touched my arm, smiled at me warmly, and went away. My sister.

"We'll get you to a hospital now," Marcus said briskly. "You need to get that wrist taken care of properly."

I sat down on the stool again and hooked my heels over a rung. I didn't feel like being sensible. I didn't want to go anywhere. I don't know what he read in my face, but he came to me and put his hand under my chin.

"Honey," he said, "I don't want anything more to happen to you. I need you in my life. You know that, don't you?"

This was what I wanted from him—something tender and gentle, something loving. I tilted my head and saw in his eyes what I'd wanted to see. Now I could slip down from the stool and accept the support of his arm as we went out to his car and drove to the hospital.

It is March again—nearly April—and once more the anniversary of Poppy's death is approaching. But this time the date has no dread for us. Perhaps she really is at rest now. There's sadness when I think of Cliff, but I have the memory of our time together at Casa Marina to comfort me. I can even think of my mother more quietly now.

All our lives have changed. Iris seems to have come through as a stronger person. For the first time, she's making her own decisions with confidence. She still lives in Cliff's house, but now she has opened it to the social life they used to enjoy when her mother was alive. She has interested herself in the problems of restoration in Key West and is helping to preserve its remarkable history. There are several men she sees, though she hasn't settled for any one. I know that shadows lie across her life, as they do with all of us, but she's learning to live with them. We are becoming more like affectionate sisters these days.

The treasure from the *Santa Beatriz* has nearly all been recovered, and historians have been gathering valuable information from its many pieces. Later it will be put on display for visitors to enjoy.

The process of law moves slowly while Derek is held for trial. Sometimes I wonder what his thoughts are and whether he has ever stopped scheming.

Fern exists mainly in her own world. She was too far removed from reality to stand trial, and she lives away from Key West in a private place where doctors care for her. Alida goes often to visit her. There is even a small solar greenhouse available, where Fern can grow a few orchids. The moments when she is lucid must be the hardest for her to endure. Alida tells me that during those times she knows what she has done, and special care must be given her. It's probably best when she is like one of her own orchids—unthinking, but no longer "murderous."

Marcus and I are still in Key West, though we've taken a house outside of Old Town. We know now that we have what we both want—the all-out commitment that marriage brings. I've let my bookstore in Bellport go to Stan Neese with hardly a qualm. I want a different life now.

Strangely enough, I am helping Marcus as he helped my father. I know books, I know how to find information, and I love on-the-spot research. Books—nonfiction books—are what Marcus wants to write, and I can help, not only with research, but also as a critic. He tells me I'm the best critic he's found so far, and whether it's true or not, I love to hear him say it. I'm even trying my skill at some short stories of my own— after all, I come by a splendid heritage.

Sometimes when I'm visiting Iris she gives me a beautiful blossom from the greenhouse that she's expanding into a business. I take it and thank her. Afterwards, I give it away as quickly as possible. I don't really like orchids, but at least I don't dream about them any more.

PHYLLIS A. WHITNEY

RAINSONG

Why should Ricky Sands, legendary pop idol at the height of his career, commit suicide?

Shattered and nonplussed, his beautiful young widow, Hollis, tries to escape the glare of publicity and seeks refuge at the Cold Spring Harbor estate. Far from discovering peace, however, Hollis enters a world of nightmare proportions as she begins to unravel the disturbing truth concerning her husband's death . . .

POST A LITTLE HAPPINESS

Post·A·Book

A Royal Mail service in association with the Book Marketing Council & The Booksellers Association

Post-A-Book is a Post Office trademark.

PHYLLIS A. WHITNEY

EMERALD

Palm Springs is a paradise for the retired rich and famous, a playground for one-time Hollywood movie-queens like Monica Warren. Journalist Carol Hamilton, driven away from New York by the terrifying threats of her ex-husband Owen Barclay, arrives in Palm Springs in despair, seeking a final refuge, a haven for herself and her small son. But the peaceful retreat that she had anticipated is not what it seems. Nor, it turns out, is Great Aunt Monica, about whom Carol plans to write a book. As she begins to delve into her relative's glamorous past dark secrets come to light – of a tragic love, a suicide, and of a precious emerald ring: secrets that threaten Carol herself with excruciating danger – and even with murder.

'Another triumph for Phyllis A. Whitney!'

Cosmopolitan

CORONET BOOKS

PHYLLIS A. WHITNEY

THE QUICKSILVER POOL

A tragic accident in the Quicksilver Pool – was Virginia's death as simple as it seemed?

Lora had looked forward eagerly to leaving her home in the ruined South and being married to Wade Tyler, the young Union officer she had nursed so tenderly.

Instead she found herself daunted by her new life in the North. She wasn't prepared for the Tyler family, for the huge dusty mansion in New York, for the jealousies of her husband's tyrannical mother or the fantasies of his bewildered son. Silence, whispers and hostility seemed to follow Lora round the house like grim shadows.

Lora was determined to unearth the skeletons in the Tyler family's past, but her quest turned out to be much more dangerous to herself than she could possibly have imagined. She found a mystery surrounding the death of Wade's first wife Virginia – and someone who wished Wade to become a widower once again.

CORONET BOOKS

BARBARA WHITNELL

THE RING OF BELLS

Compulsive, delightful and readable, the brilliantly evocative novel of a world gone by

In 1871 when Jenny Fitzgerald arrived as a child at *The Ring of Bells*, it was a simple, country inn. Seventy years and three generations later the inn had become the flagship of a thriving business. This is the story of Jenny's life and her livelihood: her passionate but turbulent marriage to Roger Leyton; her role as business woman, mother and grandmother; the First World War and the Depression; and, above all, the mainstay of her existence.

CORONET BOOKS

BARBARA WHITNELL

THE SALT RAKERS

'A dramatic story of love and loyalty'

Daily Mail

Bermuda in 1811 – a bustling, exotic island colony. A place of wealth and slavery. A time of change and danger.

Dorcas Foley, beautiful and headstrong, sets off with her new, hardly-known husband and her terrible secret: the child she is carrying is not his. Her obsession with Kit Mallory, the true father, must forever remain a secret, for the two families are bitterly opposed.

The Salt Rakers is a vivid, compelling saga of a family trying to build a life on a small, hurricane-swept island. It is a story of a growing love that is always under threat from the passions of the past.

'Sweeping romance by the author of *The Song of the Rainbird*'

Yorkshire Evening Post

CORONET BOOKS

DENISE ROBINS

ALL THIS FOR LOVE

Though cousins, Sally Browning and Philippa Frome are identical – in looks but not in character. When the spoilt Philippa persuades her identical 'twin' to pretend to be Mrs Frome so Philippa can run off on holiday with her secret lover, Sally can only reluctantly agree.

And so she embarks upon a new life of wealth and luxury, fooling all and sundry – even Philippa's invalid husband Martin. Soon accustomed to her new role and to the deceptions she is loath to make, Sally finds she has more devotion and love to give – especially to the ailing Martin – than she had dared to imagine in her wildest dreams.

'Rarely has any writer of our times delved so deeply into the secret places of a woman's heart'

Taylor Caldwell

CORONET BOOKS

DENISE ROBINS

THE INEVITABLE END

Billie Carden is one of the new breed of women: tom-
boyish and defiantly independent, she has no use for
men and no desire to marry. Nor does she need to – for
she is the lucky heiress to the fortune of her American
Uncle Silas.

But Billie's life takes a whole new direction when two
events – at first unconnected – conspire to thwart her
plans: an encounter with the impoverished Richard
Bromley, and a dramatic ultimatum from her uncle . . .

CORONET BOOKS

DENISE ROBINS

A PROMISE IS FOREVER

Fern Barrett had had a tragic personal blow, and now her integrity and courage were to be tested to the limit. She and her husband Terry were forced by circumstance to take employment in the household of powerful financier Quentin Dorey, a bachelor – and it was here Fern's troubles began. While Terry became increasingly self-centred and irresponsible, Fern found herself more and more attracted by the charm and sympathy of her employer. She also incurred the hatred of Quentin's mother who had guessed the truth about Fern's background – something Fern was desperate to conceal. What was Fern to do? Because for her a promise was for ever . . .

'Rarely has a writer of our times delved so deeply into the secret places of a woman's heart.'
Taylor Caldwell

CORONET BOOKS

MORE TITLES AVAILABLE FROM
HODDER AND STOUGHTON PAPERBACKS

PHYLLIS A. WHITNEY

☐	39496 X	Rainsong	£2.50
☐	36928 0	Emerald	£1.95
☐	17411 0	The Quicksilver Pool	£1.95

BARBARA WHITNELL

☐	32800 2	The Ring Of Bells	£3.50
☐	41222 4	The Salt Rakers	£2.95

DENISE ROBINS

☐	40675 5	All This For Love	£1.95
☐	39457 9	The Inevitable End	£1.95
☐	16218 X	A Promise Is Forever	£1.95

All these books are available at your local bookshop or newsagent, or can be ordered direct from the publisher. Just tick the titles you want and fill in the form below.

Prices and availability subject to change without notice.

Hodder & Stoughton Paperbacks, P.O. Box 11, Falmouth, Cornwall.

Please send cheque or postal order, and allow the following for postage and packing:

U.K. – 55p for one book, plus 22p for the second book, and 14p for each additional book ordered up to a £1.75 maximum.

B.F.P.O. and EIRE – 55p for the first book, plus 22p for the second book, and 14p per copy for the next 7 books, 8p per book thereafter.

OTHER OVERSEAS CUSTOMERS – £1.00 for the first book, plus 25p per copy for each additional book.

NAME..

ADDRESS ....

....